BLUE COVER UP

Chris Ward

Copyright 2015 Chris Ward
All rights reserved

The right of Chris Ward to be identified as the Author of the Work has been asserted by him in accordance with the Copyright, Designs and Patents Act 1988.

No part of this publication may be reproduced, stored in a retrieval system, or transmitted, in any form or by any means without the prior written permission of the publisher, nor be otherwise circulated in any form of binding or cover other than that in which it is published and without a similar condition being imposed on the subsequent purchaser.

This book is a work of fiction. Any similarity between the characters and situations within its pages and places or persons, living or dead, is unintentional and coincidental.

ISBN-10: 1511991925
ISBN-13: 978-1511991926

Contents

PROLOGUE 1

CHAPTER 1 4

CHAPTER 2 8

CHAPTER 3 20

CHAPTER 4 28

CHAPTER 5 33

CHAPTER 6 38

CHAPTER 7 42

CHAPTER 8 50

CHAPTER 9 54

CHAPTER 10 68

CHAPTER 11 72

CHAPTER 12 78

CHAPTER 13 90

CHAPTER 14 94

CHAPTER 15 101

CHAPTER 16 114

CHAPTER 17 122

CHAPTER 18 128

CHAPTER 19 137

CHAPTER 20 154

CHAPTER 21 158

CHAPTER 22 169

CHAPTER 23 180

CHAPTER 24 198

CHAPTER 25 204

CHAPTER 26 210

CHAPTER 27 219

CHAPTER 28 223

CHAPTER 29 228

CHAPTER 30 239

CHAPTER 31 244

CHAPTER 32 247

CHAPTER 33 280

CHAPTER 34 290

CHAPTER 35 302

PROLOGUE

The tall, wholesome, good looking young Police Officer strolled down Ashtead high street, and received a couple of bizarre looks simply because no one had seen the like for years: a proper policeman with a proper helmet on, walking the beat! At twenty-six, the constable had been in the police force since attending Hendon Police Training Centre at the age of eighteen. He adored the job and had become one of those policemen that people intuitively took to quickly. He had a comfortable manner that translated into good, effective local community policing. He was married with a four-year-old daughter, Carrie, and his wife, Georgina, was six months pregnant. They lived in a small terraced house in Leatherhead, Surrey, and although they had problems and challenges like everybody else, the family remained close-knit and joyful.

The day was gloriously sunny with clear blue skies, and being outside rather than stuck behind a desk suited him, he wore a short-sleeved, crisp, whiter than white shirt, without the jacket, and enjoyed the sun's warmth on his body. The constable popped his head into several shops and said good morning, and always received a courteous reply. He eventually got to, and walked past, the small electrical shop and turned right into the alley, which led through to the Ashtead Peace Memorial Hall car park. His predominant mood was one of peace, thinking of the new baby on the way. When he'd reached the halfway-point of the empty alley, a man entered the other end and came towards him. He wore white trainers, a green and white tracksuit, and had a flat cap pulled down over his eyes. Due to the tightness of the alleyway, the policeman prepared to squeeze over so they could both pass. They got closer and closer, now just six feet apart, and he was about to smile at the man when he got a feeling that he recognised him. When he tried to look closer, he saw who it was ...

'Hey, what are y—'

The man's arm moved in a fast striking forward motion, and then he felt it—an excruciating burning pain tore deep into his stomach—he felt and heard the ripping of his skin and further agonising pain as the man pulled the knife upwards. He heard gurgling and sucking as the weapon was then pulled out of his chest, he just caught a fleeting glimpse of the long-bladed serrated knife, and his hands automatically went to the wound. Within a second, blood covered them, and intestines, which dangled out of the gaping stomach wound. The man had long gone, and the young constable collapsed forward onto his knees—he was dying. The pain felt unbearable, but he could still reflect on his precious little Carrie. Eyes closed, he sobbed, then whispered her name, *'Carrie, I love you.'* And then his wife's name, *'Georgina, take care of them for me please, I'm sorry, so sorry I can't be with you.'* Then he thought of the unborn baby and screamed in anguish. Distantly, he heard shouting and running feet, but it was too late and he fell forward. Nothing, nothing but blackness and peace filled his world and, thankfully, no more pain.

CHAPTER 1

David Kane, sixty-eight-years old, lived on his own in Bookham—a small insignificant village near Leatherhead in Surrey. He stood at six foot three, had short grey hair, and was a well-built handsome man who dressed well and commanded respect without even opening his mouth, and he had buckets full of Gravitas. After a lifetime as a quantity surveyor, he had retired and paid off his mortgage, and had a private pension to supplement his state payment, so was comfortably off. David's wife, Mary, had died of bone cancer and he had been on his own for ten years. A classic middle class vegetarian, he led a quiet life and got on with everybody, from the local postman to the local police beat officer, and even the much despised traffic wardens. He attended the local All Saints Church in Great Bookham, and had built most of his social life around prayer meetings and Choir practices.

He was the epitome of the sort of people societies are built around. David had one son, Simon. They'd wanted more, but it just hadn't happened and, in the end, they thanked God for Simon every day. The other loves of David's life were his politics and what he called his Victor Meldrew grumpy old man's syndrome. When his beloved Mary had died he had wanted to fill up his time and so he took to writing letters of complaint. He wrote testy complaining letters to Airlines, to his local supermarkets, to his local

MP—Sheila Philips, to the Prime Minister, and to the local Council. In fact, you name it and at some time or other he would have complained about it in writing. David was a great believer in fighting injustice and had started joining demonstrations and carrying a placard. At the last one, he had joined forty-five-thousand others in central London to protest at Israeli action in Gaza. David had a full and enjoyable life, and part of that was Simon coming to visit every Saturday.

Simon, forty and single, had been engaged once and the bride-to-be, Claire, had left him at the Altar. After that he swore under no circumstances would he ever marry. Simon had female friends but no one special in his life. He lived a few miles from his father in a one-bedroomed flat in East Horsley. Simon and his father were close, and Simon had worshipped his dad from childhood. David had taught him everything he knew about life, and that included how to fix a washing machine, cut timber, and most importantly, how not to get a woman in trouble. They got on extremely well and both relished their Saturdays spent together. Simon had become increasingly concerned about his father going on demonstrations in London, but it had to be said that the organisers always looked after every one of the participants well and particularly the elderly.

There had been a downfall of snow and it was freezing cold, which wasn't unusual for early January. Still, 2012 had seen a tough winter so far. David hadn't been out of the house much and had become progressively more fed up with writing complaint letters, reading books, and watching television—a pastime he didn't like to overdo. Simon had popped in a couple of times to make sure he had enough food and essentials in the house and that he was keeping warm enough. After a couple of days the snow melted and David became his old chirpy self. He felt excited because the following Saturday he would once again don his walking boots and head to London to take part in a demonstration. This one was to complain about high energy costs and to ask the government to bring in legislation that capped the domestic price of Gas and Electricity. David was firmly committed to the cause, as he felt companies like Eon were ripping off the public and making billions in profits. He'd spent considerable time in producing a colourful placard that he would take with him and would apply the final touches to it on Friday morning. All was ready: he would take the local train up to Waterloo Station, London, then take the Jubilee line one stop to Westminster, and then walk up Whitehall past Downing Street, and meet up with the other demonstrators in Trafalgar Square. The plan was to listen to speeches for thirty minutes then walk back down Whitehall, walk round Parliament Square—where the organisers would meet up with local MP's sympathetic to the cause—and then continue by crossing over Westminster Bridge to the south of the river. David also felt thrilled and excited because he had agreed to meet up with Mary Bishop, a sixty-year-old sprightly protester whom he had taken a shine to. Mary had lost her husband and had been a seasoned campaigner for eight years. She and David had become firm friends and he hoped that, in time, they would grow into more than that.

Saturday morning dawned sunny, but still fresh and quite cold, and David made sure he was well wrapped up, and then headed off towards Little Bookham railway station. He bought his ticket and sauntered onto the platform to wait for the train, where he smiled at a couple, who were also carrying a placard and obviously heading towards Trafalgar Square. Ten minutes later, the train arrived and David boarded the third carriage. Although quite busy, he managed to find a window seat so he could enjoy the views and, five minutes later, the train pulled out.

CHAPTER 2

'Jez, you need to get ready for work—it's eight o' clock,' Sara shouted from the bottom of the stairs.

'All right. Stop fucking shouting,' came the response from the main bedroom. Jeremy pushed the jet-black duvet cover to one side and swung his legs over the side of the bed, then stopped. His head throbbed and his mouth felt as dry as a vulture's crotch. With his eyes closed, he wished to God that he didn't have to go into work. He was scheduled to be on duty at a protest march and had to get a move on if he was going to get there on time. They had financial difficulties and he had signed up for all the overtime he could get, which was usually demonstration marches, or football matches at one of the numerous London premiership clubs. Jeremy had been in the Met for four years, and been married to Sara for three. He stood up and swore to himself, 'Never again. Fuck, I feel like shit.' He staggered to the bathroom. 'Sara, leave some paracetamol on the table,' he shouted down the stairs.

'Yes, okay, I'm off. I'll see you later.' Sara worked as a hairdresser, and Saturday was the busiest day of the week. Jeremy took off his boxers and clambered into the shower cubicle. When he turned the water on full blast, the cold water hit him like a tornado, and he shouted, 'Shit,' and grabbed the heat control and turned; it soon came on warmer and he luxuriated as the hot water cascaded over his sore head. Life returned to his body, until only his head reminded him of the vast amount of alcohol he'd consumed the night before. He should never have gone to the stag party, even though he'd sworn he would only have a couple and leave early. He'd consumed a bottle of Australian Red Wine, at least seven pints of Guinness, and a couple of shots of unidentifiable strong liquor. Not until two in the morning did he stumble home and collapse into bed.

    He climbed out of the shower, and felt as though he'd been in bed for about half an hour. He brushed his teeth and scraped his tongue rigorously with the brush, then he dressed in his smart blue police uniform and trudged downstairs, where he grabbed the two paracetamol that Sara had left for him on the table, and went to the cupboard where she kept her tablet stock and took two 20mg capsules of Fluoxetine happy tablets, and swallowed them all with a handful of water. Jeremy checked the windows and locked all the doors, then exited the house and got in his two-year-old silver Ford Fiesta and drove off towards Greenford tube station.

    He parked two minutes away, down a side street, and soon stood waiting on the platform for the central line train into London. After fifteen minutes, the train arrived and he embarked, and he noticed that as usual no one would sit anywhere near him—oh the joys of being a copper. The train filled up, and soon all the seats were full. An exceptionally attractive blonde-haired young woman sat opposite him and, as she crossed her legs, he got a flash of thigh and white knickers. He looked at her and smiled, she turned away from his gaze with a look of disdain. He glanced at the flashing sign; Bond Street was the next station, and his stop.

He got off and headed for the Jubilee line to catch a train to Westminster. The noise of the trains had rekindled his headache, and he rubbed his forehead, praying the day would go quickly so he could get home and back under his duvet. The two stops to Westminster went in a flash and he was soon walking briskly up the multitude of stairs in the modern steel-and-tube chasm of a station. When he strolled out into the fresh air, a wave of nausea hit him. He struggled round the side of the road and stopped, took deep breaths, and felt a bit better. His forehead had become wet and clammy, so he wiped it and wondered whether he would survive the day. He gathered his thoughts and walked towards Westminster Road, where the Police assembly rooms were. He arrived, grabbed a coffee from the provided flasks, and heaped in three spoonful's of sugar. The heat of the brew perked him up and he felt better. He saw Max Groves, one of his friends, who had also been to the stag night.

'Max, you all right?'

Max spoke in a low voice, 'Feel like shit, mate, fucking shit.'

'Tell me about it. Never should have gone.'

'Yeah, but it was good crack wasn't it?'

Jeremy laughed. 'Yeah, it was.' He grimaced when the laughing made his head explode into renewed throbs.

'Do you want something?'

Jeremy felt momentarily startled. 'What, exactly?'

Max shrugged and glanced away. 'Just a couple of uppers to help you get through the day.'

'Uppers?'

Max whispered, 'Amphetamines. Just stimulants. They'll take care of the hangover.'

Jeremy had never taken any illegal drugs, but what the hell—anything to help him through the day.

He nodded. 'Yeah, give me a couple then.'

'Toilet.'

Jeremy followed Max to the gents'. Max took a small tin from his inside pocket, then produced three tiny white tablets and gave them to Jeremy.

He gave Max a quizzical look. 'Three?'

'You wanna get through the day or not?'

'Yeah, okay.'

They left the smelly toilet, and Jeremy grabbed another coffee then sat down at the back of the room. He popped the tablets and hoped he wouldn't fall asleep when the briefing started. It was standard stuff; they discussed the route, where there could be issues with traffic, where the back-up teams were, and the call sign for the day, which was 'energy'. Jeremy was a fully trained Taser officer, and at the end of the briefing he signed for, and collected, his Taser gun. The officers would start at Trafalgar Square and walk the march until they ended up back at the square, where there would be final speeches and then off home. The Met had scheduled it as a peaceful protest march, without any serious threat to public safety. As he left the room, he felt better and decided to ask Max for some more tablets for the future.

***

Scotty Ferguson and six of his mates had arrived at Trafalgar Square early in the morning. They were experienced Marxist protesters who had caused mayhem at various marches and demonstrations across the country and particularly in London. Before heading to the meeting point, they had disguised themselves enough to get past the police spotters and had only finally met up as a group at the square. They had decided that the energy companies needed some publicity and, although they say there's no such thing as bad publicity, violence at the protest would make all the newspaper headlines, which the energy companies would detest.

***

Jeremy had filed into one of the waiting police vans and was transported up to Trafalgar Square. The two-hundred police officers on duty would marshal an expected crowd of three thousand. Jeremy felt content to just stand about and look as though he was interested, which in reality he was not. As soon as the protesters left the square, he would be allocated a walking spot and that would be it ... dead easy money for not doing much.

***

David Kane arrived at Trafalgar Square at ten, met up with Mary Bishop by the Golden Boy Statue, and they chatted away as usual about all sorts of things. They walked around the Square admiring the other statues, Mary slipped her arm into David's, and he enjoyed that very much. Mary was petite and charming, and David felt a growing attraction to her. They chit-chatted about family, about the weather and, lastly, about the cost of Gas and Electricity. The opening speeches were boring and they could hardly hear.

Once the speeches finally ended, the march set off down Whitehall. David and Mary slotted into the rhythm of the march, occasionally waving their banners in the air and self-consciously shouting a *yes* or a *now* in answer to the leaders' shouts at the front. The march stayed well behaved as it snaked down Whitehall and onto the square outside the Houses of Parliament. The leaders at the front stopped to talk to waiting MP's, and the marchers at the back caught up and created a bottleneck. Traffic on the roundabout came to a standstill. Before anyone knew exactly what was happening, car windows were being smashed and smoke grenades had been thrown. Protesters and members of the public ran in all directions. The police reserve, parked down nearby side streets, were mobilised and headed straight to the scene.

***

Scotty and his mates had blended in with the crowd and then dispersed to different areas, they started by smashing windscreens with small steel batons they had carried for exactly that purpose. Then the smoke bombs had gone off—causing absolute chaos—car horns blared, people ran here and there, and complete pandemonium reigned. Then the Marxist individuals threw stones and rocks at the police. Two Officers went down with head injuries and faces plastered in blood. The situation spiralled out of control. The number of marchers looked to be nearer nine thousand than the estimated three. Scotty and his crew influenced others in the crowd, and scores of younger protesters united in the rock throwing and attacking of cars.

***

David and Mary felt shocked and frightened, stuck in the middle of the crowd, and desperately tried to make their way to the edge to get away from the smoke and rocks. David placed a protective arm around Mary's shoulder and attempted to guide her as best he could. Thousands of bodies pushed and shoved in all directions and it was complete bedlam. David and Mary had nearly made it to the edge of the huge swathe of protesters. Not far now.

***

The police at New Scotland Yard watched everything in real time via street and mobile cameras. They identified the troublemakers quickly and radioed descriptions and locations to the officers at the scene, who were then instructed to grab the ringleaders in the hope it would stop the chaos.

***

Jeremy's head banged. The pills had been working but, as soon as the smoke and rocks started to fly, the effect seemed to disappear. A rock whistled by his head and hit the officer next to him, and he had a huge gash in his head and looked unsteady on his feet. Jeremy shouted for assistance and two officers dragged the hurt man off. A ringleader had been identified as being near to Jeremy and he and two colleagues were tasked to go in strong, snatch the man, and make a hasty retreat back. The noise of thousands of protesters, most seemingly baying for police blood, created a maelstrom of noise and an atmosphere of danger and menace. Jeremy was suffering: he felt sick and sweated profusely. He grabbed his two colleagues and shouted to them.

'We don't stop for anyone. If there's trouble, use maximum force to get out.' To emphasise his words and to reassure them, he lifted up his baton in one hand and Taser gun in the other.

Jeremy shouted, 'One, two, three.' And they charged into the crowd towards the identified Marxist troublemaker. The crowd closed around them, trying to stop them moving, which caused even more problems as people fell and got trampled on. Jeremy and his two colleagues were stuck and unable to move forward. He was about to call off the snatch when he felt someone grabbing his leg and trying to pull him down. Mary had fallen and had grabbed at the nearest person to stop herself from hitting the floor. Jeremy thought he was under attack and kicked viciously at the person hanging onto his leg. He struck Mary in the face with his steel-toed boots and shattered her teeth and mouth. Blood flew in all directions as he leant down and hit her sharply around the head three times with his rock-hard rubber baton.

David shouted and yelled, to no avail, 'Leave her alone. It's a woman. Stop it, for God's sake, stop.'

Jeremy brought back his arm to once again smash her with his baton, but before he could, David had grabbed his hand and screamed at him to stop. Jeremy had gone—his mind told him to hurt anybody who got in his way—he pushed David away and brought up the Taser gun, aimed it at David, and fired. The prongs hit David fully in the chest, the electric shock surged through his body, and he jerked then collapsed into a heap on the floor. Jeremy didn't even look. The crowd surged towards him, intent on grabbing him, but he was strong, and pushed his way back and out of the crowd and was soon safe behind police lines.

***

David and Mary got trampled on even more as the crowd went wild, seeking vengeance for the perceived inappropriate and unlawful force the police were using.

***

The control room at New Scotland Yard was calm but still on edge. A fair number of the demonstrators had dispersed in all directions, which made it easier for the police officers. A sudden shout had all eyes centred on one of the camera shots, where a crowd of people were on their knees tending to two injured demonstrators. Some of them jumped up and shouted at police officers. The camera zoomed in and a man was seen pumping the chest of an elderly man lying prostrate on the concrete road. Next to him laid an elderly woman who looked unconscious and whose face was covered in blood.

'Shit,' Commander Fellows said as he pushed his hair back from his forehead. 'Just in case no one's done it, call an ambulance and be quick about it.'

Fellows went back to studying the film, still showing the man on the ground, and thought he was dead. He couldn't be sure about the woman, but she looked seriously injured. Police officers made their way to the scene and arrived a minute later. They pushed the crowd back and cleared a path so that the ambulance could get through as quickly as possible. First to arrive was a paramedic on a motorbike; he jumped off his bike and a policeman was seen to speak to him, he then went straight to the man lying on the ground. He felt for a pulse and shook his head, then grabbed his box and took out the defibrillator, turned the machine on, ripped the shirt off the body, and held the two pads. He tensed his hands and applied the pads to the man's chest. He held them for a second, and then the man jerked up as an electric current surged through the body. The paramedic applied the pads again, and the body once again jumped into the air, but still no change could be seen. The paramedic tried one last time, but to no avail—the man was gone. He shut the eyelids and covered his face with a towel. It was over. The paramedic glanced over to the woman. Two ambulance men tended to her. The first paramedic shouted something, which Commander Fellows couldn't hear on the silent camera feed. All he could do was watch while a brief conversation shot back and forth between the ambulance men.

Commander Fellows was beside himself. 'Everybody out of the room, now. Apart from you, Philip. Some fucking quiet demo about energy costs. Rewind that film. I want to see what happened, from the beginning.' Everyone left, except Philip Black and the video operator.

The room felt eerily quiet while the film rewound, and the two men's eyes stayed fixed on the screen. The operator stopped the film, and the elderly man and woman could be seen clearly as they moved through the crowd towards the edge of the demonstration. Anyone watching the film would assume they were trying to get away from the violence and the huge swaying crowd. A group of police officers then appeared, heading into the crowd just in front of the couple. Fellows turned to Black and said, 'They're going in to extricate a troublemaker.' Then to the operator, he said, 'Slow the film down.' The crowd pushed in every direction and the old woman fell. The police officer in front reached her at the same time and she grabbed at his leg for support. Fellows was shocked when he saw the officer bring his leg back and kick the woman in the mouth, smashing her face. He then bent down and hit at the woman's head with his baton. The horrible sight looked even worse seen in slow motion. Fellows watched while the old man grabbed the officer's hand to stop him hitting the woman any more. The officer pushed him away and drew his Taser gun. A gasp came from behind Fellows, and Philip shouted, 'Oh God.' The Taser prongs hit the man and, a second later, he lay prone on the ground.

'Shit,' Fellows said. 'I want the original in my office, *now*. No copies. I want to know the name of the officer who fired the Taser and I want him here at 9am tomorrow morning.' He looked at the operator and Philip Black.

'Nobody is to breathe a word of this—do you understand?' He eyeballed each in turn.

They nodded and whispered affirmatives.

'Get back to work.' He strode from the room and went towards his office.

CHAPTER 3

Simon Kane had become slightly concerned that he had not heard from his father. His dad would always phone when he got home from a protest to say he was all right and to tell him how it had gone. Seven o' clock had crept around, and he had been expecting a call at about six. He told himself not to worry and sat down to eat his late meal: a Birds Eye frozen Roast Chicken TV Dinner. He sat at his tiny Formica-topped table in the small lounge that served as dining table, jigsaw puzzle table, map table, war games table, and everything else table. Halfway through his meal, the doorbell rang. Who the hell could that be at this time of night? He took the two short steps to the front door, undid the double lock, and pulled it open. Blue police uniforms met his shocked gaze. A female and a male officer stood on the step, looking apprehensive.

'Good evening. What can I do for you?'

The male officer spoke in a subdued, concerned voice, 'Good evening. Are you Mr Simon Kane?'

This startled Simon—what the hell was going on? 'Yes, I am. What's happening, officer?'

'Can we come in, please, Sir?'

The way the officer had spoken unsettled Simon, and he stood aside to let them in.

The police officer took a deep breath. 'Your father is Mr David Kane, of Kneads Close, Bookham?'

'Yes, that's correct.' Simon had a terrible feeling that dreadful news was coming.

'I'm afraid there's been an accident. There is no easy way to tell you. I'm so sorry to tell you that your father suffered a massive heart attack at the energy demonstration in London today and died at the scene.'

Simon just stood there. He couldn't speak. Couldn't move. Time had stopped. Life had stopped. He laughed.

'I think there has been a misunderstanding. My father left home this morning to go on a peaceful demonstration and he'll be phoning me any minute.' He looked at his watch. The female police officer put her hand on his arm and guided him to a chair.

'I'm so sorry, Mr Kane, but it's true that your father has gone. I know it's so difficult to take this in, but it's the truth.' The officer rubbed his arm in an attempt to comfort him.

'We need you to identify your father,' the male officer said.

Simon was in another world, looking around the room but not seeing it. 'Dad was coming over for some dinner tomorrow—I got some mince in. I was going to cook a cottage pie with cheese on the top. It was one of his favourites.'

The female officer looked at her partner. They had seen it all before. Some people accepted it straight away, some screamed and collapsed, and some talked complete rubbish; you could never tell.

She tried to get Simon's attention, 'The car is outside. We can take you now—it would be for the best, if you're up to it? Is there someone who could accompany you? Perhaps a friend, a neighbour, or another member of the family?'

'There's no one.' Simon closed his eyes and thought of his father lying in some chilled steel draw, or on a table with a white sheet draped over him.

'Was it quick? Did he suffer?'

The female officer answered softly, 'I can't say anything, because we don't know the details. Do you want to put a coat on?'

Simon couldn't move. The male officer looked around, grabbed a coat hanging on a peg on the back of the front door, and helped Simon into the jacket. He took hold of Simon's arm and led him toward the exit. The female officer checked that the back door and windows were locked, and joined her colleague and Simon just as they left the property.

Simon revived enough to ask, 'Where are we going?'

The male officer answered, 'To the Westminster Public Mortuary on Horseferry Road. It'll take us about an hour.'

'Is Mary with him?'

The female officer asked, 'Is Mary his partner?'

'No, just a friend. They would have been together at the demonstration.'

They looked at one another, before the policewoman said, 'I'm sorry, Mr Kane, we have no reports on other individuals.'

'Dad was a good man—one of the best.'

The policewoman smiled. 'I'm sure he was. How old was he?'

'Sixty-eight. At least he had a reasonable innings, I suppose. But he was fit … a heart attack seems unbelievable.' Simon shook his head.

'We'll soon be there, and then you can say goodbye properly.'

That set Simon off and he couldn't stop the tears; floods poured down his cheeks as he sat and sobbed for his lost father.

'The worst thing is …' He paused. 'I would like to have said goodbye, told him I loved him, and thanked him for all he did for me.' He looked at the female officer. 'You said he didn't suffer, and that it was quick?'

'I told you exactly what I was told, and that was that your father suffered a heart attack at the demonstration. A paramedic attended the scene but, unfortunately, he could not be saved.'

Simon sat back and shut his eyes, seconds passed, and he wanted to wake up. Perhaps it was all a bad dream. But when he opened his eyes, he saw the two police officers and knew it was real.

The policeman spoke from the front of the car, 'Five minutes and we'll be there.'

Simon took a deep breath and tried to calm his nerves; he shook at the thought of seeing his naked father laid out on some slab.

Not long after they passed the Horseferry road sign, they pulled into a courtyard in front of a small hospital-type building. The male officer parked the car, jumped out, and opened the back door for the policewoman and Simon to vacate. Simon didn't want to move: if he didn't go in then he might still wake up. Lights shone from the building and illuminated the darkness. Simon shuddered at the thought that dead bodies would arrive throughout the day and night—every day and every night—a conveyer belt of endless dead bodies.

'Mr Kane, are you ready now?'

Simon collected his thoughts. 'Yes, of course.' He climbed out of the car, determined to be strong and show some British stiff upper lip. The policewoman took his arm and walked him to the entrance, where they entered into a reception area, which looked as though they had tried to make it a friendly environment with quiet calming blues, but nothing could take away the fact that he'd come here to view a dead loved one. Simon sat in one of the chairs and looked around. An elderly woman was seated close by, quietly sobbing, and dabbing her face with a pink floral hanky. He felt an arm on his shoulder.

'This way, please, Mr Kane.'

Simon stood and the tears started again. This was it: the moment of truth. Maybe, when they pulled the cover back, it wouldn't be him. He walked next to the female officer. Well, he wasn't so much walking as staggering along, white faced. They reached a door marked 'Mortuary. Authorised personnel only'. The cold hit him as soon as he entered. It felt like a walk-in fridge. He supposed it kept the bodies from decomposing, and looked at the wall of draws along the right-hand side. A man in a white coat approached.

'This way, please,' he said as he checked his clipboard.

He stopped and held the handle to drawer number 34, but waited until Simon stood next to him.

'I'm going to open the drawer and pull the sheet back. Please identify the body. Do you wish to have a moment with the deceased?'

'Yes, on my own, please.'

'Of course. Ready?'

'Yes.'

The drawer rattled when the man pulled it open, then he pulled the white sheet away from the face.

Simon gasped, then composed himself. 'Yes, it's my father.' More tears flowed. He looked peaceful, serene, in his death—even with his colour changing almost in front of his eyes, the ash-grey taking over. The man in the white coat disappeared and Simon stood looking at his father.

'Dad, I love you so much.' The tears continued to pour. 'Why did you have to go? We had so much still to do.' Simon pulled the sheet down slightly, leant down, and kissed his father on the forehead. He felt cold and slightly clammy to the touch. He lifted the sheet to pull it back up and saw some marks, so he pulled the sheet back down and was shocked. He jerked back when he saw his father's chest and stomach covered in black, yellow, and blue bruising. 'Jesus.' He couldn't take his eyes from the awful sight. How on earth did he get such terrible bruises? Then he realised that they would have worked on his chest to try to get the heart started again, and that would have caused it. Of course, that was the obvious explanation.

Simon turned and walked towards the exit. He met up with the policewoman in the reception area.

'What happens next?' he asked.

'I've been told there will be an autopsy to confirm the cause and manner of death, then the body will be released to you for burial. You'll need to contact a funeral director to pick up and store the body. It will all take a few days. Shall we get you home, then?' She took hold of his arm and steered him towards the exit and their car.

Simon slumped back in the rear of the car, mentally exhausted.

'I never finished my chicken dinner, you know?'

The policewoman took it in her stride. 'We could always stop and pick something up, if you like.'

Simon didn't answer, he was away somewhere else. Then he noticed a Kentucky fried chicken. 'Let's get some chicken!'

The male officer looked pissed off, but did stop on the double yellow lines right outside. Simon dashed out and ran into the shop. He came back with a huge bucket of chicken.

'Who wants some chicken?' he shouted, and laughed.

The two officers said they had meals to go home to and declined. Simon ate two mouthfuls and threw the bone back into the bucket.

'I'll eat that later.'

They eventually arrived back in East Horsley. The female officer saw Simon into the flat.

'So, Mr Kane, the Public Medical Examiner's Office will be in touch with the date of the Autopsy, and will let you know when you can arrange to pick up the body. Keep your chin up, eh, time is a great healer.'

CHAPTER 4

Jeremy Hope sat in a secret meeting room on the fifth floor of New Scotland Yard. He had gotten home from the demonstration aware that he'd injured someone with the Taser Gun, but without realising the result. He had slept for ten solid hours. His wife had answered the phone at nine p.m., and someone from Scotland Yard wanted to speak with her husband on a matter of great urgency. She'd woken him and he was told to report to New Scotland Yard at nine a.m. the next morning. Now he sat sweating and waiting for whomever to turn up. Eventually, someone came and took him to a meeting room where he found two senior officers seated behind a desk. The curtains had been drawn and darkness cloaked the room, so he couldn't see them very well.

Jeremy sat in a hard, straight-backed chair in front of the desk.

One of the men spoke, 'The first thing we are going to do is watch a tape.'

A television on the wall burst into life and Jeremy watched, transfixed. It took him a second to realise that he was watching the demonstration. Jesus, something terrible must have happened. Then the film went into slow motion and he saw himself pushing into the crowd, he then watched himself kick the woman in the mouth, shattering her teeth, and then he commenced hitting her in the face with his baton, and a man then grabbed his arm to stop him attacking the woman. God alive, he shot him at point blank range with the Taser Gun and the man went down. The man didn't move, and then the paramedic turned up and rushed to assist. He watched, dumbfounded, as the paramedic placed the pads on the man's chest, and him jerking, and then it was over. The man had a sheet over his face … dead. Jeremy held his head in his hands. *God, what have I done?*

'Please, wait in the other room. We'll call you when we're ready.'

***

Jeremy left the room and, as the door shut, Commander Fellows spoke to his Deputy, Philip Black.

'Do you think he's up to it?'

'Christ, I have no idea, his record is good, the crux is he will either be kicked off the force and could even go to prison, or join us.'

Commander Fellows sat in quiet thought then eventually spoke, 'Look, if this becomes common knowledge, my transfer to a political life will be over before it's even begun, and you can kiss your promotion to Commander goodbye. You'll be counting paperclips for the rest of your career.' He paused for a moment. 'So, we'd better ask him, then.'

Black walked to the door and said they were ready for him.

***

Jeremy wondered what was happening, but one thing he did feel was that things were not exactly going through official channels.

'Officer Hope, I am Commander Fellows and this is my Deputy, Philip Black. You've been a right fucking idiot, haven't you.'

'I'm not sure what ...'

Fellows raised his voice and eyeballed Jeremy. 'Let me explain to you a couple of facts: there is a dead body in the morgue and a lady in the hospital with horrific facial wounds because of you.' He raised his voice even more. 'You are a menace. You were totally out of control.' Fellows then thought of something else, 'We know about the drugs, and that you were as high as a fucking kite, you prat.'

A silence followed, until Jeremy broke it. 'So what's going to happen to me?'

Commander Fellows looked at him and moved his head forward.

'Now that is the fucking question, isn't it?'

More silence.

'Well, we can suspend you right now, pending an investigation by Internal Affairs—there's no doubt you will be kicked out of the force and could even go to prison.'

Jeremy held his head in his hands, thinking about the disgrace, his family, and that they could lose the house. Then it hit him that something else was up, and that's why he was here. There was something else; he looked up.

'Or … ?' was all he said, but the look on Fellows' face said he knew they had their man.

'Or, you could cooperate with us in making sure the Metropolitan Police retains its good name and continue with your work as a police officer.'

Jeremy was shocked at the cover up; they were saying they would hush the whole thing up.

'And what do I have to do? You obviously want something from me—what is it?'

Fellows spoke in a much friendlier tone, 'Jeremy, there are reasons of national security why this should not be all over the newspapers, and you will have to play your part in ensuring that such publicity does not happen.'

They had him lock, stock, and barrel. If he said yes, he had some idea of what they could ask and he would have no choice but to do their bidding.

'It looks like we'll be working together then.' He gave a half-smile, half-grimace.

'Good, then we understand each other. Now, as to the future, you go back to work as normal, all contact will be through Philip. Do not even think of ever contacting me again, is that clear?'

'Very clear.' He got up and left, knowing that in the future he would have to pay the price. As he left, he overheard the commander speaking, 'Philip, there are numerous things you have to do and do quickly. Call in favours, get our people working on this as a matter of urgency, and I'll get on with

Blue Cover Up   Chris Ward

my part. Call me tonight at, say, seven and we can see where we are.'

CHAPTER 5

Detective Inspector Karen Foster was flying high; it had been six months since she'd solved the Surrey Serial Killer case. The two psychopaths, Duncan Fowley and Terry Boxer, languished in Broadmoor high security psychiatric hospital with no hope of ever being released. Toby Moore, the green-snake-in-green-grass Police Constable at Epsom, had received ten years for Paedophile activity but would probably only do five, and would serve his time under protective administration, as he would be a target for violence from every other inmate whilst serving every minute of his sentence.

Things had certainly quietened down since the bloody killings that summer, and Karen had gotten what she'd been after: six months of policing the local community where the gravest crimes were bike and mobile phone thefts. Karen met her ex-partner, Chau, in the town centre occasionally and it always brought back painful memories of the terrific times they'd had in the past. Chau was still with Roberto, the café owner, and they made a splendid couple living and working together twenty-four-seven. Karen had split up with Roger Carter and had been single for months, although not without sexual gratification, which she acquired from several sources. She had become firm friends with Geraldine, Chief Inspector Gary Park's wife, and they often met for coffee at the weekends. Karen liked to think she had won over the male officers at Epsom Police Station, and was now firm colleagues with Sergeants Mick Hill and Fergus O'Donnell, who she considered to be her right-hand trusted lieutenants.

Karen still lived at the flat in Alexandra Road near Epsom town centre. She had found the money to have it decorated in beige and cream colours, and splashed out on a new multi-shades blue three-piece suite, which she had bought on credit from DFS. She cooked Asian meals—a throwback to the Chau days. The big problem had been, and still was, booze; she enjoyed a glass or three of red wine and had also taken to knocking back Pernod and Orange squash with ice like it was going out of fashion. She drank to excess when at home on her own, drank to excess when she went out to a club, and had even been known to get stuck into a bottle of red in the office during the afternoon. When she weighed up her life, she always felt thankful for a job she loved, so all she had to do was sort out her personal life and all would be well, but that was far easier said than done.

Today, Karen was sitting on the side of a hotel bed while Friday stood undressing. He had removed all his clothes apart from his white boxers, and Karen admired his muscular physique. She stood and went to him, crouched down, tucked her thumbs into the sides of his shorts, gripped them, and pulled them down nice and slow.

'Jesus, what the hell?' She found herself looking at the hugest cock she had ever seen, and it wasn't even erect.

With a grin, she took hold of it and felt its weightiness, then she lifted it towards her mouth, took him in, and filled herself as much as she could. She stroked it in and out, in and out, then dribbled saliva on the head until it became slippery, and then she continued to pump it.

Karen Foster had met up with Friday, a six-foot-four black Ghanaian man, at the Travel lodge in South Croydon. She'd been drinking one night at home and messing around on sex dating sites when she stumbled upon Friday advertising himself as an available stud for hire.

Friday moaned as Karen continued to suck and caress his cock with her mouth.

While she masturbated him, she looked up into his eyes. 'I won't be able to take all this in my pussy you know, it's too big.'

Friday smiled, which showed his fabulously perfect white teeth. 'Don't worry, you're going to love it, especially when I stick it up your arse.'

Karen didn't say anything, but she was *not* having that thing up her arse and that was for certain.

Friday grabbed her shoulders. "Bout time you showed me what you got.'

Karen stood up, moved a step away, pulled her dress over her head, and threw it onto the bed. She wore a matching set of sexy black underwear. Friday seemed to be impressed, and it showed, as his cock stood up and saluted when Karen pulled her knickers down to reveal a beautiful shaved pussy.

She lay on the bed, opened her legs, and played with herself. Friday climbed onto the bed and went down on Karen, licking and slurping. Apparently, he was so excited he couldn't wait, and he moved between her legs then held his cock at the entrance to heaven. Karen felt more than a little apprehensive when she saw he was about to enter her. She lifted her arse and moved it provocatively in front of his massive weapon.

'Gently, please.'

He smiled, and then gently pushed his swollen cock into her entrance. Her muscles stretched and it felt slightly painful but not unpleasant. He pushed in oh-so-slowly until she was filled, then pulled back and began the rhythmic in and out that would soon have Karen screaming with pleasure.

They fucked for three hours and Karen had definitely had enough. She would be sore, but what the hell?—It was so good that she didn't mind, and it would remind her later so she could remember it all over again until the next time. She'd told Friday she wanted to see him again and he was all for it, of course, as Karen had given him a really good time.

On Saturday afternoon she headed back to Epsom. Her personal life was more of a mess than ever. It seemed that since splitting up with Chau, things had spiralled downhill. She drank far more than was sensible, and the only way she could get a fuck was to contact strangers on the net. Being on her own, she would probably hit the bottle when she got home, and wake up in the morning with a very bad head. Perhaps she would contact Geraldine, Chief Inspector Park's wife, and see if she was free for a drink. Surely that had to be better than drinking alone?

CHAPTER 6

Mary Bishop had lost four teeth, had nasty cuts to areas of her gums, her left eye had swollen closed, and the rest of her face had been severely bruised. She had been admitted to St Thomas Hospital in central London and, although badly shaken, she was recovering quickly. The Monday morning after the Demonstration, a man arrived to see her. He looked smartly dressed, in a dark blue suit complimented by a crisp light-blue shirt and dark blue spotted tie, and he even had a blue handkerchief hanging out of the top pocket. He was handsome, and spoke very well with an upper class accent and, she felt, would have generally been described as a good sort.

'Reasons of National Security, you say?'

'That's right, Mrs Bishop, or can I call you Mary, please?'

It was difficult for Mary to speak because her mouth was a mess; broken and lost teeth, gum damage, and severe bruising all over her face.

'By all means, call me Mary,' she stuttered.

'We feel that we have let you down, Mary, and would like to make it up to you. The Government would like to provide you with a luxury stay in the South of France for a couple of months to recuperate and then enjoy a holiday. How does that sound?'

'The South of France sounds wonderful, but I still don't understand why the Government should ...'

***

Theodore Taylor was a fixer, he had connections throughout the Conservative and Labour parties. He had done jobs for numerous business leaders, MP's even, and for the Prime Minister's office. He didn't need to know why wealthy Commander Fellows wanted to lavish luxury on the woman—all he had to do was make sure she accepted the offer and he would be handsomely paid.

'Because you deserve it, Mary. You've had a terrible time and the Government recognises its duty of care. A few months in France will do you the world of good. If you like it out there a great deal, maybe you could even stay.' Theodore hoped that would be the final carrot that pushed her and he was right.

'Well, whatever, I accept the Government's hospitality and am already looking forward to the good food and even more the excellent wines I shall be drinking.'

Theodore allowed himself a salacious smile; another big cheque would soon be landing in his account, plus a visit to the South of France—all expenses paid.

He sat with Mary for an hour and talked a great deal. That afternoon, a private ambulance left St Thomas and took Mary Bishop to Heathrow. An air ambulance, which resembled a private jet, flew her to the South of France, then a chauffeur drove her to a lovely townhouse in a quiet part of the town. Her no-expense-spared recuperation had begun.

Simon Kane had stumbled to his local shop to pick up the *Daily Mail* newspaper. The front-page headline transfixed him: *Protester dies at Energy Demonstration.* A picture of the demo crowd stampeding across the green outside the Houses of Parliament took up most of the page. Simon read the article ...

A sixty-eight-year-old man, David Kane, died of a massive heart attack at the London demonstration against Energy prices. He apparently had a weak heart and the stress of the violence brought on the attack.

Massive heart attack? The papers always liked to dramatize an event. *Weak Heart*—where the hell did they get that idea from? He was as strong as an ox. Simon felt bewildered and angry as he read on.

Several well-known Marxist agitators were present at the demo and are being blamed for the riots. The police are investigating and wish to speak to anyone who has information on the troublemakers and their possible whereabouts.

Simon had been in a nightmare-like world ever since the two police officers had knocked on his door that Saturday night. He wasn't a heavy drinker, but he had bought some whisky and had polished off most of the bottle—a huge amount for him. He still couldn't take it all in and, he reminded himself, he had to contact Mary Bishop to find out if she had been with his father when he died. The next news stated that the Autopsy had been carried out and that cause of death was a heart attack, and that nothing could have been done to save him. The body had been released to W H Truelove & Sons, the funeral directors in Leatherhead.

Simon had taken a week off work to arrange the funeral and it had been planned for three days later on the Thursday. He had tried to get hold of Mary Bishop at least three times, but she wasn't answering her phone. There would be no one at the funeral, and he was upset about that, but the thought that his father wouldn't know, somehow comforted him.

Simon's flat was a disgusting mess; he'd been living on frozen ready meals, he hadn't cleaned, and hadn't even thrown away the packaging that littered the floors. Two new full bottles of whisky replaced the empty one. Simon sat in his chair drinking whisky from his favourite small tumbler. In between the tumblers of whisky, he scratched his wrists and they soon became red raw and bled, so he had to wrap them in bandages. He had to go to his father's house ... there were things that needed to be done ... but he couldn't face it. Every time he thought about touching his father's clothes, he collapsed in a heap of sobbing. He wasn't ready. In truth, he didn't know if he would ever be ready.

CHAPTER 7

Jeremy Hope had gone home from New Scotland Yard knowing he had sold out to the devil in the name of Fellows and Black. One day there would be a call, or a package would arrive, telling him someone needed a chat: in other words, someone needed silencing. It seemed incredible to him that a man's death could be forgotten so quickly and that life had returned to normality as fast as it had gone haywire. He had nightmares and would wake up shouting, imagining that he was back in the middle of the demonstration, surrounded by a crowd baying for his blood, and trying to rip his arms from the sockets. He never told his wife anything other than that during his visit to New Scotland Yard he had been asked to do some secret work infiltrating Marxist organisations. He'd done that in case at some time he had to disappear quickly without a reasonable explanation. He returned to his beat in West London and got on with his job as best he could.

Now, in mid-February, smatterings of snow had fallen throughout London, creating picture-postcard images in parks and leafy lanes. The package had arrived by hand and been put through the letterbox at around nine p.m. Although Jeremy knew that this would happen at some time, it still came as a shock. He went up to his bedroom and sat on the bed, opened the large canvas envelope, and tipped the contents onto the duvet. One by one, he picked up the items. The first thing he picked up, a photograph, showed a young man, who must have been early-to-mid-twenties, scruffy, and a bit hippie looking. Without checking any further, he guessed this could be one of the troublemakers from the demonstration. He picked up the next item, a sheet of A4 paper, with a list of details down the side. He read the first paragraph, which stated that a Mr Mark Heenan, an unemployed Marxist revolutionary, had made a complaint by letter to his local police station. He questioned why no police officer had been brought to justice for the unlawful killing of the elderly man at the energy demonstration in London, in January. The letter had gone to the demonstration investigation team and had then been passed onto Deputy Commander Philip Black. Jeremy read down the list, which gave an address in Camden. It had a short handwritten note attached …

Jeremy, your first assignment: have a word and, if that doesn't work, then deal with the problem permanently. PB

Jeremy sweated as he read the words over and over again: *deal with the problem permanently.* He had no choice; he was—as they say—in a rowing boat without a fucking paddle. He collected the papers together and put them back in the envelope. He would buy a safe and keep them there; after all, you never knew if they might come in handy in the future. It would be easy for him to get time off, as Commander Fellows had included him in a new secret undercover team who were supposedly infiltrating Marxist and other agitator groups.

He disappeared from normal duties and thought about the best way to handle the situation. He also thought about disappearing permanently abroad with his family, but they would come for him and he couldn't risk putting his family in danger. When he thought about what he had to do, he shook … he'd never killed anybody in cold blood, and the prospect frightened him. He just had to hope he could find a way to reason with Mark Heenan, and persuade him to keep quiet or disappear for a year or two. The first thing he had to do was to establish contact, and the next morning he set out for Camden.

Soon, he found himself seated across the street from 36 Leicester Road. It never ceased to surprise and amaze him that children of middle class British parents turned into Marxist revolutionaries. He felt sure Heenan would not have a job, so he hunkered down for a possible long watch.

He got lucky at lunch time, after three hours of waiting, when the long-haired, scruffy, jean-and-duffle-coat-wearing young man came out of the house and started walking down the road. Jeremy felt undecided for a moment, follow or … no, he wouldn't: he had a feeling that Heenan was going to the local shops and would be back soon. He jumped out of the car, walked across the road, and climbed the steps to number 36. He rang the doorbell, and his copper's intuition was confirmed when no one answered the door. He laughed: the parents were out earning money to keep their middle class Marxist son in middle class comfort. He returned to his car and waited, praying that the boy wasn't off on some jolly, and would return soon. He only waited half an hour, then he saw Heenan striding up the road, eating what looked like a Dona kebab, and that was when it hit him and his breaths came rapidly, while tremendous panic overcame him. What exactly was he going to do? Did you play it by ear when you might have to kill someone? He wasn't ready. He couldn't go through with it. *'Fucking shit,'* he said out loud as he wiped his sweaty hands on his trousers. He thought of his wife, and Carrie, the new baby, and then reached into his pocket and felt for the three tablets he kept there. He pulled them out and threw them into his mouth, working to get some saliva to help swallow them. He had a regular supply of amphetamines from Max, which he popped on a regular basis, along with his wife's Fluoxetine for depression. He took deep breaths and calmed down: he would go and talk to the man and, if he wanted, he could walk out of the house at any time and deal with the problem later. He drove two roads away and found a parking space, then walked back to the house.

He knocked on the bright red door, and the man opened it. 'Hello, are you Mr Mark Heenan?'

'Yes, I am, what do you want?'

'I'm detective Jeremy Hope. I've come to talk to you about the letter of complaint you sent to Camden Police Station.'

Heenan looked edgy. 'Let me see your ID.'

Jeremy took an instant dislike to the man. He took out his badge and warrant card and presented them to Heenan, who took them and studied the details for a full ten seconds. Then Heenan opened the door wide and stood to the side.

'Thank you,' Jeremy said, and made his way into the house.

'Go straight through—the lounge is on the right-hand side.'

Jeremy turned into the lounge and sat on a single chair next to the door. Heenan sat opposite him and just stared.

Jeremy eyeballed Heenan. 'So, you made a complaint about an officer at the energy demonstration.'

'That's correct. I know what I saw, and the greatest purveyor of violence in the entire world, my own government, has covered it up. I cannot be silent.'

Jeremy took a deep breath. 'Are you sure of what you saw? Apparently, there was a lot of trouble and chaos at the time.'

'I've thrown my whole life on the scales of destiny. I saw an elderly man, one of our socialist brothers, shot down like a dog by an officer with a Taser gun.'

Jeremy didn't understand the scales of destiny bit, but assumed Heenan was spouting forth some Marxist bullshit, and he already felt pissed off.

'There are reasons of national security as to why it would be better if you forgot about what you saw.'

'Within a Socialist community there is no room for personal freedom and choice of spirit: what I saw is what I saw. Class exploitation has to stop. I am a proletarian revolutionist, a dialectical materialist, and thus an irreconcilable atheist, and people *will* hear my voice.'

Jeremy had fast become sick of this idiot who thought he was so fucking clever.

'The reasons of national security make it impossible to pursue your complaint and, if you take my advice, you will just forget it.'

'The group is superior and more powerful than the individual. I belong to a group, and our voice will be heard in every city, every town, and every marketplace.'

Jeremy reeled; he hated this moron, and couldn't stand his voice. He had no idea what he was talking about and wanted him to shut up. His body swayed, he was tired—even though the tablets should be keeping him alert—and he shook his head.

Heenan continued his rant, 'You are part of the establishment, the ruling class, but don't you see you are being exploited? Break free of your shackles; join us in the struggle ...'

Jeremy reached into his side jacket pocket and felt the knife, but his vision had blurred, he shook his head again and he saw that Heenan was about to start speaking again. *No, I will not let him. I can't stand any more.*

He jumped up, took one stride towards the man, plunged the knife into his left eye, and pushed with all his strength. The six-inch razor-sharp blade slid through the eye and into the brain. Blood and brains trickled out while Jeremy held the knife in place, the man's legs thrashed, and he lifted his arms to push Jeremy away, but he had no power. Jeremy pulled the knife out and stuck it into Heenan's chest, aiming for the heart. Heenan stopped struggling, took one last breath, gurgled, and died. Jeremy heard the man's bowels open, and then the stench hit him. He stepped back and closed his eyes. Thank god it had gone quiet.

He stood still, and couldn't believe what he saw in front of him. Heenan sat in his chair with his head slumped over, and blood and brains oozing from his eye socket. Jeremy looked around: had he brought anything into the house? He didn't think so … everywhere was clean … he wore gloves … so, no fingerprints and no DNA. Time to go. He opened the front door an inch and looked out onto the street: all quiet, so he walked down the steps, turned left, and made towards his car.

By seven o' clock that night, Jeremy had been drinking heavily. He told himself it was a dream, until he heard the television news reporting a gruesome murder in Camden. It was real enough. He had done it, he had actually killed someone, and he took another gulp of neat Tequila. He sat back, and felt strong—even invincible—if he was asked to do it again, yes he could. Another slug of Tequila; anybody who got in his way would suffer just as that stupid bastard Marxist prat had; he drained his glass and reached for the bottle.

CHAPTER 8

(TWO YEARS LATER)

The thirty-something, short-haired brunette still looked attractive, with good legs, pert breasts, and that quintessential English-rose look that captivated so many men, young and old. The booze problem had not, as yet, affected her, but it could only be a matter of time. Detective Inspector Karen Foster sat in the lounge bar of the Leg of Mutton and Cauliflower pub in Ashtead Village. Her usual large red wine kept her company, and she was—of course—waiting for a man to appear. Karen had met him three months before, and he seemed an enigma to her. She loved his quietness, his apparent gentleness, and strength, in equal quantity. He always treated her kindly—a result of a troubled past that he had survived and come through stronger. He was a little older than her, but that didn't matter—she'd had to teach him about a woman's body as he was inexperienced, but she had enjoyed that—as only a teacher (whose pupils got brilliant end of year exam results after a hard year's studying) would understand. He'd listened and learned, and could now satisfy her every lustful requirement. He was five minutes late, which was unlike him. Karen took a sip of her red wine and looked towards the door just as it opened and he appeared. She smiled, stood up, and went to him, threw her arms around him, and gave him a hot kiss on the lips.

'Simon, you're late,' she said with a smile and a soft laugh.

'Sorry, got held up at work, but I'm here now.' He took her into his arms and kissed her fully on the lips, pushing his tongue into her mouth, while his hands wandered down to her bottom and he gripped each cheek and squeezed.

'Hmm, that's nice. So, you like my arse, then?'

'Karen, I love your arse more than ... more than all the tea in China!'

Karen laughed out loud. 'And that's a lot.'

'Yes, a lot, but you still haven't let me, you know, up the bottom.'

She squeezed his buttocks. 'Don't worry, it'll be soon. I'm looking forward to it.'

'Oh God, stop it, I've got a hard on already.'

'I'll take care of that for you later,' Karen whispered, as she squeezed his balls and cock with her hand.

They had, of course, met in a bar, and were thrown together in a whirlwind of wine and whisky and, when that ran out, anything alcoholic they could get their hands on.

The relationship had been difficult at first. They both drifted like flotsam in a huge rough sea, not knowing where they were or where they were going. It had been a massive struggle but, eventually, they had understood each other enough to establish a relationship. Both were good people who had allowed events, circumstances, and booze to dramatically affect their lives. Karen had taken time but had eventually given herself completely to Simon, fed up with the one-night stands, the empty feelings, and the low self-esteem that had almost driven her to suicide. He still had his flat in East Horsley, although he spent a lot of time at Karen's place in Epsom.

Simon had told Karen about his father's death and she had been suitably sorry. He'd come to terms with the loss, and actually felt happy that he'd had his father for such a long time when many didn't. Although he'd fallen in love with Karen, if you'd told him he would end up having a strong relationship with a woman police officer, he would have laughed and said it could never happen. They did all the usual things couples do: lunch and dinners out, sex in the flat, sex on the downs, sex in the car, sex on the bonnet of the car, sex in the layby, and even sex in the ladies' toilet at Epsom Library.

'So, what's new?' Simon asked.

'Same old. Locked up a couple of drunks, spoke to President Obama, ... a pretty quiet day really. What about you?'

'Same as you, quiet, had breakfast with David Cameron, spoke to gangster boy Putin, so not much to report.'

They both laughed and both were about to speak, but Karen got in first.

'So, we've both had the same old days we had yesterday and the day before that and—'

Simon butted in, 'Yes, and the day before, bla, bla …' they both continued to laugh and anybody watching them would have thought them a happy couple.

Simon went to the bar, got a pint of Carlsberg lager, and returned to Karen.

'So, it's back to your place and get the kit off then?'

'Simon, please, can we have some meaningful conversation about politics, religion, the economy?'

Simon stared at her with a huge cheesy-grin on his face, because he knew what was coming soon.

Karen continued, 'The local elections? I could go on, you know.'

He grinned some more. 'I'm well aware you could go on for a very long time if you wanted to.'

'Well, how about some sexy seduction? Some gentleness? Some loving whispers in my ear?'

Simon didn't answer, just smiled.

Karen threw her hands in the air. 'Okay, you win, we go back to my place, I rip my clothes off, and you fuck me senseless for hours.' She gave him a stern look, and finally laughed.

'Sounds perfect to me.' Simon raised his pint and clinked glasses with Karen.

CHAPTER 9

The end of February arrived, and everybody enjoyed the yellow daffodils and purple crocuses shooting up all over leafy Epsom. A bit of colour always cheered up the residents and Karen was no exception. She almost bounded into the police station on a bright, but still fresh, Monday morning. She said good morning to numerous civilians and police officers as she made her way to her first-floor office. Once settled, she asked Janet, her personal assistant, to organise a latte and she went to work on some paperwork.

Her mind soon wandered back to the previous night with Simon; she shook her head and smiled, the carrot had been huge and sooo bloody hard but it had been fun. Quickly, she dismissed those thoughts before she got completely horny again and would have to disappear to the toilet to masturbate. Instead, she worked her way through a boring pile of reports and almost wished for something serious to happen that she could get her teeth into.

Lunchtime came, and she felt like being sociable, so went down to the canteen. The homemade chicken and ham pie appealed to her, so she had that with broccoli. Karen left the till and looked round the tables, where she saw Fergus O'Donnell and Mick Hill, her trusted lieutenants, and headed for their table.

'Room for a small one?'

Mick piped up, 'Of course, boss, have a seat.' And he pulled the chair out for her.

'So, how are you two, and what's new?'

Mick and Fergus looked at each other and then at her and said in unison, 'Nothing.'

Karen wasn't surprised, because she would have heard of anything interesting coming in. While she looked at the two officers, she wondered if they were motivated and on top of things.

'Who's in the cells at the moment?'

Mick took the lead, 'No one of any consequence, that's for sure, although the guy who came in last night for being drunk and disorderly is quite entertaining.'

Karen smiled and, between mouthfuls of pie, managed to speak, 'So, there is some action. Tell me more.'

'Are you sure, boss? It's all bull … you know.'

'He's right, boss,' Fergus said. 'The bloke is a nutter, telling tall stories.'

'We haven't got anything else happening, so if nothing else we can all have a laugh.'

'Well, he talks non-stop about Marxism and Trotskyism. I swear I haven't understood a word he says.' They all laughed.

Karen was interested. 'So what's his name?'

'Scotty Ferguson, and he's a trouble maker with a capital T. He's been involved in trouble at demonstrations and marches all over the country.'

As soon as Karen heard that, her ears pricked up and she thought about Simon's father who had died at the energy demo in London two years ago.

'So what are the tall stories then?'

Mick waved his hand in dismissal of what Scotty had been saying.

'Firstly, he says there's been a massive cover up by the Met, and that at a demo a couple of years ago in London, a guy was supposedly murdered by a police officer and it's all been hushed up. Plus, wait for this, a friend of his has been murdered and he swears that was done by the Met as well to keep him quiet.'

Karen didn't think anything of it, but asked the question anyway, 'Did he mention what the demonstration was about?'

Mick looked thoughtful for a moment. 'Yes, he did ... what was it now? ... Oh yes, it was called the Energy Demonstration.'

Karen felt a chill down her spine; there was something in this—she could feel it and she hardly ever got it wrong.

'Are you all right, boss?' Fergus and Mick were surprised by the look on Karen's face.

'Yes, I'm all right, but I do want to interview this Scotty character. Fergus, go and organise it ... full taping, the works. Mick, come with me.' Food lay forgotten on the table as the three of them left the canteen.

Karen and Mick went up to her office, and she went straight onto the internet and Googled *Energy Demo.* A long list came up within a second. She chose one and clicked on it, a headline appeared on the page: *Man dies of massive heart attack at Energy Demo. A Mr David Kane died after suffering a massive heart attack at the chaotic and violent Energy Demonstration held in London today.*

Karen sat back, shocked. Why on earth would this Scotty be making such serious allegations? It felt nothing short of astounding, and she couldn't take it all in, but stood up and looked at Mick.

'Let's go. We may have something interesting to do after all.'

Mick looked confused, but followed Karen back out of the office to interview Scotty.

Karen and Mick plonked themselves in the CID office, waiting to hear that Ferguson had been taken to the interview suite. Mick Fidgeted, and couldn't wait any longer. 'So, what the hell is going on, boss?'

Karen thought for a second—no need to make a fool of herself. 'I want this interview conducted in a professional manner. At the moment, I'm not going to say anything else, but these accusations have to be looked at seriously and recorded.'

Fergus stuck his head through the doorway. 'Ready to go, boss.'

Karen and Mick stood and made for the door. Karen spoke to Fergus as they left the office, 'Watch from the viewing room and concentrate on exactly what he is saying. Think about what he isn't saying as well.' Karen turned to Mick. 'Don't speak unless I ask you to, okay?'

Mick nodded, a disbelieving look on his face. She had surprised the two officers by getting so involved. Karen strode into the interview room, then looked straight at Scotty Ferguson, to get some sort of measure of the man. He appeared scruffy, with long hair, jeans, and a tee shirt. She looked at the writing on the shirt: *Marxism rules.*

Not in here mate, she thought. 'Mr Ferguson, good afternoon, I am Detective Inspector Karen Foster of Surrey Police, and this is Detective Sergeant Mick Hill. We wish to interview you in connection with your complaints against the Metropolitan Police, and we will tape the meeting. Did you understand what I have just said?'

'Jesus, I've been to university. I understand simple English.'

'You would be amazed at the people we see. I … anyway, it is thirteen twenty-three and the interview is commencing.' She looked at the detainee. 'Mr Ferguson, you have made some references to the Energy Demonstration, held in London some two years ago. Would you repeat those, please?'

Karen put the ball squarely in his court, and wanted to hear what he had to say. She sat back, and Ferguson took a deep breath.

'We'd travelled up separately, so as not to get spotted—six of us. We were there to add, shall we say, some grit to the proceedings. Thousands more turned up than anticipated, so the police presence was inadequate, to say the least. The six of us split up into different areas and we confronted the police lines peacefully.'

'By chucking bricks at police officers?' Mick interrupted, angry.

Karen just glanced at him and he lowered his head, remembering what she had said.

'Please, carry on, Mr Ferguson.' Karen offered him a smile.

'The crowd was running, stampeding in every direction, I was caught up in it, and was making towards the edge of the square to safety. I saw the man and woman running together. He had a protective arm around the woman, trying to keep her up and moving. The next thing, I saw her fall, and it was only then I saw the three policemen pushing through the crowd towards me. She'd fallen next to the officer in the front and I think she must have grabbed his leg, because he started kicking at her, then he smashed her in the face with his baton. Believe me, the copper was high on something, and it was a horrible sight, that poor woman.' He took a breath. 'Then I saw the man, who I know from the papers as David Kane, grab the policeman's arm to stop him attacking the woman. The officer lifted up his Taser gun and fired at near-point-blank range. It was murder, fucking murder.'

'Carry on, please.'

'The man collapsed to the floor and got trampled on by people running for their lives. The coppers just retreated back to their lines. The papers said he died of a heart attack, but that was a lie, he was killed by the copper who beat the woman senseless.'

Karen was thoughtful before she spoke. 'And what did you do the next day?'

'I knew they were after me, so I lay low. I could hardly start shouting about the Kane man and his girlfriend and drop myself in it.'

'Who else saw this happening?'

'I don't know. You have to remember it was chaos, and people were running for their lives; it was fucking madness.'

'You said a friend of yours was murdered recently, and that you think it was the Metropolitan Police?'

Ferguson nodded. 'He saw some of it and made a complaint to his local nick; next thing I hear is someone has shoved a knife through his eye, … police said it was a bungled burglary.' He laughed. Ferguson leant forward and looked Karen straight in the eye. 'You think this couldn't happen? Well, it has. I'm telling you the truth. You know what's going to happen when I leave here, they'll find me, I'll be killed or, more likely, it'll be a car accident or something similar.'

More than shocked, Karen actually believed him. 'What was his name?'

'Mark Heenan—a good, sound bloke.'

'Do you have any idea what happened to the woman? By the way, her name was Mary Bishop.'

Mick looked startled. Probably wondering how the fucking hell Karen'd known that. He sat up straighter in his chair and concentrated even more than he had been. Karen didn't miss it.

'All I know, is that she was taken to St Thomas Hospital. I heard rumours she was killed as part of the cover up.'

Karen had taken so much in, she was on overload.

'Mr Ferguson, I think a break would do us all good. Would you like some tea and biscuits, perhaps?'

'Yeah, cup of char would be great.'

'I'll organise it for you. We may well want to talk to you again.'

'I'm not going anywhere.'

Karen left the suite and went to the viewing room, where she all but collapsed into a chair. 'Fucking hell. What did you make of that?'

Fergus spoke first, 'I thought he was just trying to cause trouble, but the more you listen to him the more convincing he is.'

'Mick?'

'How did you know the woman's name was Mary Bishop?'

Karen thought of what to say. 'I have an interest in this case, that's if there is one, and that's all I can say at the moment. He is either the best liar I've ever met or there is some truth in what he says. How much, exactly, is another question. For instance, what's happened to Mary Bishop? How on earth someone could cover up something like this, as big as this, … it doesn't seem possible, and the death of this Mark Heenan seems suspicious.' Karen shook her head. 'I need to think.' She stood. 'I'll be in my office. I suggest you both get to work on finding out all you can about the Energy demo, but do not, I repeat, do not alert anyone to the fact that you are doing so, understood?'

Both Mick and Fergus said yes, and Karen left.

While Karen sat at her desk, twiddling a pen in her fingers, the phone rang.

'What? I'm on my way down now.' Karen leapt out of her chair and rushed to the stairs, took them two at a time, and smashed the door open into the CID office. Fergus and Mick were already there, deep in conversation.

'What the fuck is going on now?'

Mick looked up in shock as he answered. 'A special operations officer from New Scotland Yard is in reception.

Says she's come to collect Scotty Ferguson to help them with some enquiry.'

'What is going on here? Jesus, this is getting crazy. What on earth do Scotland Yard want with Ferguson? I tell you, I don't like it. The more I think about this the more it stinks. Well, she's not having him because I haven't finished with him. Mick, can we stop her taking him?'

'I don't know, but she can't just waltz in here and disappear with him. There are procedures, for God's sake.'

Karen ran her hand through her hair. 'Shit, I don't want to be too dramatic, but I'm worried for the boy's safety if we let him go.'

Mick looked unsure. 'This is Scotland Yard, for God's sake—surely he'll be safe?'

Karen shrugged. 'I'd better go and see her then.'

'I'll come with you,' Mick said. 'She's got two huge gorillas with her as back up.'

Karen shook her head in dismay. 'Let's go.'

Determined to be friendly—after all, they were all colleagues—Karen swept into reception. The woman and two huge, bear-like men sat on the blue chairs laid out for the public. Karen looked at the woman and made an instant decision that she was one of those hard-nosed, career-type Scotland Yard bitches that she detested. Karen gave her best smile as she approached the woman. 'Hello. I'm DI Karen Foster. I'm sorry, someone should have taken you through and given you some coffee.'

The woman stood up, her stature short and stocky. She wore a severe dark-blue trouser and jacket suit that looked far too tight.

'Carla Westburgh. No problem. We need to get away quickly, so no need to worry.'

'Okay, we need to have a quick chat. Can you follow me, please.'

The woman smiled and followed Karen into the small interview room next to reception. Mick hung around. The two women sat down opposite each other.

Karen studied Carla for a few moments, then asked, 'So, do you have a rank, Carla?'

'I'm a commander on secondment to a special operations team.'

'And what exactly do you want with Ferguson?'

'It's not your concern, but we need him to help us with some enquires.'

'To do with the Energy Demonstration a couple of years ago?'

Carla did not look happy. 'As I said, it's not your concern.'

The two women sat and stared at each other.

'Well, I haven't finished interviewing him, so perhaps you could come back in a couple of days.'

'That is impossible, I want him right now.' And with that she opened her bag, pulled out a piece of paper, and placed it gently on the table. 'My authorisation.' Her smile didn't reach her eyes.

Karen picked up the paper and read the first few lines ...
In the interests of National Security.
By order of the Commissioner of Police signed ...
By order of the Home Secretary signed ...
The individual, named Scot Ferguson, is required to be handed into the custody of New Scotland Yard ...
And so on and so forth ...

'Mr Ferguson has made certain accusations against the Metropolitan Police, which have been recorded. I hope he will be safe in your custody, or there could be repercussions.'

Carla leaned forward. 'Are you threatening me, you cunt? Be careful, very careful. You're out of your depth, love, so mind your own fucking business and get my prisoner.'

'No police officer has ever called me a cunt. You're dam lucky I don't put my fist in that ugly fat mug of yours, now go back and sit with your muscle while I check the authenticity of this document.' Karen opened the door and Carla marched back out and sat on another of the blue chairs. Karen went through to the offices, where she stopped to collect her thoughts. What was she doing? She'd almost attacked the bitch, which would have seen her lose her job. She had to get a grip of herself, and quickly.

'Boss, what's happening?' Mick asked as he joined Karen.

'What's happening, Mick, is that that bitch Westburgh, if that's even her real name, is going to take Ferguson and there's nothing we can do about it.'

Fergus appeared and seemed out of breath. 'There's a call for you from Guildford, Chief Inspector Park.'

'Fuck.' Karen went into the nearest office and grabbed the phone. She put the phone to her ear was about to speak but stopped.

'Yes, Sir, I understand. Yes, Sir, I'll do exactly that.' She put the phone down and said in a loud voice, 'Shit.' Then looked at her two fellow officers. 'Mick, get Ferguson signed out and given to that bitch Westburgh. There's nothing we can do, … hold on.' She thought for a second. 'Except, make sure you tell Ferguson to contact me the minute he is released by Scotland Yard.'

'Will do, boss.' He disappeared towards the custody suite.

Karen wanted to go back out and give that Westburgh woman a real mouthful, but decided against it. She would ignore her and hope that they would meet again one day in different circumstances. *Cunt … that bitch—she actually called me a cunt.*

Karen went back to her office and stood looking out of the window. She wanted to phone Simon, but thought better of it—she would have to think seriously about what she was going to do next in this unbelievable turn of events. Mick appeared an hour later to confirm Ferguson had gone, and that he'd had to be dragged into the car by the two goons, while he screamed that they were going to kill him. Karen was determined that this wasn't the end of it. She would make sure she found out what happened to Ferguson, no matter what it took. One thing was painfully obvious; powerful people were involved and she would have to tread with utmost care.

CHAPTER 10

'We have to be careful. Carla said DI Karen Foster at Epsom interviewed Ferguson and it was taped.'

Philip Black had sailed in the slipstream of Commander Fellows for twenty years, and he was his man. Black had performed jobs and covered up for Fellows for years and his future was inextricably entwined with his. Black always looked for the angle, and his first thought when meeting someone for the first time was always, *what can I get from this person? How can I use him to further my career and prospects?* Selfish in the extreme, he was a small, short man with stubby hands, and a face that was longer than normal, which gave him a strange appearance.

Commander Fellows twisted his mouth in a sneer and was without question in a foul mood.

'Who the fuck is this woman? Get the fucking tape. I want it destroyed, … wait, do it all officially through channels—part of the investigation. You know what to do. I've spoken to Park at Guildford—Surrey police will give us all the official help we need.'

'Okay, but what about the Foster woman?'

'Leave it for the moment and let's see if she makes a nuisance of herself, and if she does, then we can get Hope to deal with her. What's happening with Ferguson?'

'He's in custody. We haven't even interviewed him yet.'

Fellows laughed. 'What's the point in interviewing him? We know exactly what he's going to say.' Fellows smiled. 'I know exactly what's going to happen to that little shit. Now, listen carefully ...'

***

Commander Fellows stood at six-foot-two. A thin, wiry man with a small weasel-like head, he had piercing grey eyes, a larger than normal nose, and overly thin lips. He could be scary at the best of times, and terrifying when angry. He had disappointed his well-to-do parents by choosing the police force as his career of choice. The only reason he chose the police, was because he got off on power: raw, unadulterated power. Even when he'd been walking the beat as a young copper, he loved the feeling of power when he walked into a shop or onto a train. Everybody would look at him with respect or they would be frightened of him. The sensation felt remarkable, but he lost it whenever he wore his civilian clothes. He always carried his badge and warrant card, and would flash them at any excuse. The only time he should have flashed his badge and didn't was when a gang of thugs were threatening a couple with knives in Tottenham Court Road. Darkness blanketed the empty streets, and he could have gotten seriously hurt, which was not part of his plan and journey to New Scotland Yard.

His parents had known people who knew people, and he progressed up the ranks at an incredible rate—patronage from serving officers, politicians, and old school pals worked exceedingly well. He eventually got where he wanted to be, a commander's job at New Scotland Yard, and he planned to do that for a maximum of three years before parting for a political career. He'd been given the wink that a safe conservative seat would be found for him as soon as possible. It just went to show that huge donations to political parties could oil the wheels. He'd done two years and nine months, so only had three months to complete. The Energy demonstration, which he was in charge of, had gone tits up and he was desperate to get it buried before he left office.

***

'Officer Hope, how are you?'

Jeremy gripped the phone with white knuckles. 'Fine.'

'Well done on the recent visit to our friend; the boss was thrilled with the outcome.'

Black was talking about the killing of Mark Heenan, and the boss was Commander Fellows.

'Yes, well, I hope there won't be any more of those.'

'In our line of work, we can never say never.' Black gave a sick chuckle.

Jeremy held his voice steady, 'So, what can I do for you?'

'Oh, yes, the purpose of my call. Good news for you, young man, you're to be promoted.'

Jeremy was shocked. 'Promoted to what, exactly?'

'Well, we'll start with the rank of Sergeant and, hopefully, rapidly move on from there. How do you feel about intelligence work?'

'Never thought about it really, sounds fascinating.'

'Oh, it's very interesting, believe me. I assume you know about SO15?'

'Yes, it's the Counter Terrorism unit.'

'Yes, but it's a lot more than that. It is our main weapon in dealing with Terrorism, but also has fingers in many other pies.' Black slowed down and spoke with care, 'We have an interest in domestic extremism, which is what you will be doing initially. And, to facilitate that, you will be working in the sticks.'

'Oh, where exactly?'

'I'll let you know soon. You will be on secondment as a Counter Terrorism Liaison Officer, I'll get all the paperwork done, and you will start your new role on the first of March. I'll be in touch. Good luck.' And with those words, the phone went dead.

CHAPTER 11

Scotty had a deep, broad Scottish accent and when he spoke in London some people looked at him as though he was from outer space. He loved Scotland—no, in fact, he worshipped Scotland to the point of absurdity. His favourite film was Braveheart, which he must have watched at least twenty times, and when drunk (which was quite often) he had been known to stand up and recite the battle speech by Mel Gibson, Ad Infinitum, much to the chagrin of some. Whenever back home in Scotland, he wore a kilt—he belonged to the Fergusson clan. He wouldn't hear a bad word said about the glorious highlands, and God help any Scotsman who slagged off his homeland in his hearing.

At twenty-six, he had been living in London for three years, after leaving Aberdeen University where he had studied Political History. He was a fanatical member of the Scottish Nationalist Party and still viewed the English as an occupying Military force. Moving to London had only exacerbated the hatred of all things English. Scotty had recruited a band of like-minded individuals and was well known to the Metropolitan Police as a serious agitator who had been present at numerous Marches and Demonstrations throughout the UK. He had eventually received a banning order, which meant he was not to participate in any demonstration or march within London. He got round that by travelling incognito on his own and keeping in contact with his team by untraceable Blackberry messages. He had a low opinion of the average police officer, which he considered to be stupid and without imagination, and enjoyed goading them whenever and wherever he could.

Scotty had taken the time to call Epsom CID to inform Fergus that he was alive and kicking. Fergus said they would like to keep in touch, as Surrey Police were looking into his complaints. Scotty told him to fuck off and hung up.

Then Scotty made his way to one of the many squats that existed in London. One of his mates, Kenny, lived in a dirty, rundown council flat in South Norwood, and it had plenty of room, even if the place was a shit heap. Scotty arrived with his haversack and made himself as comfortable as he could—he was used to it and thought nothing of going days or even weeks without a bath or shower. He immediately made phone contact with his team and found out where they all were and what they were doing. As usual, someone had decided to go back home to Scotland, while another wanted to experience life and had gone off to Peru. Scotty could never understand why anyone would want to do anything other than fight for Scottish Independence and the cause of Marxism: his Peru would have to wait. He'd dabbled in drugs. If you lived the lifestyle he did, you were always going to mix with people who smoked Marijuana, took Crack, or even Heroin. He had avoided the serious drugs like the plague, had seen to many lives destroyed by addiction, and swore he would never go down that path. His life was simple: as long as he had a roof over his head, food in his belly, and the occasional half-decent shag, he was content.

Scotty decided to have a week off and spent time lazing in his smelly sleeping bag, going to the post office to draw his benefit money, having a pint in the local boozer, and eating his favourite Kentucky fried chicken.

***

In all the time since he had been released, he hadn't clocked the surveillance team watching him. He'd been designated a threat to national security, and Black had allocated two of his team to track and manage the target. The breakthrough came when Kenny was seen to leave the squat with his travelling bags, which meant that Scotty was on his own, and they had to act quickly before anyone else turned up to complicate matters.

Matt and Tony had done several jobs for Philip Black. While they detested the man, he had looked after them in their hour of need. Both would have been kicked off the force if not for Black, but they were repaying that debt in spades. This one would be messy and unpleasant, but orders were orders, and the bonuses came in handy.

Matt and Toby sat in the parked car, two hundred yards away down a side street. It was time, so they made their way to the squat and soon stood outside the front door. Matt carried a small holdall, which contained everything they would need.

The front door of the squat was damaged and weak, and they could hear noises—probably Scotty moving around inside. They looked at each other and, without saying a word, knew instinctively what to do. They each raised a leg and kicked the door, and with a mighty crash, it fell to the side, hanging on by one of the hinges. They marched in and yelled, *'Police. Stand still. Do not move.'*

Scotty froze on the spot. Matt came across him in the lounge, grabbed his arms, and pinned them behind his back while Tony put on a plastic tie.

'What the fuck do you two want? I've just been fucking released, you know.'

'Language, Mr Ferguson, please.' Matt gave a cold grin.

Matt pulled and lifted Scotty, then deposited him on the cat-urine-smelling, dilapidated green sofa.

'Jesus, you people live like fucking animals.'

'What do you bastards want?' Scotty glanced over to where Tony was taking a rubber tube and syringes out of a holdall.

'You fucking ...' He knew what was going on, so he leapt from the sofa and charged for the door. The move caught Matt unawares, but Tony reacted quickly, and grabbed Scotty by the arm and threw him to the floor. Then he took a handgun from a holster inside his jacket, and struck him on the back of the head. Scotty, out of it, collapsed to the floor in a heap.

'That'll make things easier then,' Matt said as he dragged the body back to the sofa.

Tony had finished setting up, and he checked to make sure he had everything he needed. Six dirty, used Syringes, a large plastic spoon, a rubber hose, a bottle of mineral water, a big chunk of Black Tar Heroin wrapped in a plastic bag, a near empty bottle of whisky, and a lighter. He nodded to himself; he was ready. 'Untie him.'

Matt undid the tie on Scotty's arms and pushed his head back onto the arm of the sofa. Tony moved the small table next to the sofa. He took the Heroin out of the plastic and the usual slight smell of vinegar hit his nostrils. He placed it on the plastic spoon. He then drew sixty units of water out of the bottle with one of the syringes, squirted the water into the spoon with the heroin, and applied heat from the lighter underneath the spoon.

Matt took the rubber hose, wrapped it round Scotty's right arm above the elbow joint, and tightened it. Tony found a beautiful vein sticking out of Scotty's arm like a lighthouse beacon at night. Ordinarily, you would then place cotton in the spoon to remove all the particles of rubbish that you didn't want to inject but, in this instance, Tony didn't bother. He took one of the syringes and drew the heroin in.

Scotty's eyes opened and he looked up at Tony. 'No, please.' He shook his head but was too drowsy to move.

Tony smiled then quickly pushed the needle into the vein and withdrew the plunger. When blood came out, he knew it was a good connection and pushed the plunger down, injecting the heroin. Matt and Tony stood back and watched Scotty die, he closed his eyes and appeared to be asleep, but was in fact in a deep coma within minutes. His heart stopped five minutes later.

Matt turned to Tony. 'Not a bad way to go, really.'

Tony just nodded in agreement. He then took the empty bottle of whisky and removed the top, tipped the small amount of whisky onto Scotty's lips, and threw the bottle onto the floor next to the sofa. He then threw the remaining syringes over the floor, creating a scene that would point straight to an overdose of heroin as the cause of death. They dusted themselves down and left the squat as though nothing important had happened; life was cheap in their hands.

CHAPTER 12

Fergus O'Donnell landed at Nice Airport at three in the afternoon. He'd dressed sensibly for cold English weather, but not for the wall of heat that hit him as he walked to the terminal building from the plane. He started sweating straight away, and decided he should visit a clothes shop to get some tee shirts and shorts as soon as possible. He sailed through customs and was soon in a taxi on his way to the Hotel Nicea—a three star budget establishment. He enjoyed the views and imagined how great it would be to live in a place like this all year round. He arrived at the white painted hotel, which seemed to glitter in the sunshine, surrounded by beautiful pink and crimson flowers, which Fergus couldn't name for love nor money. The hotel was at least three miles from the sea, thus the reason why it was so reasonably priced.

He made his way to the third floor, having to use stairs, and found room 31. It appeared clean and had everything he needed, so would be adequate. He sat on the bed and thought about how lucky he was to be in the South of France and travelling on expenses. Detective Inspector Foster had contacted the French Police Nationale and arranged for an officer to meet and support Fergus in his hunt for Mary Bishop. The French officer would arrive at the hotel that evening at about seven thirty. Fergus had been up early and decided to have a sleep. Instead of an afternoon sleep, he always referred to it as a 'power nap' so he didn't feel guilty. Fergus slept for two hours, longer than he had wanted, then got up and showered. When he'd dried himself off, he dressed in his usual conservative clothing of grey trousers and white shirt. He also squirted on lashings of deodorant. He wanted to give a good impression to the French police officer.

At ten past six, he took a short walk. It was a beautiful evening and he strolled down the road, taking in the sights and sounds of a vibrant and bustling community. He didn't want to go too far, so stopped at one of the many cafes to enjoy a small glass of chilled white wine. He loved the holiday atmosphere, and sat people watching as he sipped his drink. A woman walked towards the café and she caught his eye, maybe forty years old, but such grace, such movement. With short brown hair, she looked like a classic French beauty (whatever that was), and when she got closer he studied her even more: a short black skirt which, when she put her left leg forward, rose to show a glimpse of thigh and stocking top. He was in love. God, what a woman. She passed close to his table and smiled as she passed; he was totally dumbstruck, like a boy at his first time of asking a girl to dance. She sashayed past and Fergus felt a stirring in his groin. He sat a further ten minutes and enjoyed his wine. Oh God, imagine a night with the French beauty? He wished he knew her name so he could whisper it as he masturbated that night while thinking about her. A little later, he strolled back to the hotel. The receptionist called him over and said in broken English that he had a visitor who was waiting for him in the bar. It was only seven o' clock, so the French liaison officer was early. Fergus entered the bar fully expecting to see a man leaning on the bar waiting for him, but no such sight greeted him. The French beauty sat at a table right in front of him and she was the only person in the bar. The woman stood up and took two paces towards him.

'Good evening, Monsieur O'Donnell. I am Esme Delon, Police Nationale, and am your liaison officer during your stay in France.' She smiled. Fergus said nothing—he couldn't speak. Eventually, he managed to splutter, 'Good evening, Mademoiselle, it is a pleasure to meet you.' Then he held out his hand.

Esme looked at the hand, ignored it, and leant forward and air-kissed his two cheeks. 'Shall we sit down?'

While they seated themselves, Fergus only thought of the stocking tops and the white thigh. Esme had been speaking but he hadn't heard a word she had said.

'I'm so sorry, Esme, what were you saying?'

'I was saying, I saw you sitting in the café. I knew it was you because of the upright way you were sitting. No Frenchman sits that way and, of course, no one wears tie-up black brogue shoes in this heat.' She finished the sentence with a warm smile.

'Really, how interesting.' Fergus took a closer look at Esme and she didn't disappoint: slim, pert breasts, and long legs. He couldn't put his finger on it, but there was just something about French women that he found incredibly exciting. 'Your English is so good. Where did you learn?'

'Of course, it has to be good, I am a liaison officer with the British.' She laughed, showing her almost-perfect white teeth. 'I spent two years living in Cambridge. A lovely City, which I enjoyed so much.'

Despite her English being excellent, Esme spoke it with a slight French accent, which Fergus found so thrilling he hardly knew which way to look. Fergus thought it would be a good idea to stay on safe ground, so he spoke about work. 'Okay, Esme, so have you made any enquiries as to the whereabouts of Mary Bishop?'

'Enquires? My dear Fergus, I know exactly where you can find Mary Bishop.'

Fergus gave Esme the best possible smile he could. 'And where might that be, exactly?'

'She has a small but agreeable town-house in the Avenue De Grasse. Oh, which is in Cannes, of course. All foreigners must register, so it was one call and that was that.'

Fergus wasn't concentrating, but wondering instead what Esme thought of him—did he have any chance?

'Great, so we can just go and knock on the door.'

'It is not quite as simple as that.'

Fergus felt confused. 'Is there a problem with that?'

'Well, not really, but the bodyguard might not be very happy.'

Now Fergus's confusion morphed into surprise. 'Bodyguard? Are you sure? Could be a relation or friend, perhaps?'

Esme laughed. 'When … if … you see him, you will know he is a bodyguard. How do you say? … He is scary and very muscular!'

Fergus' mood became slightly glum—he wouldn't be able to take on a massive bodyguard, even with his training.

'I only want to speak with this woman. Do you have any ideas?'

Esme smiled. 'As a matter of fact, I do. She visits the post office once a week, the guard disappears for an hour, and they meet up back at their car. I suspect he has a woman somewhere that he, well ...' She laughed again. 'You know you men cannot live without us women for very long.' Esme said all this matter-of-factly, and Fergus had not only fallen rapidly in love, he was also impressed with her professionalism. He cursed. For some reason he blushed and felt like a bloody schoolboy again. 'So, we can talk to her then?'

'Yes. It is Tuesday today, and Mary Bishop will go to the post office on Thursday at eleven a.m., so we have all day tomorrow to prepare.'

Fergus liked the sound of that; all day with Esme would be incredible. He surprised himself by gushing out, 'What about dinner tonight?'

Esme laughed again. 'I thought you would never ask. Of course, it would be my pleasure. I will take you to my favourite fish restaurant on the seafront. You will love it.'

Fergus was so happy he couldn't speak.

Esme placed her hand on his arm. 'Fergus, are you all right? Are you ill?

'No. No. I'm, eh, very well, thank you.'

'It is just that you are, how do I say this, red faced.'

Fergus couldn't believe this—he was making a complete fool of himself. 'I'm hot, that's all. I'll be fine.'

Esme looked unconvinced and gave him a sultry, sexy look that melted his heart and gave him a slight erection at the same time.

'Okay.' Esme got up. 'I will pick you up at eight thirty.' She turned to leave, but then turned back. 'Fergus, no need to be so formal tonight. Casual clothes will be fine.' She gave him another one of those delicious smiles.

***

Fergus waited in reception at eight fifteen. He'd remembered what Esme had said about dress code, and wore a smart pair of denim jeans and a blue shirt, which the hotel maid had ironed for him. He had also bought an expensive pair of leather sandals. He sat purposefully, so he could see the entrance. When she appeared, his heart leapt into his mouth. She wore a country-style, white lace dress that set off her slight tan to perfection. Her legs went on forever and she had a fabulous pair of leather sandals with tiny bells on that jingled as she walked, drawing more attention to herself. Fergus couldn't stand—she was so far out of his league, she should be on the arm of a Hollywood movie star.

She stood close. 'Fergus, you are looking so much more relaxed in your jeans and nice new sandals. Bonsoir comment allez-vous?' Esme wanted to know if he understood or spoke even the simplest of French.

Fergus gave her a resigned look that declared he had no idea what she had said. 'Esme, I really think we should stick to English.' He paused and looked her in the eye. 'You look stunning, absolutely beautiful.'

Esme stood close to him, and appeared to be waiting for … Fergus leant forward and kissed her lightly on the cheeks.

'Good. You are too kind, Fergus O'Donnell. Shall we go? I am very hungry.' And, suddenly, so was Fergus.

Esme drove one of those popular little French Fiats and she tore through the streets towards the seafront. Fergus couldn't talk, because he was holding on for dear life as she swerved round corners at what seemed like dangerous breakneck speeds. Then he saw the sea and prayed that they would arrive soon so he could get out of the car. They pulled up outside a white painted, quaint, small restaurant, and he looked at the sign above the door: *Poisson Esme.* The entrance had hanging lobster pots and pictures of fish on the walls. He got out of the car and took a deep breath to collect his thoughts, then went to smooth his shirt, but Esme was already moving.

'Come on, Fergus, let's go, I'm starving.'

As they entered the restaurant, he was a step behind her. The inside looked beautifully French, with white tablecloths, and fishnets and more lobster pots on the walls. Uproar ensued, as seated customers shouted 'Bonjour' to Esme, then a waiter hugged and kissed her, and a minute later a big cuddly-looking man, dressed in chef's whites, approached.

Esme squealed and ran into his arms. 'Papa, Papa.' They kissed and hugged, and then her mum appeared. Esme looked so excited and grabbed her in a tight, warm embrace. 'Mama, comment allez-vous?' Kisses flew in every direction and Fergus assumed that Esme had not seen her parents in quite a while. Little did he know, she had popped in at lunchtime as well. Once it had quietened down, Esme stood back and introduced Fergus. 'Papa, Mama. Ce est le Celebre detective de Scotland Yard a Londres.'

Fergus heard 'Scotland Yard' and smiled, then asked, 'What did you say? I am not from Scotland Yard.'

'I know that, Fergus, but let us have some fun. It is not every day the restaurant has a famous detective from Scotland Yard through its door.'

Fergus just smiled. Well, why not?

The father looked at Fergus quite sternly, and in stuttering English, said, 'You, you survive in car? Yes?'

Fergus laughed. 'Yes, but only just!'

Then Esme said something and the restaurant laughed in uproar.

'Now what did you say?'

'I told them that you said I was a brilliant driver.'

Fergus broke into a beacon of a smile and laughed heartily. He was falling more and more in love with this woman every second.

Esme explained that she had worked in the kitchen and served in the restaurant as a child from an early age. Papa and Mama had been unhappy when she had chosen not to follow them and run the restaurant, but when they saw how happy she was as a police officer they understood. Time flew by and soon they were sipping coffee, having had a superb fish dinner prepared by Papa and served by Mama. Fergus had never enjoyed himself so much in months or even years.

'Esme, I've had the most wonderful time, I ...'

Esme stood suddenly, as a man approached the table, shouting at her.

'Vous Salaud donc ce est qui ta putain maintenant?'

[You Bastard, so this is who you are fucking now?]

The man went to lift his arm to strike Esme, and then her Papa was there, meat cleaver in hand.

'Sortez avant que je vous ai arête.'

[Get out, before I have you arrested.]

The man stepped back, looking at Fergus as though he wanted to kill him. Fergus accepted the challenge, took two steps, and stood next to Esme. He touched her arm to let her know he was with her and that he would protect her if he had to.

'Do not worry, he is going.' She looked at the man and pointed to the door. The man had obviously been drinking, but he turned and strode out of the door without any more fuss.

As the door shut, a sigh of relief shot through the restaurant. Esme and Fergus sat back down.

'My ex-boyfriend. He is upset that we split up. He's a good man, really.'

'So, do you live on your own?'

She smiled coyly. 'Is that a chat-up line, Fergus?'

'Oh God, no.' Fergus could feel his face reddening. 'I just think maybe you should stay at your parents tonight.'

'So why the hell isn't it a chat-up line?' Esme looked tearful.

Fergus was confused, and couldn't tell whether Esme was being serious or not.

He stuttered, 'You're in an emotional state. I like you more than you can imagine, but I don't want to upset you or say something I shouldn't.'

Esme took a large gulp of pinot grigio. 'Fergus, I love your quietness, your Britishness, and your stiff upper lip.' Then she began to cry.

Fergus wasn't good with distraught women, but this one was special beyond belief. He took her hands in his and kissed them several times, and then he heard loud tumultuous clapping. When he looked up, the whole restaurant was laughing, clapping, and cheering. He swore under his breath as he blushed again.

Esme stayed with her parents that night and, although Fergus was disappointed not to spend the night with her, he was glad she was safe and that he was going to spend all the next day with her. He went back to the hotel Nicea, got to his room, undressed, and collapsed onto his bed, exhausted.

At six the next morning, Fergus heard a tapping at the door. He rubbed his eyes and hobbled across the room. When he pulled the door open, he expected to see a member of staff, and was shocked to see Esme. She gave him a glorious smile. 'Are you going to invite me in then, or am I to stand here all morning?'

Although shocked, Fergus felt over the moon, and pulled the door open wide. She swept in, threw her arms around him, and proceeded to kiss him plumb on the lips. He responded and, soon, passion overtook them. Esme stepped back from the embrace, and took off her coat to reveal herself in matching white stockings, knickers, and bra. Fergus gasped. She was the most beautiful woman he had ever seen. 'Esme, Esme, you are so beautiful.'

She slipped her knickers down, then undid her bra. She was so beautiful: naked with firm breasts and a gorgeous smooth pussy. He groaned when she pushed him onto the bed gently and sat astride him, then their bodies melted together.

CHAPTER 13

'Karen, are you thinking straight? Have you gone completely fucking mad?'

'Sir, I'm telling you that something is not right.' Karen felt confused and frustrated beyond belief, not to mention angry—very angry.

'Jesus, he died of a fucking heroin overdose and he was pissed, having downed a whole bottle of whisky.'

'I apologise in advance, Sir, but that's bollocks. Something's going on. I believe he was murdered, and I strongly suspect that certain officers in the Met are responsible.'

Chief Inspector Park couldn't believe what he'd heard. 'Your association with the son, Simon Kane, has scrambled your brains. The Metropolitan Police do not go around killing people … this is insane!'

'He told me, … he sat in front of me and told me he would be killed.' Karen was almost screaming. 'He knew what was going on. God, can't you see it, for Christ's sake?'

'Be careful, Karen, you are overstepping the mark.'

'I'm truly sorry, Sir, but I'm sure, positive, that David Kane died as a result of police action. It has been covered up for over two years until now. We will know more when officer O'Donnell gets back from the South of France.'

'The South of France? Who the fuck authorised that?'

'I did, Sir. It is critical to the progress of the case.'

Chief Inspector Park couldn't speak for a second, while he took all this in. 'Apart from enjoying the weather, the food, and the wine, what exactly is he doing on tax-payer's money in the South of France?'

'He's contacting a woman called Mary Bishop, who was at the Energy demonstration with David Kane. Apparently, she was beaten severely by a police officer, and then mysteriously whisked off to France to recuperate.'

Chief Inspector Park shook his head. 'Jesus, this is … ' He couldn't find the right words. '… this is unbelievable. Okay, let's calm this down and see where we are. Who exactly are you saying is involved in this at Scotland Yard?'

'I don't know, except for the special ops woman, Carla Westburgh, who came to Epsom and took Ferguson off. A right bitch, that one.'

'I don't know her, but there's been a request through channels for the tape of the Ferguson interview. They want it sent to Scotland Yard with a special order that no copies are kept.'

'I was unaware of that. Doesn't that strike you as rather strange, Sir?'

'There are things you don't know. I had a call from Commander Fellows, a man with huge influence. Bloody hell, the rumour is he's going to be an MP and government minister in the near future. He asked for full cooperation in the Ferguson matter and anything appertaining to it. He also said that you should be muzzled, as you were in over your head and you could compromise an on-going investigation into Marxist agitators.'

'Commander Fellows? ... Mmm, this is more serious than I thought. Sir, we have to do something, to sit back and do nothing would be a dereliction of our duty to uphold the law.' And then an idea came to her. 'If it should come out later, we will be seen as having been complicit.'

Karen could tell immediately by Park's anguished face that he did not like that one bit.

'Complicit? Complicit in what?'

'A monstrous cover up by the Metropolitan police, Sir.'

Park rubbed his face. 'Shit, I remember telling you I was very happy you had joined us, but now I'm not so sure. .... Okay, this job is about tough decisions and this is what we, or more to the point, you are going to do. O'Donnell must find this Bishop woman and get a statement. I want to see it as soon as it's available, and once we see that, we can then decide the next step. Secondly, I'll make some enquiries about this Westburgh woman and see what she's up to. You will make some discreet enquiries about the Heenan murder, and the Ferguson—' He stopped. Gathered himself. Continued, 'Well, whatever it was, you did hear the *discreet,* didn't you?'

Karen was delighted that, at last, Chief Inspector Park was taking it seriously. 'Don't worry, Sir, discreet is my middle name, and exactly what my enquiries will be.'

Park looked at Karen, raised his eyebrows, and half smiled, which almost made Karen laugh, but she managed to keep quiet.

'Yes, well, carry on then, Inspector.'

Karen noted that Park had not used her name, which he normally would have. Should it all go horribly wrong, they both had their heads in a noose.

'Thank you, Sir. I will keep you informed.'

CHAPTER 14

On Wednesday evening at seven o' clock, Karen and Simon met at the Woolpack pub in Banstead high street.

Karen told him, 'Bloody hell, it's all happening.'

He looked interested, but said, 'You grab a table, and I'll get the drinks, … usual?'

'No, I'll have a Pernod and orange squash, with ice, in a long glass.'

Simon got back to the table, drinks in hand. 'I'm desperate to know what's happening. Spill then.'

'Where to start? Okay, the meeting with Park was, eh, how shall I say, interesting, to say the least. He's sort of on side …'

Simon cut in, 'Sort of?'

'He knows something's going on and he's agreed to discreet enquiries being made—we can't ask for more than that. Fergus will hopefully see Mary Bishop in the next couple of days, and then we may know more. I'm positive Heenan and Ferguson were both killed by officers involved in the cover up of your father's death.'

'Even now, this doesn't seem possible. Perhaps I'll wake up and it will all have been a dream.'

'Imagine Scotty Ferguson being held down or drugged while they injected him with an overdose of Heroin. No, Simon, this is no dream, and we both need to be extremely careful.'

Simon sat quietly and considered what Karen had said. 'Jesus, do you think we're in danger?'

'Not at the moment, but they have killed already, so my guess is they wouldn't hesitate to do it again to cover their tracks.'

'Bloody hell, it's beyond comprehension, these people are pure evil. Are you sure you're going to be safe?'

'Yes, so let's change the subject. Are you staying at my place tonight? I'm a woman and I have needs.' Karen laughed. 'I think I need another,' she said, draining her glass and holding it out to Simon, who took the glass.

'In answer to you, yes, I am staying and, believe me, I am going to fulfil all your needs and more.'

'I can't wait,' Karen said with a sexy smile. She thought she would give Simon her arse—he'd been waiting long enough and he deserved a treat.

***

Karen strode into Epsom police station and made towards her office. Every step she took reminded her of the night before; her bottom was sore and she made a mental note to get some Vaseline at lunchtime, which would help. Even with the soreness, it had been worth it. She loved the feeling of being totally taken and dominated. With a shake of her head, she got back to thinking about work. Eventually, she waded into the vast pile of relentless paperwork that she had grown to hate with a passion. Mick had called and requested a meeting and he arrived at the office at eleven.

'Good Morning, boss.'

'Morning, Mick. Fancy a coffee?'

'Thanks, but just had one, I was after an update on the Ferguson case.'

'Good timing, because I wanted to talk to you about that today. There are some things I want you to do, but they have to be done with discretion—we don't want certain people to hear that we are poking around, you understand?'

'Yes, of course, when do you want me to start?'

'Straight away. I want some people found, and then you'll be going to visit them. It could well mean being away for quite a few days.'

'Great, a holiday is just what I need.'

'Good.' Karen took a folder marked 'Secret' out of her drawer and opened it. 'So, the first name is …'

Karen had lunch and was back looking at the paperwork when, at three thirty, reception put a call through to her office. She listened for only a second. 'Okay, send him up, please.' With a slight frown, she stood and moved round from her desk, then smoothed down her grey pleated skirt and black shirt. A knock sounded on the door and she said, 'Come in.' A handsome young man, dressed in a dark suit and white shirt, entered the office.

'Good afternoon, Ma'am.' He approached Karen with his hand held out, which she shook warmly when they met in the middle of the office.

'Jeremy Hope. I'm the new Counter Terrorist Liaison Officer, on secondment from Scotland Yard.'

'Detective Inspector Karen Foster, welcome to Epsom.'

'Thank you, Ma'am, it's a pleasure to be here.'

Karen smiled. 'Well, first thing is that everybody calls me "boss", so I'm sure you can get used to that?'

'Of course, Ma'am, I mean, boss.' They shared a laugh.

'Did you find us all right? And where are you from?'

'Easy journey, thanks. I live in Greenford, West London.'

'Well, sit down for a minute. I appreciate you have a certain amount of confidential work to do, so we've given you an office on your own at the end of this corridor. I guess you would have been at Guildford, but they seem to have run out of office space. We have secure comms with Guildford and Scotland Yard, so I'll leave you to get on with your highly secret work. Just one more thing, if there's anything we can do to help, please just pick up the phone or knock on the door. I'll get one of the constables to give you a tour of the station tomorrow morning, if that's all right.'

'Yes, of course. I don't officially start 'til tomorrow, but I wanted to see how long it took me to get here. Epsom seems a really lovely area.'

'Yes, it is. I was at Bermondsey before here, and Epsom is heaven compared to there. Okay, so we'll see you in the morning.'

'Yes, thanks, see you in the morning.'

Karen liked him: a good looking, young, respectful, and intelligent copper. *How big is his cock?* she wondered. *And is he any good in bed?* She smiled to herself and got back to work.

***

At eight thirty in the morning, with spring in the air, Jeremy pulled into Epsom Police Station car park. He parked his sparkling clean, silver Ford Fiesta and took a deep breath, then got out and made for the entrance. He arrived at the same time as a young constable and said good morning. The constable replied with a smile and a nod. Jeremy went up to the third floor and knocked on Karen Foster's office door.

'Come in.'

Jeremy almost marched in. 'Good Morning, boss.'

'Ah, our latest recruit. Follow me, then.'

Karen took the stairs back down to the ground floor and walked into reception. A young police constable, Robert Young, stood waiting and smiled as Karen and Jeremy approached.

'Jeremy, this is Robert; Robert, this is Jeremy.'

'Robert, if you could give Jeremy the guided tour? Make sure he sees everything.' She looked at Jeremy. 'And then I'll see you back in my office, Okay?'

Karen departed back upstairs, leaving Robert and Jeremy to it.

***

'Would you follow me, please, Jeremy.' Robert led him out of the reception and headed towards the canteen.

'That's a very good idea.'

'What idea is that?'

'Coffee and a donut, of course.' Jeremy grinned.

Robert smiled. 'Well, you are the senior officer, so what can I say except, of course, Sir.' They laughed and both got the feeling that a good friendship could have started. Robert and Jeremy discussed police life, police women, and a bit more about police women. Robert laughed a lot and said that he wasn't into the typical tall, well-built female police officers, and preferred petite slim women. Jeremy said he was happily married with a daughter and another on the way. They walked through the entire station, with Robert pointing out various interesting facts. Robert even took him to the room in the basement where Phil Hogan had hung himself.

Eventually, the tour ended and they stood outside DI Foster's office. Robert and Jeremy were now firm friends and agreed to meet for lunch in the canteen. Jeremy knocked on the office door and, when he heard the *'come in'*, he pushed the door open and took one step in.

'All finished, boss, so about time I did some work.'

Karen came round from her desk and Jeremy noted the way she moved, which was incredibly sexy. He took a close look and liked what he saw.

'Good, I'm sure we'll bump into each other now and then, … break a leg, then, eh.'

'I hope not, but thanks for the good wishes.' And with that, he shut the door and strolled down the corridor to his office. He unlocked the door and went in. The spacious room housed a large oak desk, some cupboards, and an empty bookcase. The swivel chair looked expensive. He gazed around and thought he would like to add a touch of colour, as it was so damn like a typical boring police station office. He sat down and opened the desk draws, which were all empty except for some pens, paperclips, and a notepad. He shut them and relaxed back into the chair.

Black had explained to him that he would not be very long in Surrey and that he should not be worried about actually doing any serious work. The plan was for him to do a couple of months and then be transferred to Scotland Yard, where he would be of far more use to them. He had been provided with a file that gave him an insight into standard counter terrorism activity and, as long as he stuck to that, he couldn't get in trouble. Black had stressed to him that he was an intelligence officer, and that what he did was secret, and no one—not even the ranking officer at Epsom—had the right to query what he did or where he went. Any problems of any sort were to be referred to Black at Scotland Yard. Jeremy took a porn magazine out of his brief case, relaxed, and leafed through it.

CHAPTER 15

The lovemaking had been an experience Fergus would never forget. Esme had awakened a sexual appetite in him that he didn't realise was there, and it was without question one of the most passionate moments of his life. They had just made it down to the restaurant buffet for breakfast, and it was a good job as Fergus was starving. Esme had some fresh melon and a small croissant, while Fergus had four sausages and a mountain of scrambled eggs, followed by toast washed down with buckets of coffee. Esme's foot rubbed up his leg towards his cock, and he looked at her and smiled.

'So, now you have, you say, re-charged your battery? It is time for us to go back upstairs and continue where we left off, no?'

Her toes had reached his balls and she rubbed them. An erection stirred. 'I think that is a very, very good idea, but I must tell you that once you enter the room you may never leave. I think I will kidnap you forever.'

She giggled, then rubbed some more. 'That would be so wonderful, let's do it.'

'You forget we have some work to do.' And, all of a sudden, Fergus became worried. He'd forgotten about work completely. Mary Bishop was the focus of why he was in France, and here he was with his beautiful Esme, enjoying himself. He shuffled his legs and Esme's foot slipped away from his balls. She stiffened, startled.

'What is wrong, Fergus?'

'Nothing, but we need to talk about and plan how we are going to meet up with Mary Bishop tomorrow. I also want to visit the post office and find somewhere we can talk without being disturbed. Once work is finished, then we can play, you understand?'

'You British are so professional and, of course, we must do as you say. Let us shower, get dressed, and then we can go to see the post office and surrounding shops.'

They left the breakfast table and went back to Fergus's room. Fergus watched Esme undress and go into the shower cubicle, when she turned the water on, it cascaded over her beautiful body. She soaped her breasts and between her legs, and Fergus felt sure she was being provocative for his eyes. He watched her closely and she glanced at him as she began to masturbate with the bar of soap. She spread her legs and stroked herself with the soap. Fergus was transfixed. It was the most erotic thing he had ever seen. Esme gasped as she moved in time with her hand thrusts. Fergus got up from his chair and stripped off, his erection huge and standing up, then he went into the shower and got onto his knees. Esme took her hands away so Fergus could kiss and lick her.

***

It had been another hair-raising driving experience getting to the post office. Esme brought the car to a screeching halt just around the corner and placed a Police Nationale badge on the dashboard. They walked back round the corner and Fergus followed Esme into the Bureau de Poste.

Fergus looked around the small building and imagined Mary entering and going to the counter; she would collect her cash and then turn and leave. They would have to talk to her just as she came out. He nodded at Esme and walked back outside, where he stopped on the pavement and looked for somewhere close by they could sit and talk. He saw a café, three doors away, which appeared to be perfect. He walked towards it, followed by Esme. The café had a few tables outside with red and white striped umbrellas to shade customers. Fergus went in. Six tables filled the small space, and it looked picture-perfect. They could sit inside in comfort and chat over a coffee. Fergus sat down and Esme ordered coffees. He thought through what they would say to Mary as she came out from the Bureau de Poste, and what they would do if she refused to speak to them. If she walked off, they could hardly grab her and cause a scene. Perhaps they could trick her somehow into having a coffee with them. The issue, as far as Fergus saw it, was that they would get one chance and one chance only. Fergus had a sudden thought: did Mary even know that her friend David Kane had been killed? And was she paying for the stay? If she wasn't, who the hell was? Esme had kept quiet while Fergus deliberated in silence.

'What are you thinking?' she asked at length.

Fergus felt concerned. 'I'm thinking that something I thought was very simple, could go terribly wrong for all sorts of reasons.'

'She is a woman. I am a woman. I can help, it is not a problem.'

'Hmm, sounds simple, but I don't want this messed up. And what happens if the bodyguard decides not to see his girlfriend and is with Mary?' Bloody hell, he'd better calm down. He cleared his throat, then said, 'Esme, we go as planned, she'll be on her own, and when she comes out of the Bureau de Poste, I will tell her I need to speak to her about David Kane. That is it, simple.'

They drank their coffee, then took a stroll through the pedestrian shopping area, where they found somewhere agreeable for lunch. They got back to the hotel at four p.m., and Fergus told Esme he needed to rest. Esme understood that Fergus had been swamped with emotional situations and suggested he get some sleep while she went to see her parents at the restaurant. They agreed that Fergus would go to the restaurant at eight for dinner.

Fergus did have a sleep and it did him the world of good. He showered at seven thirty, dressed ten minutes later, and sat in a cab five minutes after that, with his eyes shut, hanging on for dear life, and praying that it would all be over as soon as possible. They screeched to a halt outside the restaurant in a hail of dust and flying stones. Fergus opened his eyes and thanked the Lord he had arrived in one piece. He paid the beaming driver and gave him a hard stare. It made no difference, as the man kept smiling. Fergus turned towards the restaurant entrance and stopped. *Why on earth did I give that maniac a tip?* He shook his head, smiled, opened the door, and immediately saw Esme sitting at one of the tables with her mother. Esme waved, jumped up, and wrapped her arms around him and gave him a ferocious hug.

'Hallo, gorgeous,' he said, then he kissed her on the lips.

'Is everything okay?' she asked.

'Everything is perfect, thank you, Esme. Hmm, something smells good.'

'Papa is preparing a special meal for you. I'll tell you in English, so you understand better. First, we have freshly harvested mussels in a white wine and cream sauce—very delicious and one of the restaurant specialities—then a fish soup, Mediterranean style, then a delicious Halibut with brown butter and lemon then a—'

'Crikey, stop, that will be enough.' They laughed and held hands.

'Fergus O'Donnell, as if you didn't know, I am very much in love with you.' She stared into his eyes, and Fergus became tearful.

'Esme, you are the woman of my dreams. Now, where's all this fish? I'm so hungry, I could eat a horse.'

'Horse,' she said quietly, looking at him.

'No. No, it's an expression, it means I could eat a lot.'

They laughed again and Esme headed off to the kitchen to check on progress.

***

On Thursday morning, Fergus awoke early. He felt nervous, and wasn't used to this sort of cloak and dagger stuff. He just prayed it all would all go smoothly without any hitch. Esme would arrive at the hotel at ten and they would drive down to the Bureau de Poste, arriving at ten thirty, in case Mary Bishop was early for a change. He showered, got dressed, and was waiting in reception by quarter to ten. Esme strolled in at five to, and they kissed. They went to walk out of the hotel and, as Esme turned towards the door, Fergus saw she had a gun in a holster inside her short jacket. He grabbed her arm and pulled her back, led her over to the side of the reception, and spoke quietly, 'What are you doing with the gun?'

Esme looked shocked. 'It is normal practise that if we are working, we carry a gun. It is for protection, as you never know what could happen.'

Fergus thought for a second. 'Of course, I'm sorry, I was shocked because, as you know, we don't carry guns in England.'

'I am used to it, so do not worry. It is purely a precaution, okay?'

'Yes, okay, let's go.' Fergus laughed; it wasn't as if having a chat with Mary Bishop could turn into a gunfight at the OK corral. Fergus relaxed a little in the car, he had grown use to the crazy driving, and now had his eyes open, although he still hung on to the strap above his head to keep from flying around. They parked in the road next to the post office. Fergus looked at his watch: ten thirty five. They sat in the café across the road from the post office, and ordered coffee. Fergus felt on edge, made worse by the apparent relaxed state that Esme was in.

'What shall we do tonight, Fergus?' she asked.

He looked at her, taken aback. 'I've no idea. Do you think she'll be early?'

'I have no idea. We will find out in a minute.'

They sipped their coffees, watching the taxis spill out passengers all down the road.

'There she is, in that taxi just pulling up now. Good, she's on her own.'

Fergus looked and saw a smartly dressed, elderly woman get out of the taxi and stroll into the post office.

He stood and made his way across the road, with Esme next to him. Just outside the post office entrance, they stopped and waited. Anxious sweat coated his body. Then she appeared. He took a step across to her and looked her in the eye.

'Mrs Bishop, good morning, I am a police officer from London. I need to talk to you about David Kane and the energy demonstration two years ago.'

Mary Bishop put a hand to her chest, shocked. She took some seconds to react. 'If that is the case, why didn't you just come to the house?'

Fergus felt lost, and then it clicked: of course, she must think the police were her friends.

'David Kane was killed, did you know?'

Mary's face turned a white colour. 'Dead? What are you talking about? He's in America.'

'Believe me, Mary, he is dead. He was killed at the Energy Demonstration.'

Mary became agitated. 'I don't understand. I'd better phone Alex.' She went to get her phone out, but Fergus couldn't let her make the call, as he was sure Alex was the bodyguard. Before he could say or do anything, Esme stepped in and held Mary's arm gently. She whispered quietly into her ear.

'Mary, I am Esme, and I work for the French Police service. Everything Fergus has said is true. Please, come to the café next door, and we will explain why we are here. All we want to do is talk to you for five minutes.'

Maybe it was because Esme was a woman, or that she just had a way with her, but she got the result she wanted.

'Yes, okay then, a quick coffee and let's clear this up.'

Fergus led the way to the café, with Esme guiding Mary by the arm. They settled into seats at a table at the back with a good view of the door. Fergus spoke, and Mary was all ears.

'I'm sorry we had to contact you like this, but there are reasons. It is important that Alex, and I assume he is your bodyguard, does not know we have spoken.'

Mary looked astonished. 'Bodyguard? Don't be ridiculous, he is my companion … a friend.'

Fergus didn't know what to say, so continued, 'Did you know your friend David Kane died at the Demonstration?'

'I'm truly shocked. When I came round from surgery, they told me he was injured but that it was not serious. Later on, they said he'd gone to New York to recuperate, and the next thing I know is I'm on a flight here, all expenses paid.'

'Who are they, Mary? It's very important.'

'A nice, well-dressed man came to see me, from the government. Said I needed a rest, some sunshine, and a holiday. He said I had been let down by the authorities and that they wanted to repay me somehow. He said I could stay in this townhouse for three months, all expenses paid. What could I say, other than yes please?'

'And you are still here, Mary.'

'Yes, when it came time to go home, I said I would like to stay, and they agreed. I sold my house and bought a little flat for cash with a some extra help from the government.'

'What was the man's name, the one from the government?'

'Gosh, it was such a long time ago, I have no idea. I'm not even sure he told me at the time. I'm sorry, it sounds feeble now, but I was injured and my face was a mess. I love it here so much.'

'Why do you think Alex is here with you?'

'People are so kind, he's very helpful round the house, and we get on well.'

Fergus began to think that Mary had mental issues, which could be true after suffering such a serious attack. He couldn't think of any way forward, and then Esme spoke:

'Mary, you were attacked and David Kane was killed by a police officer, and it has been covered up by the authorities. This man Alex is not here to help you, he is here to make sure you do not speak to anyone about what you saw at the demonstration. Have you spoken to the man who came to see you, the well dressed man, recently?'

'Oh, goodness me, no, it's months since I spoke to him.'

Esme asked, 'Do you have a phone number for him?'

'I have an emergency number that I can call if needs be. For instance, if something happened to Alex.'

Fergus was excited; this could be of extreme importance. 'And do you have that number with you now?'

'Of course, it is in my diary.' She opened her handbag and took out a green coloured, small diary, then opened it to the notes page at the back. 'Do you want the number?'

Fergus took his pen out of his inside pocket, and his hand shook a little. 'Please, read the number out, Mary.'

'0208 653 3476,' she read slowly.

'May I?' Esme took the diary and read the number out again, which Fergus checked against the one he had written down, it was correct.

Fergus desperately tried to think of anything else he should ask, anything else that could help, but he couldn't think of a thing.

'So, Mary, you have been very helpful.' Fergus took a gamble, and played on the suspected brain damage. 'I expect David is having a wonderful time in America, and we wish you a happy life here in the sunshine.'

'Oh thank you, I knew everything was all right, after all.'

Esme spoke again, 'Mary, funny that we should just bump into each other like that, it's been so nice to have met you. We don't want to worry Alex, do we? So no need to tell him you met us.'

'No need at all,' Mary exclaimed. 'Well, I must be off, I have a little shopping to do, it's been such a pleasure to meet you.' Mary stood and wandered away from the café and disappeared into the crowd.

'Poor lady, she's suffering from some kind of brain damage or dementia, I think. The good news is that she has probably forgotten she met us already.'

Fergus hardly heard what Esme said, as he was looking at the phone number. 'We need to get this number over to Karen as soon as possible.'

'It's about time you visited a French police station. You can talk to London and transmit a message at the same time. Then we can have some lunch.'

Fifteen minutes later, Fergus and Esme sat in an office at the local Poste De Police drinking coffee. Fergus had drafted a message and it had been sent to Epsom. He was desperate to talk to Detective Inspector Foster, but he left it ten minutes so she could read and understand the situation. The ten minutes seemed like an hour.

'Boss, its Fergus, did you read the message?'

'Yes, how are you?'

'Very well, thank you. I—'

'Okay, that's enough small talk, the phone number is very interesting. We're running checks now to see whom it belongs to. Aside from that, you are saying Mary Bishop will be of no use to us?'

'That's correct, boss. I'm no doctor, but she seems to be suffering from dementia.'

A moment of silence fell, then Karen said, 'Okay, well, in that case, get yourself back here as soon as possible.'

'It might be a couple of days, boss. I think I'm coming down with flu or something.' He looked at Esme and shook his head.

'Flu in the South of France? Are you sure it's got nothing to do with that Liaison officer, Esme Delon?'

Fergus' face reddened and he cursed to himself. The bloody woman always knew everything. Then he laughed. 'Esme, God, she's twenty stone and built like a brick … you know what.'

'Make sure you're back in the office come Monday morning, nine a.m.' The phone went dead. Fergus replaced the handset, looked at Esme, and gave her a huge smile. He had three whole days before he had to leave, and boy was he going to make the most of it.

CHAPTER 16

'Morning, Mick, come in and have a seat,' Karen said.

'Thanks, boss.' Sergeant Mick Hill sat at one of the chairs set round the conference table.

'How are you?' Karen asked as she shuffled the papers on her desk into a pile and pushed them to the side. Then she picked up a blue plastic folder and joined Mick at the table. A minute later, Janet came in with two coffees, and Mick laughed.

'How did you know I was dying for a coffee?'

'Ah, woman's intuition, or is it Detective Inspector intuition?' They all laughed. Then Karen grew more serious. 'Right, let's get down to it.' She opened the blue folder and picked up a sheaf of paper, studied it for no more than a minute, then slipped it back into the folder.

'So, Chief Inspector Park has reported that the Carla Westburgh bitch is a gofer for Commander Fellows. Apparently, if he needs something sorting, she's one of his favourites. Nasty piece of work that woman. Can you believe she called me a cunt, right to my face in my nick?'

Mick shook his head. 'Couldn't agree more. A right nasty piece of work.'

'Well, she'll fucking regret that one day, believe me.' She paused and looked up. 'Fellows is smart, he has people like Westburgh who don't actually have real jobs with real responsibility, they just float around, and are available to him twenty-four-seven. So, let's move on. Anything from the Heenan and Ferguson murders?'

'In a nutshell, no. It's impossible to make enquiries without alerting Scotland Yard. Anything to do with the Energy Demonstration goes straight to deputy Commander Philip Black.'

'Another one of Fellows' cronies, so where does that leave us now? The good news is that we have some progress from France. Fergus has done a good job and got some serious information for us. Mary Bishop is elderly and, according to Fergus, has dementia, so she will be of no use to us whatsoever, but she had a phone number for emergencies and we now know whom that number belongs to.'

Mick sat wide-eyed and waiting. 'Yes, who is it then?'

'We are dealing with fire here, and we will have to be very careful we don't get burnt. It belongs to a Mr Theodore Taylor, who lives in Hampstead, and is a political facilitator.'

'What exactly is that?'

'He does jobs for people, very senior people in Politics and business. So many rumours, it's unbelievable. But if only ten per cent were true, he's had more fingers in pies than we've had hot dinners. He's connected. Very well connected. Park says he could even have a line into Downing Street.'

'Are you sure?'

'Listen, Mick, they all went to Eton together. They are the establishment, all in the same club, a big boy's club where they compare cock sizes and eat spotted dick with custard, and more importantly they look after each other.'

'So what the hell are we going to do then? I like my job.'

'Chief Inspector Park is not without influential friends, but we need to get more information before we can use them to good effect. This could need to eventually go direct to the PM. By the way, is Jeremy in today?'

'Yes, I saw him earlier, he's been in his office for the past couple of hours.'

Karen stood and moved to her desk, where she picked up her phone and asked the switchboard to transfer her to Jeremy Hope's office.

Mick looked concerned. Karen asked him, 'What's wrong?'

'There's something fishy about him that I can't put my finger on, but ...' Mick stopped talking when Karen listened intently.

'Jeremy, it's Karen Foster, can you spare a minute? Oh good.' She hung up and looked at Mick. 'What do you mean by fishy?'

'Sergeant's intuition, boss.'

'Look, we have an intelligence officer working right here who we can use. He may well have heard of this Theodore character and could help. It would be silly not to take advantage of that.'

Two minutes later, a knock came at the door and Jeremy entered the office.

'Good Morning, how are you, boss? And what can I do for you?'

'Have a seat, Jeremy. You don't mind helping us out for a moment?'

'Not at all, but I'm not sure I'll be able to help.'

Karen rubbed her chin. 'Have you heard of a character called Theodore Taylor? He's some sort of political gofer in London.'

Jeremy answered truthfully, 'Never heard of him—should I have?'

'No, not at all. That's a shame, but if you don't ask ...' She paused. 'Okay, sorry to trouble you Jeremy, but that's it.'

'Oh, okay, that was quick. Anything I can do to help, let me know.' And with that he got up and made toward the door.

***

He pulled the door open slowly, so as not to make any noise, and heard Karen speak.

'You know what, it's funny isn't it? We start with the Energy Demonstration and now we're almost at Downing Street, ... it's a funny world.'

Jeremy hurried back to his office. Had he heard correctly? Did Detective Inspector Foster just mention the Energy Demonstration? What was the name of the man she'd asked about? ... Theodore Taylor, that was it. He sat down at his desk, and it suddenly hit him: that's why he was in Epsom. Karen Foster was on to something and he was there in case she had to be silenced. Jesus, a fucking Detective Inspector, no less. Five minutes later, Jeremy called Philip Black on the secure line. He told him the story, then listened to silence at the other end. Finally, Black spoke.

'You've done well, Jeremy. The situation is more serious than I thought, especially now she knows Taylor is involved. I wonder how the hell she found that out! Carry on as normal, and I'll be in touch.'

***

Black called Commander Fellows and arranged to see him that evening. He then called Alex, in France, and asked him if there had been any visitors or strangers asking questions. Alex said nothing had happened, and that all was well as usual. He did say he would talk to the stupid cow and see if she knew anything, and get back to him.

***

'Mary, did you meet anyone new recently?'

Mary looked thoughtful. 'I don't think so. No, I'm sure I would have remembered.'

She probably wouldn't have remembered, but Alex wondered about when she was last on her own.

'What about the person you met at the post office the other day?'

'Oh, it wasn't a person, Alex, it was two. A very nice policeman from London and a French girl ... such a nice couple.'

Alex couldn't believe his fucking ears.

'What did they talk about? Do you remember their names?'

'Eh, no, I'm sorry, Alex. I can't remember anything at all, I'm so very sorry.'

Alex felt like beating it out of her, but the fact was she could remember what she had for breakfast thirty years ago but not that morning. Alex relayed the information to Black.

***

Philip Black worked out that they must have gotten the emergency number from Mary Bishop and traced Taylor with that. He visited Fellows in his office at six o'clock. Fellows looked at him and held his finger to his mouth, signifying he should keep quiet. Black heard a noise to the side and, when he turned, saw a man sweeping the office with what looked like a small metal detector. Fellows was having his office swept for bugs. The man soon finished and declared it clean.

'You can never be too careful, eh. Have you had yours done recently?'

'No, but I'm going to.'

'Sit down and give me some good news.'

Black took a seat. 'Sorry to say, it's all bad, but manageable.'

Fellows raised his eyebrows. 'Go on.'

'The Foster woman at Epsom asked Jeremy Hope if he knew of Theodore Taylor.'

Fellows jumped to his feet, shaking. 'How the fucking hell did she find out about Theo? He'll be fucking furious.'

'Perhaps Theo should take a well-earned holiday?'

'Probably a good idea. See to it. That DI Foster is becoming a fucking nuisance. Doesn't she know when to leave things alone?' Commander Fellows sat back down.

'It would appear not. I had another piece of information from Hope that you will not believe. DI Foster is going out with Simon Kane, the son of the man who was killed at the demonstration.'

Fellows looked as if he couldn't quite take that in. 'What? Jesus, this is getting more bizarre by the minute. I wonder if there's any leverage in that fact? We'll see. What else?'

'The Bishop woman has dementia. She's become a liability.'

Fellows spoke quietly. 'She is of no further use to us, so deal with her.'

'I guess the good news is that Foster trusts Hope, so we can keep tabs on exactly what she's doing.'

'Good. Now, I have a cocktail party to go to.'

Black left the office and got straight on the phone to Alex …

'That's exactly what I said, Alex. Deal with it as soon as possible.'

CHAPTER 17

On Saturday morning, Alex told Mary to dress smartly as he was taking her out to lunch. Mary got all excited, as she couldn't remember when she'd last been out for a meal. In fact, it had only been a couple of days prior, but she'd forgotten. She dressed in one of her most fashionable outfits: a white, sleeveless, short dress with blue spots, and she also sported a white cartwheel sunhat, perfect for the Cannes hot weather. At eleven, Alex drove Mary to a multi-storey car park near to Le Grand Hotel. He drove up six floors, right to the top. When he parked, they got out of the car, and Mary stood and looked at the sea view—the sun reflected on the water and made it so bright that she had to squint her eyes.

Alex took her arm and she assumed he was going to lead her to the lift. He didn't. What he did do was hold her arm tight and take her the two steps to the safety fence, then he gripped her waist with both hands, lifted her, and threw her over the fence. She opened her mouth to scream, but not a sound came out. The hat fell from her head, a gust of wind caught it, and it flew off into the distance. Mary fell, arms and legs flailing, until she hit the concrete pavement below with a sickening thud. She was just a bag of bones, and hitting the concrete from that height and at that speed, broke most of them. She died instantly as her head caved in, and within seconds her white outfit had turned crimson.

***

Before she'd hit the bottom, Alex had gotten back into the car and drove to the exit. He departed the car park just as passers-by ran along the pavement to the body. Alex had already filled the petrol tank and loaded the boot with his belongings, so he was soon speeding along on the road to Lausanne, Switzerland, where he had agreed to meet a rather sexy young lady for a week's holiday.

Alex—real name Trevor Banks, ex metropolitan police officer—stopped at the first motorway services and used the public telephone. He rang Philip and told him it was done. He said nothing more, and put the phone down. The job looking after Mary had done his head in and he looked forward to unwinding, fucking Jesse, and drinking plenty of whisky.

***

Fergus and Esme were so happy they were worried, as neither had fallen in love so quickly before, and both were worried that it could fall apart as quickly as it had grown. Fergus still couldn't believe that he had pulled such a beautiful woman as Esme, and marvelled at her character as well as her ripe body.

They had taken walks in the sunshine, eaten fantastic meals at the restaurant, and sat in street-side cafes watching the world go by. It was midday on the Saturday when the dark shadow cast itself over the sunshine. Fergus and Esme had got up early and gone for a run. They arrived back at the hotel at nine and ate a hearty breakfast, or at least Fergus did, Esme seemed to live on titbits and fish. They finished breakfast, went back to their room, and made love in the shower before collapsing on the bed and cuddling. At exactly midday, Esme's mobile rang. Not long after picking up and listening, she turned white. Fergus couldn't understand what was being said, and wondered if perhaps something had happened to one of her parents. Esme took the phone away from her ear and cried.

Fergus grabbed her arm. 'What is it? What has happened, Esme?'

Esme looked up, wiped her face, and then spluttered, 'Mary, Mary Bishop, she's dead. Jumped off the top floor of a multi-storey car park. Oh God, the poor woman.'

Fergus was in shock. 'Jumped off? Did anyone see her do it?'

'I don't know. We need to visit the Poste de Police for further information.'

'Esme, … the townhouse … let's go straight there now.'

Esme thought for a second. 'Alex.'

'Exactly,' Fergus said.

They rushed to get dressed and soon the pair of them stood in the lift heading to reception. Ten seconds later and they were in Esme's car careening out of the hotel car park, en route to Mary's townhouse.

Ten minutes after that, they pulled up outside the property in the Avenue de Grasse. The drive had been worse than usual, and Fergus had to collect his thoughts before he opened the car door and got out. He glanced back. Esme took a gun out of the glove compartment. She shut the car door and they strode to the blue painted front door. Fergus thumped on the door with his knuckles. They waited, but there was no answer. Esme took a large bunch of keys out of her pocket and started trying them in the lock. Fergus was shocked when he heard a click and the door opened. Esme held the gun out in front with two hands and entered the house at a cautious pace.

'Police Nationale! Anyone there?'

Fergus followed in. The house was empty, completely. Everything had gone: no chairs, no carpets, no nothing. They made their way to the kitchen and opened some cupboards—empty, nothing. Then they checked upstairs and found it to be the same. Fergus looked around and found it hard to believe two people had apparently been living in the house only hours before.

Fergus voiced what they were both thinking, 'So, where is Alex then? Interesting that he seems to have disappeared at the same time as Mary jumps from the sixth floor of a multi-storey car park.'

Esme fumbled for her phone. 'It is more than suspicious. I must put out a call for this Alex.' She called the local police station. Alex understood when she mentioned the name

Alex, but other than that he couldn't tell what was being said. Half an hour later, a police technical team arrived. After conducting tests, they couldn't even find one fingerprint in the very sanitised property. Fergus and Esme headed for the police station.

'He'll be gone by now. We won't find him. We don't even know his surname, and Alex could well be fictitious. We have no images.' Esme thumped the steering wheel, causing the car to swerve, and Fergus to hold on tighter. 'It is, as you say, a pile of shit!'

'Yes, doesn't look good. I must tell London.'

Prior to sending an official report, Fergus rang directly through to Karen and explained what had happened, adding that he was sure Mary Bishop had been murdered by her bodyguard.

For the rest of the day, the mood remained somewhat subdued. They went to the family restaurant and picked at some food, but Mary's death and the fact Fergus was leaving the next morning had put a bit of a dampener on things. They made tender sweet love that night, not knowing when they would see each other again, although it was suggested that Esme should reacquaint herself with the UK by flying over as soon as possible. Fergus had never had feelings like the ones he was now experiencing, and he ached with pain that he had to leave her. He'd even considered just not returning home, but thought that a bit drastic, considering they had only just met.

The parting at Nice Airport on Sunday morning was heart breaking. Esme would not stop crying, and sobbed that she would never see him again, that he would meet a beautiful English girl, and that he would forget her the minute he got on the plane. Whatever he said ended up being wrong, and he eventually had to drag himself away from her arms to go through security, otherwise he could have missed his flight. He, too, felt upset at the parting, but he would move heaven and earth to see her again very soon.

CHAPTER 18

'How's the steak?'

'Tender and delicious, thank you, Sir.'

'I wanted us to have a chat, and what better way than over a glass of half decent wine and a good steak.'

Chief Inspector Park had invited Karen to lunch at the Argentinian Grill in Guildford town centre. He was a regular and Karen observed the extra special service they got. Karen wasn't sure which she enjoyed most, the delicious filet steak with pepper sauce or the exquisite bottle of Saint Emillion, but eventually decided that both were equally magnificent, and she devoured the steak and wine with gusto.

Chief Inspector Park gave her a piercing look. 'Things have changed. As were you, I was shaken by the death of Mary Bishop. The French Police have labelled it a suicide, but you and I both know it wasn't, and that this Alex character was almost certainly the perpetrator of this heinous crime. The French police are totally inadequate, almost as dreadful as the Italians, so don't think anything else will be done. In fact, I expect the case has already been closed.'

Karen nodded. 'Fergus O'Donnell is back and I had a long chat with him; he's totally convinced that Alex or whatever his real name is, was responsible for Mary Bishop's death. The dead bodies are piling up: David Kane, Mark Heenan, Scot Ferguson, and now Mary Bishop—where in God's name is it going to end?'

Chief Inspector Park leant forward and lowered his voice. 'We're dealing with the most ruthless individuals you have ever come across. Commander Fellows will soon be sitting in the House of Commons and I can guarantee you that Philip Black will be a new commander at Scotland Yard. There are already rumours that Fellows will get a ministerial post within a couple of months. God forbid, one day he might even be Prime Minister.'

Karen couldn't believe what she heard. 'Prime Minister? You're not serious, Sir?'

'I'm deadly serious, these people are capable of anything, and the old-boy network will protect them. Have you thought about your personal safety?'

Karen didn't speak for some seconds as she took in what Chief Inspector Park was saying. 'No, they couldn't, a serving Detective Inspector, surely even they would balk at that?'

'I don't think so, Karen; of course, it would be an accident, so you had better take extra care. Where are you with the enquiries?'

'At a dead end. There's nothing we can do with Heenan, Ferguson, or Bishop.'

Park looked thoughtful and rubbed his chin. 'Yes, well, they're covering their tracks very well. You know what I always say, if you can't get anywhere then go back to the beginning, which means you need to find the rogue police officer who killed Kane.'

'How the hell am I going to do that? Even this Theodore Taylor has disappeared, everywhere just dead ends.'

'Oh, yes, sorry, I should have told you that I heard this morning that our friend Taylor is in Brussels working for the UK Permanent Representation Organisation to the EU.'

'What the hell is that?'

Park leaned back with a soft chuckle. 'God, don't ask, it would take me a week to brief you, suffice to say he is out of our reach for now. So let's move on. Scotland Yard would have filmed the demonstration, but there is no way you'll be able to get your hands on that. Why don't you contact the newspapers and ask for all the images they have?—There will be thousands, so it will be a long job but could give you something.'

'That's a good idea, thank you, Sir. I'll get right on it.'

'I've told you before, Karen, I'm glad you are here.' He laughed. 'Even if trouble seems to follow you around like a ...' He didn't want to say 'bad smell' so he just let it trail off, but Karen guessed his words anyway. 'Right, anything else?'

'Thank you for the steak, Sir,' she told him with a grin.

Park gave a hearty laugh. 'Army marches on its stomach.' He cut a large piece of steak and shovelled it into his mouth.

Later, back at her office in Epsom, Karen got Fergus and Mick contacting the newspapers asking for copies of all images from the Energy Demo. At four O' clock, Jeremy

Hope knocked on her door and asked if she could spare a minute.

He leant against the doorframe. 'Afternoon, boss, how are you?'

'Well, thank you. What can I do for you?'

'Oh, I just wondered if you had made any progress with Theodore Taylor.'

She smiled. 'Only that he disappeared to the EU.'

'I looked him up, you know, through channels, bit of a fixer.'

'So I heard.'

'If you need help with anything, you only have to ask, okay?'

'Great, thanks, Jeremy, I may well take you up on that offer sooner than later.'

'Good. Okay, so see you later.' Jeremy left the office.

Karen twiddled the pen in her fingers; Jeremy could well be very useful in the future.

The next day, thousands of Energy Demonstration images arrived, a few every minute from every newspaper in the country. The plan was to capture an image of every single police officer at the event. This collection would then be whittled down by taking out officers who were working away from the scene of Kane's death. Karen had said that if they were left with thirty officers it should be considered a success. Of course, they then had to identify those officers, and how they did that and what they did with them afterwards, still remained conjecture.

Robert Young was drafted in to help, as he had good reliable eyes and was a dab hand with computers. Robert was keen to get stuck in and he began the laborious job of identifying and logging each officer at the scene. When it got to lunchtime, Robert logged out of his computer and went to grab a bite to eat. He wandered into the canteen and joined the queue. While he looked up at the specials board and decided to have the fish pie with broccoli, someone nudged him and he turned around.

'Hey Jez, how are you?'

'Very well. What's happening?'

Robert laughed. 'Fish Pie and Broccoli is as exciting as it gets.'

Jeremy laughed. Their friendship had remained strong since Robert had shown Jeremy around the station on his first day.

'I think I'll join you—it sounds healthy.'

They bought some cokes, collected their meals, and Jeremy led them to a table some way away from where anybody else was sitting. The pair made for a serious contrast: Robert wore his clean sparkling uniform, while Jeremy had on jeans and a red sweatshirt.

'So Jez, what's happening in the secret world of Terrorism and espionage?'

Jeremy burst out laughing. 'You've been reading too many books. Most intelligence work is reading reports and trawling the internet.'

'Have you done surveillance work on terrorists?'

'Who do you think I am, James Bond? And even if I had, I couldn't talk about it.'

Robert deflated a bit. He'd hoped to hear some exciting report of chases through the underground, ending in shootouts and terrorists dying gruesome deaths.

Jeremy looked around and spoke in a quiet, conspiratorial whisper, 'Okay, I tell you what we'll do, I'll give you some interesting snippets of information and you do the same. Quid-pro-quo, what do you say?'

'That would be okay, but I'm afraid you'd be disappointed with news from me, I know nothing.'

Jeremy smiled. 'You might be surprised what I'm interested in; for instance, Karen Foster: I would, what about you?'

Robert blushed a little. 'She's at least ten years older than me, but she does have a nice figure.'

Jeremy leant even closer. 'Rob, she is the fucking business. Next time you see her, take a close look, she's well put together. I tell you, I'd be there like a shot. So, unfortunately, she must have a boyfriend?'

'Yeah, a bloke called Simon Kane.'

Jeremy was prepared for that, as he knew about the connection from Black.

'Jammy bastard. I wonder if she likes younger men.'

Robert spoke slowly, 'There are rumours ...'

Jeremy was instantly all ears. 'Yes, go on then ...'

'Well, rumours are ... she's a bit of a nympho—loves it, apparently.'

Jeremy leant back. 'What! Are you sure?'

'Totally rumours, nothing else.'

'Are you sure you haven't been there, Robert?' Jeremy asked with a knowing grin.

Robert bristled. 'Yes, I'm bloody sure. She likes a drink, too.'

'You mean a bit more than she should?'

'Only rumours, Jez.'

'Hmm, the DI is an interesting woman.' Jeremy looked as if he gave serious thought to having a pop at her and seeing what happened. 'Last thing then; what are you working on at the moment?'

Robert spoke through his grin at Jeremy's transparency regarding the DI, 'God, something very boring, believe me. I don't know all the details, but someone was killed at a Demonstration in London a couple of years ago, actually it was Karen's boyfriend's father, bit strange that really. Anyway, it's all very hush hush, but the rumours are that it was a Met copper—'

Jeremy interrupted him. 'A Met copper? Are you serious?'

'That's what I hear, but as I say, I have nothing to do with the case.'

'So what are you doing looking at the computer screen all day?'

'Oh, waste of time if you ask me—I'm collecting and referencing an image of every officer who worked at the demo—what for, I have no idea.'

***

Jeremy was shocked but hid it well, they were further ahead than he or Black knew about, and it was all being done in secret.

'Well, that's all very boring, I wish I hadn't asked now.'

'I told you boring is the word, so now it's your turn.'

Jeremy lowered his voice even more, 'You must never mention a word of this. In fact, we have never had this conversation.' Jeremy stopped, and looked so serious that Robert thought he was going to divulge something extraordinary. 'There's a new Al Qaeda terrorist cell operating in Surrey. I'm monitoring them from here and in a mobile vehicle. They're planning to bomb a major railway station, but the problem is, we don't know which one yet.'

'Jesus, that's incredible, OMG—so exciting.'

Jeremy couldn't believe Robert had been taken in so easily. 'You can see why my work is so secret.'

'God. Yes. Do you think …' He hesitated. '… do you think it will end okay? I mean, they won't actually get to detonate you know … ?'

'We could pick them all up now, but we want their contacts. I'm always talking to GCHQ, we're listening to every word they say, and it's only a matter of time before we get them all.'

Robert looked jealous of Jeremy's job. 'Can you put a good word in for me? I wouldn't mind working in intelligence.'

'Robert, life is about "you scratch my back and I'll scratch yours", of course I'll help, but I can't do anything until we have this latest terrorist case sorted, you understand?'

'Of course, I understand, we're talking national security here. You know, when you're able to, I'd really appreciate your help.'

'You and I have to stick together; we could be working on the same team soon, hunting terrorists.'

Robert had been sucked in, and all the GCHQ, terrorist stuff had gone to his head. Hope mused that if Robert had seen him in his office reading his books and watching porn on his laptop, he might have thought differently.

Lunch over, Robert went back to his computer and Jeremy back to his office. Just as Jeremy got to the third floor landing, Karen came out of her office. She didn't say anything, just smiled at him, and that was enough. He watched her walk to the stairs and knew he had to have her. He wanted that prim-looking English rose screaming as he fucked her, and he couldn't wait.

CHAPTER 19

Karen met with mick in her office, and asked him, 'How is the work on the demonstration images progressing?'

'Slowly, boss. I keep getting dragged away to do other things, so Robert's the only full-timer and there are thousands of images; it's a long and laborious job.'

'Typical police work then. Is Robert all right?'

'He's doing a respectable job, but it's going to take weeks.'

'Keep him at it, and I'll come back to you later.'

Karen slumped back into her comfortable swivel chair, and thought seriously about asking Chief Inspector Park for some more manpower, but was loath to, as it wasn't an official enquiry. She sat up and decided to take the bull by the horns and get stuck in herself, and there was no time like the present.

She marched into the office being used by Robert on the ground floor like a whirlwind. 'Robert, the cavalry has arrived, show me what to do.' Then she rubbed her hands together and smiled. 'Lets crack on then.' Robert gawped at her open mouthed.

When Mick came back to the office an hour later, Robert and Karen were hard at it and chatting like best friends. It was painstaking work once you had identified an officer. You then had to check that he had not already been logged and, if he had, whether or not it would be useful to have another image perhaps from a different angle.

All the officers had been allocated numbers, and they were collectively on thirty-seven. Karen had already worked out that they were talking months not weeks. When she thought about that, she decided to take a broader look at it. So, instead of taking time on every image, they would delete the dozens that were obviously in the wrong location. That would still leave them hundreds, but it might not seem such a daunting task.

Exhausted from concentrating and looking at a computer screen for hours, which was tiring, at four thirty Karen decided she'd had enough. She trooped back upstairs and turned into the corridor to her office. Jeremy stood by a window, she approached him, and saw him blatantly looking her up and down, and it thrilled and aroused her in equal measure. Karen looked him in the eye.

'So, what are you going to do about it?'

Jeremy grasped her hand, pushed open the door to her office, and led her in, shutting the door with his foot. He turned her round and shoved her against the door, his hands travelled quickly to her white blouse and he ripped it open, scattering buttons all over the floor. Then he lifted her bra to reveal firm ripe breasts, and he bent down and sucked at a nipple that was soon hard and sticking out and begging for more.

'No, not here, no, please.'

His hand slipped down her knickers.

She soon lost control. 'Oh God.'

She couldn't stop, and grabbed at his belt and undid it, then fumbled with the trouser catch, eventually opening it. She pulled the zipper down and tugged at the trousers. They slipped down and she had it, a fully erect, hard cock in her hand. She masturbated it up and down, up and down. They both breathed loudly, hands grabbing at cock, breasts, and arses. Jeremy stood back and pulled his trousers off, Karen followed suit and, within a second, stood naked. She moved and put her hands on the back of one of the chairs, splayed her legs, and stuck her backside into the air. Jeremy was there in a second, and he entered her from behind with a deep thrust. She gasped when he slid in and out. It was over quickly, but had been frantic, spontaneous, and electrifying.

Without a word, Jeremy got dressed. When he'd finished, he looked up at Karen and said, 'We must do that again, it was fantastic.'

'I'll see. Now hurry up and go.'

Jeremy left and Karen felt near to tears. She'd enjoyed it, such passion, but in her office in the fucking police station? What was she thinking? Next time, if there was going to be a next time, she would take him back to the flat. And unprotected ... God, he'd better not have given her anything. And she was seeing Simon later. Oh well, no time to feel guilty. She opened the bottom drawer in her filing cabinet retrieved a bottle of screw-top Cabernet Sauvignon, and then drank from the bottle. Just before she left the office, she pulled on her suit jacket to hide her nearly button-less blouse, and ten minutes later she was on her way home, still enjoying the hot tingly feeling she had from the sex.

***

Jeremy still sat in his office, with his feet on the desk, relaxing. Robert had been right, she loved it, and there must be a next time. She was so fucking hot and sexy. Then it hit him: he'd just had sex with a Detective Inspector who was hunting him—talk about being closer to your enemies than your friends. He couldn't get any closer, which made him laugh. Then it occurred to him that he had fucked the woman who was going out with the son of the man he'd killed at the London demo. Imagine if Simon Kane found that out. He smiled even more.

***

The pace remained relentless: image after image—it was never ending. Robert found himself more and more on his own. The office walls seemed to have closed in and he felt more and more claustrophobic. His eyes were worn out, he was worn out, and he had to finish early—he needed to rest. But then something caught his eye; he looked closely at the screen. Just to the right side, three police officers pushed their way through the crowd, the one in the front being Jeremy Hope. 'What the fuck?' he said out loud, and then he sat back and wondered what the fuck Jeremy Hope was doing at the Energy Demo. Robert came up with one or two answers. He'd never asked him how long he'd been in intelligence, so he may well have been an ordinary copper then, or more interestingly, he was doing some Intelligence related work. He jumped up from his seat … this would be fun.

***

'Jez, you still here? Come down to my office, I've got a surprise for you.'

A couple of minutes later, Jeremy knocked and entered the office.

'Hi Rob, what's the surprise?'

Robert didn't speak, he just looked at Jeremy and then at the screen, and then nodded at Jeremy. Jeremy followed his eyes and saw the image on the screen, then he went closer, and to his horror he saw himself right there, right there on the fucking screen in the middle of the Energy Demo. His eyes bulged almost out of their sockets and he felt a deathly chill course through his body.

Robert challenged him, 'What the fuck were you doing at the Energy Demo?'

'Undercover work. We were after some Marxist agitators.' It slipped off Jeremy's tongue so easily.

Robert nodded with bright eyes. 'I knew it would be secret stuff.'

'Has anybody else seen this yet?'

'No, everybody left ages ago.'

Jeremy thought, desperate to know what to do. 'You'll have to delete this and anymore you find.'

Robert sat up straight, shocked. 'I can't do that, not without official approval.'

'This is secret work, Rob. It must be deleted. No one should know I was working at that Demo.'

'I can't delete it. You'll have to clear it with Detective Inspector Foster in the morning.'

'Okay, no problem, I'll talk to Karen. I presume you're on shift in the morning?'

'No, I'm having a change of scenery, I need some fresh air, a morning on the beat in Ashtead, and back on the computer after lunch.'

'Okay, catch up with you lunchtime.'

Jeremy flew back to his office and stood looking out of the window. Five minutes later, he saw Robert leave the station, so he dashed back downstairs to the office and tried the door—miracles of miracles, it was unlocked. He went straight to Robert's computer and turned it on. He navigated to the picture files, and when he saw *Energy* he realised that must be it. He clicked it open and he almost jumped for joy as the screen lit up with hundreds of images of police officers. He went back to 'pictures' and found a new file: *collated officers Demo,* then scrawled down and came to number eighty-two, Hope J. He opened it and there he was. Next, he right clicked and deleted it and closed the file. He went to the recycle bin on the computer and deleted it again. Then he rested, he needed to think, Robert would see straight away that his computer had been compromised and that his image had been deleted, and of course, he would have to tell Foster. Shit. He panicked, then pulled himself together, rushed back upstairs to his office, and called Philip Black—that bastard always knew the answer.

He listened to Black and, after five seconds, the call ended.

***

The tall, wholesome, good looking young Police Officer strolled down Ashtead high street, and received a couple of bizarre looks simply because no one had seen the like for years: a proper policeman with a proper helmet on, walking the beat! At twenty-six, the constable had been in the police force since attending Hendon Police Training Centre at the age of eighteen. He adored the job and had become one of those policemen who people intuitively took to quickly. He had a comfortable manner that translated into good, effective local community policing. He was married with a four-year-old daughter, Carrie, and his wife, Georgina, was six months pregnant. They lived in a small terraced house in Leatherhead, Surrey, and although they had problems and challenges like everybody else, the family remained close-knit and joyful.

The day was gloriously sunny with clear blue skies, and being outside rather than stuck behind a desk suited him, he wore a short-sleeved, crisp, whiter than white shirt, without the jacket, and enjoyed the sun's warmth on his body. The constable popped his head into several shops and said good morning, and always received a courteous reply. He eventually got to, and walked past, the small electrical shop and turned right into the alley, which led through to the Ashtead Peace Memorial Hall car park. His predominant mood was one of peace, thinking of the new baby on the way.

When he'd reached the halfway point of the empty alley, a man entered the other end and came towards him. He wore white trainers, a green and white tracksuit, and had a flat cap pulled down over his eyes. Due to the tightness of the alleyway, the policeman prepared to squeeze over so they could both pass. They got closer and closer, now just six feet apart, and he was about to smile at the man when he got a feeling that he recognised him. When he tried to look closer, he saw who it was ...

'Hey, what are y—'

The man's arm moved in a fast striking forward motion, and then he felt it—an excruciating burning pain tore deep into his stomach—he felt and heard the ripping of his skin and further agonising pain as the man pulled the knife upwards. He heard gurgling and sucking as the weapon was then pulled out of his chest, he just caught a fleeting glimpse of the long-bladed serrated knife, and his hands automatically went to the wound. Within a second, blood covered them, and intestines, which dangled out of the gaping stomach wound.

The man had long gone, and the young constable collapsed forward onto his knees—he was dying. The pain felt unbearable but he could still reflect on his precious little Carrie. Eyes closed, he sobbed, then whispered her name, 'Carrie, I love you.' And then his wife's name, *'Georgina, take care of them for me please, I'm sorry, so sorry I can't be with you.'* Then he thought of the unborn baby and screamed in anguish. Distantly, he heard shouting and running feet, but it was too late and he fell forward. Nothing, nothing but blackness and peace filled his world and, thankfully, no more pain.

***

While Karen sat in her office, Mick Hill took the call and ran to the stairs, then took them two at a time, and was gasping when he got to the top. He ran to the office door, knocked, and went straight in. Karen looked up and was instantly worried. Mick took a deep breath.

'Robert Young's been killed, stabbed to death in Ashtead, car's ready.'

Karen stood up and stumbled, grabbed the table to steady herself, and stood still for a moment. Robert was one of her favourites—a lovely young man, it wasn't fair, he had a pregnant wife, children—she welled up and could feel the tears coming.

'Boss, lets go,' Mick urged.

Karen pulled herself together and strode towards the door. Mick opened it and followed her as she quickened her pace.

A police car had arrived four minutes after the 999 call, an ambulance from Epsom got there in eight minutes, but Robert was already dead and nothing could be done—he'd bled to death through the terrible knife wounds to his stomach and chest.

Karen and Mick arrived at the same time as the ambulance. Karen, back in command, felt delighted to see that the high street had been closed and strict procedures were being adhered to. She had officers combing the immediate area asking for witnesses, and they quickly found out that a man had been seen leaving the alley at the same time as the murder was committed. He'd apparently been dressed in a green and white tracksuit and white trainers. This information was sent to all mobile officers who were pouring in from all over Surrey to help in the search.

Karen rubbed her eyes. 'Why would someone want to kill Robert? It doesn't make sense.'

Mick had also become fond of Robert and felt upset and distressed. 'We're going to catch the bastard who did this, and when we do—'

Karen spoke loudly, 'We'll arrest him, and he'll spend the best part of his life in prison.' She understood Mick's feelings, but couldn't have any personal vendettas messing up the investigation. 'I want search teams here in the next ten minutes; crime scene should be here soon. Mick, get to work.' Karen said it with such force that she startled the officer and he jumped to it.

'Yes, boss.'

Karen looked around her, lights flashing in every direction, so many emergency services, and he couldn't be saved. Such a waste of a precious life. Who would want to kill a young police officer in the middle of Ashtead village? She couldn't understand it. Karen already knew they were up against it—random killings for no apparent reason were always difficult to solve. Oh God, she'd have to go and see his wife. With a shudder, she got his address from her phone contacts. It was in Leatherhead, not far away—she found Mick.

'I'm going to see his wife before she hears it from somewhere else. It's only ten minutes away. I'll see you back here.'

Karen found a female police officer to take with her, who she would leave with Robert's family. They located the house and Karen didn't want to get out of the car. It was the worst thing she'd ever had to do. She eventually got out and walked to the door. A woman stood behind the kitchen window, and as soon as the woman saw the officer's uniform she looked worried, and within moments she flung the door open.

'What's happened?'

Karen tried to sound gentle, 'We'd better come in, Mrs Young.'

'Oh God, no, please.' She burst into tears.

Karen stayed for five minutes, and left as the police officer was putting on the kettle. She was soon back at the crime scene and talking to Mick.

'So, what have we found?'

'Nothing, fuck all, all we have is the green and white tracksuit and white trainers—perhaps he was fucking Irish.'

Karen shook her head. 'Nothing will stop me finding the bastard that did this. Nothing.' Then she shouted, 'Mick, do you hear me? NOTHING.' Then in a more normal voice, 'I want all the reports on my desk first thing in the morning.' Then she turned away.

Tears streamed down her cheeks while she drove back to Epsom nick. She parked and entered the back entrance. The station was in mourning—a colleague had been killed doing his job—it was deathly quiet, no one spoke, no one needed to speak, and the silence said so much.

She made towards her office, and colleagues lined the way, nodding in commiseration, some openly crying—oh what a terrible day. More officers lined the stairs and the landing. Jeremy looked distraught—she knew he and Robert had become firm friends, so she smiled at him, and a tear fell down his cheek. Finally, she made it to her office and shut the door, then made straight for her booze drawer and took out the red wine. She knocked it back, and it felt good, but she needed something stronger—she'd get a new bottle of Pernod and maybe some whisky on the way home. The she collapsed into her chair and the tears flowed.

***

Jeremy went back to his office. He felt proud of his performance, and the tear when Karen was looking at him had been a piece of magic. He put his laptop into his satchel and went to pick up a blue holdall by his feet. He stopped and pushed the green-coloured tracksuit arm into the holdall and zipped it up tight. He opened the door, turned the light out, and was soon on his way home.

***

Karen was still in shock as she drove home, and could very easily have had an accident. She just couldn't understand why someone would apparently randomly stab an officer to death in sleepy little Ashtead village. They needed to check if he had enemies, who had he arrested that might have come out of prison looking for revenge, but the theories all sounded too farfetched for Karen to really consider. Perhaps it had been a nutter who had something against the police in general, and Robert had just been unlucky to be chosen for the retribution. Karen jumped as the driver behind her pressed his horn viciously; she was sat at traffic lights that had turned green. She pulled away, swung across the road, and parked in front of the Co-op. Two minutes later, she got back into the car, with a bottle of

Pernod and a bottle of Bells whisky. She did a U-turn and headed for home.

While she drove, she had another thought: could it be a contract killing by a professional? But why? He hadn't been working on anything remotely contentious. Then it hit her, like someone had smashed a brick in her face. Robert had just started work on the Energy Demo investigation. No, there couldn't be a connection—surely not. He'd only worked on collating images, … maybe that was it, and there was something someone didn't want him to find. No, it was all too tenuous. She would speak to Park to see what he thought. But would that be a bad idea? Maybe he would say there was no evidence. She could imagine his enumeration on the subject: questionable, feeble, unconvincing, weak, and shaky—no, she wouldn't say anything, not just yet.

At last, she pulled up at her flat, parked, and strode into the building, gripping the Co-op bag underneath to make sure the bottles couldn't fall through and shatter—she desperately needed them. Once she'd opened her front door, she made straight for the kitchen, where she plonked everything on the small table and grabbed the whisky bottle. She opened it in double quick time, then took a heavy cut-glass tumbler out of the cupboard and poured a good measure. For a second or two, she twirled the whisky in the glass, deep in thought. Then the smell hit her and she poured it down her throat. Its hot, burning sting gave her a warm comforting feeling. She put the empty glass down and gave herself a refill, then walked towards the bathroom for a shower, still sipping the whisky.

When Simon arrived at eight that evening, Karen answered the door in a completely drunken state. He kissed her on the cheek and held her.

'Not like you to be drunk on a weekday, and this early—what's happened?'

Karen had drunk three-quarters of the whisky, and slurred her words. 'It's not every day a polite, considerate, kind, charming and everything else you can think of, young copper gets stabbed to death in a small Surrey village.' And with that, the floodgates opened. Within a moment, Karen was crying hysterically.

'He was a good copper—never hurt a fly, such a kind, nice young man. Why, Simon? Why did he have to fucking die like that?' Simon almost carried Karen into the lounge and laid her on the sofa. 'Wife and children, Simon. He bled to death on his own in a fucking alley. God, sometimes I despair, I'm not even sure I can go back. I've had enough, really had enough. I need a drink.' She staggered back to her feet and headed to the kitchen.

Simon followed her. 'Karen, the booze, it's not going to help, you know we've both been there before.'

Karen raised her voice, 'I don't fucking care. I don't want to remember. I want to blot it all out.' The hysterical crying started again. Simon went to her and helped carry her back to the sofa.

'Don't worry, I'm here now, everything will be all right, I'll look after you.'

And then she remembered fucking Jeremy Hope and she fell further down the black hole that went on forever and ever. She jerked up and screamed at the top of her voice, 'Give me a fucking drink, right now!' Then she collapsed.

Karen opened her eyes at nine o'clock the next morning, and had never felt so ill. Her head throbbed, she felt nauseous, and her mouth was as dry as the Sahara. Initially, she wondered where she was, and then saw the familiar surroundings. Thank God, she said to herself. She had no recollection of the night before and, on other occasions, had woken up naked next to a strange man she didn't even know the name of. She glanced round the room and spotted Simon—he slumped, fully clothed, asleep in a chair. Now the day and night before began to focus … Robert being killed, buying Whisky and Pernod at the Co-op, … that sick feeling of not knowing what she'd said and done that haunted her so often was back.

She threw the blanket off and slipped off the sofa, then made for the kitchen. Each step was a triumph over body and soul as her shuddering movements told her she was ill and should lie back down. She made it to the sink and turned the cold tap on, then let it run for a short time to make sure it was as cold as possible. Next, she filled a beaker and drank until it was empty, then filled it again and drank more slowly.

'So, you're up?'

Karen turned around—Simon stood in the kitchen entrance. 'Not for long, I'm going to bed.' She ambled past Simon, touching his arm gently, and made her way to the bedroom. Simon followed, and watched as she clambered into bed and pulled the duvet up tightly round her neck. He sat on the side of the bed and smiled. Karen was still tearful. 'I'm so sorry, Simon, I ...'

'Don't worry. No harm done. You got drunk, end of story.'

'I didn't say ... or do anything terrible?'

'Nothing, you were upset about Robert, which is only to be expected.' He ruffled her hair.

'Except that most of the staff at the nick will turn up for work this morning. I can't go in, ... maybe this afternoon.' She closed her eyes, and Simon touched her cheek tenderly.

'You need to stay at home today and get fit so you can go back tomorrow.'

She fell asleep within moments.

CHAPTER 20

Commander Fellows had invited Philip Black to his club, Raffles, for lunch. The club was old fashioned, with book-lined rooms and one-hundred-year-old, huge comfy leather chairs. The members liked tradition and opposed change and modernisation with a passion. The restaurant had served the same food for generations: liver and onions, shepherd's pie, steak and ale pie, and everybody's favourite—bangers and mash with bubble and squeak. Desserts were called puddings and, again, were traditional: spotted dick, treacle roly-poly, and chocolate sponge with chocolate sauce. Commander Fellows felt in good humour. A massive cheeseboard had arrived at the table and the Taylor's vintage port was going down a treat.

He gave Philip a genial smile. 'So, everything is working out as we planned.'

'It would appear so, Sir, but I'm still watching the situation and the people closely. I don't want any surprises at the last moment.'

'Good, that's what I like to hear, and that's why you'll make an excellent Metropolitan Police Commander. My congratulations, Philip.'

It was a done deal: Philip Black would move up a rung on the ladder to Commander, something he had dreamt about for twenty years.

'Thank you, and of course, we will keep closely in touch.'

'It was terrible, Freddie Thompson popping off in that awful car accident, but he has left me with a majority of twenty-three thousand, which I intend to take full advantage of. I will be the new Member of Parliament for Kingston and Surbiton—almost the safest conservative seat in the country.'

Black chuckled. 'I'll drink to that, Sir.' He held up his glass of port. 'And after that, Sir? Downing Street?'

Fellows laughed and his eyes bulged. 'If the country needs me, I would have to answer that call.'

They both grinned and sipped their port.

'Back to work, Philip—what's happening with that bloody Foster woman?'

'Apparently, she's off sick. The terrible and tragic death of the young police officer in Ashtead has upset her tremendously.'

Fellows shook his head. 'No guts. The woman is weak. Hope has turned out well.'

'So much better than we could have hoped for—no pun intended—yes, he's doing a good job.'

Fellows spoke in a murmur, 'Is there much in the slush fund at the moment?'

'At least a hundred-thousand. You need some?'

'Not at all, but might be a good idea to send Hope a bonus, … say, ten grand.'

Philip nodded. 'Yes, a good idea. I'll see to it immediately.'

The slush fund was a secret account in Switzerland, used to reward team members who had done something helpful for the organisation. Matt and Tony, who had murdered Scotty, got a twenty-grand bonus each, and now it was Jeremy's turn. The money came from two drug barons, who Fellows protected in exchange for huge amounts of money. There was nothing that Fellows and Black wouldn't do to forward their own positions of power and influence.

***

Jeremy sat watching Masterchef, one of his favourite programs. He had a glass of Beaujolais, which he sipped while alternately stuffing Doritos into his mouth. He heard the thud as something hit the floor, having been posted through the letterbox. He put the glass down on the small coffee table at his side, and made for the front door. He picked the package up and thought it would be for his wife Sara, but when he looked at the name it was addressed to him. Surprised, he headed back to the lounge. He sat down took, a further sip of wine, and then opened the package. It was well sealed and he had to fight to get the sellotape off. A little nervous at what he might find, he eventually got it open and pulled a plastic bag from the cardboard package. When he looked closely at it, he couldn't believe it, … a huge wedge of twenty-pound notes, tied with an elastic band. He sat back and passed the bag from hand to hand. Then his mobile rang.

'A little present for a job well done, and there's plenty more where that came from.' The line went dead.

Jeremy felt ecstatic. He looked at the wedge of cash—must be a few thousand. Plenty for a fantastic holiday abroad. He opened the bag and counted out fifty notes ... a grand.

'Sara, come here, good news,' he called.

He hid the package underneath the seat cushion, and Sara walked in a minute later. 'What's the good news, then?'

Jeremy threw the buddle of cash at her and she caught it with a wide-eyed look. As soon as she saw what it was, she yelped, 'Oh my God.' A huge smile lit up her face and eyes.

'Treat yourself, you deserve it.' Jeremy felt like the big man.

Sara was over the moon and couldn't take her eyes off the notes, and then suddenly her demeanour changed. 'Eh, where exactly did you get this?'

'Don't worry, one of the guys knows a racing tipster, and he gave me the nod on an outsider. Brilliant, isn't it?'

The smile reappeared on Sara's face. 'Just be careful.' She looked at him, probably to judge whether he was telling the truth or not, but must have decided to give him the benefit of the doubt, because she laughed as she slipped the money into her bra and skipped out of the room, so much happier than when she went in.

CHAPTER 21

Fergus had been waiting for over an hour. The information board said the plane had landed, and he stood watching the arrival doors like a hawk. Gatwick seemed really quiet—he couldn't believe how few people were in the North Terminal—the only busy place was the Costa coffee outlet, which sat opposite the arrivals. Mind you, it was eleven at night. He'd already had two coffees, and felt as nervous as hell. Would she be pleased to see him? He shook his head and told himself off. If she didn't want to see him, she wouldn't be on the plane a week after they'd met in Cannes.

A sudden rush engulfed the large space when the doors swung open. Several French-looking people scampered through, and there she was. God, she looked beautiful. French women had a way of wearing simple clothes, while still managing to look like film stars. He ducked under the silver bars and ran to her. She saw him, took one step, and they were in each other's arms. They hugged tightly and then kissed, and they were stuck like glue for what seemed an inappropriate time, as the taxi drivers with their name boards, and other passengers and visitors to arrivals stared.

'Esme, Esme, I'm so happy to see you.' He refused to let go of her.

Esme looked and sounded near to tears. 'Not as happy as I am to see you, believe me. I've missed you so much.' More hugging and kissing followed.

Eventually, they'd professed their love for each other to exhaustion and Fergus felt it was time to move. He took Esme's bag and they left arm in arm towards the short-stay car park, just across the road. Fergus drove and Esme talked. She told him about her Mama and Papa, how the restaurant was doing, and how the flight had been good and on time. Fergus loved to listen to her, and within an hour or two he would be kissing every centimetre of her gorgeous body—he couldn't wait. After Esme stopped talking for a second, Fergus got in quick and asked about the Mary Bishop case. Esme laughed.

'What case? It has been closed. The official view is that it was suicide, end of story.'

Fergus had thought that would be the answer. 'I'm telling you that Alex was responsible, he'll turn up, he's British and probably English, and he'll be back here sometime. By the way, can you give our e-kit people a description? It would be good to have something on file.'

'Of course, it is easy. He is big, and has a … what you call? … I think, a crew cut.'

'Anyway, it would be helpful. Now, are you hungry? Thirsty?'

'Only for you.' She moved her hand to his crotch. This caught Fergus by surprise and he blushed. 'Fergus, you are going red again.' She leant over and kissed him on the cheek and, at the same time, squeezed his swelling cock.

'We'd better get home quickly or we may have to stop the car,' he said with a chuckle.

Esme smiled, and spoke seductively, 'You want to do it in the car?'

'No, I said we'd better hurry home because—'

'Yes, let's stop the car somewhere, it will remind me of my teenage years.' She rubbed and squeezed some more.

Fergus felt flustered. Aroused as he was, he tried to calm the sexual tension a little. 'It'll be more comfortable at home, and we're only twenty minutes away.'

'Live dangerously. I will suck your cock and swallow.'

Fergus was shocked, but got busy looking for somewhere to stop.

Three minutes later they came off the M25 at the A3 turnoff and Fergus turned left into a dark wooded area with a car park, where Esme did exactly what she said she would, and Fergus got his first ever car blow job. The rest of the journey back to Fetcham was uneventful, but Esme got her voice back and didn't stop talking the whole way. They got home and went straight to bed, where they made love for hours, finally collapsing in each other's arms and falling asleep. Fergus had taken the Friday off, so they could make a long weekend of it, with Esme flying back on Sunday night.

They woke up late and cuddled some more. Esme was insatiable and soon sat on top of Fergus, riding him like she was bucking in the saddle of a Grand National winner.

Fergus hadn't been sure how Esme would take to the somewhat dingy one-bedroom flat. The whole place needed decorating, and the furniture, what there was of it, was hand-me-downs and from the British Heart Foundation charity shop in Wallington. But Esme said she loved the quaintness, even though it could do with a lick of paint and a woman's touch. Fergus thought she was being kind but, seeing as she spent most of the time in bed, it didn't really matter what the rest of the flat was like.

On Saturday, he eventually got her to go out for lunch in Guildford town centre. He surprised her by taking her to the Thai Terrace, a modern, contemporary rooftop restaurant in Sydenham Mansions. She had never eaten Thai food, and immediately fell in love with the décor, which featured Buddhas and oriental tapestries. Fergus ordered for her and the table soon groaned under the weight of countless delicacies such as Bami Haeng Pet (Egg Noodles with Dry Braised Duck), Phat Si-io (Rice Noodles with Pork and Soy Sauce), and what turned out to be Esme's favourite: Chuchi pla Kaphong (A red curry with Fried Snapper fish). After lunch, Fergus took her to the Tunsgate Square shopping centre, which had a large number of designer fashion stores, which he felt sure she'd love. Just as they came out of the

Ralph Lauren store, lo-and-behold but whom should they bump in to, other than Detective Inspector Karen Foster and a man.

The DI greeted them warmly. 'Fergus, how are you enjoying your weekend?' While she spoke, she smiled at Esme, and didn't give Fergus time to answer. 'And you must be Esme Delon. So nice to meet you, and thank you so much for all the help you gave Fergus in Cannes.'

Esme returned the smile. 'It was my pleasure.'

Fergus went red. How did she know his friend was Esme?

Karen introduced herself, 'I'm Detective Inspector Karen Foster.' Then she turned to Simon. 'This is my friend, Simon.' Then, to Esme, she said, 'You have a good young man in Fergus, and he has a bright future in the force. I'm so happy to meet you, Esme.'

Karen seemed to have taken an immediate liking to the young woman. Fergus looked on, bemused, as Karen asked, 'Esme, when are you returning to France?'

'Sunday night.'

'Oh, so soon. That's a shame. Look, what are you doing tonight? Why don't we all go out for dinner?'

Fergus went to open his mouth, but Esme beat him to it. 'We would love to.' She turned to Fergus. 'Wouldn't we, my sweet?'

Fergus could hardly speak. 'Y-yes, love to, sounds like fun.' He shoved his free hand into his pocket, while Esme held firmly to the other one.

Then Simon pitched in. 'Sounds lovely. Do you like Greek food?'

Esme raised her eyebrows. 'I don't think I've ever had Greek. Sounds wonderful, though.'

Simon looked at Karen and Fergus. 'So, the Greek Tavern, Chapel Street, eight p.m.?'

Once the arrangements were made, they parted company and Fergus was not best pleased.

'Esme, I have to tell you my idea of a great night out does not include dinner with my boss.'

Esme grabbed his arm and smiled. 'I like her. In fact, I might fancy her a bit.'

Fergus just looked at her in amazement.

She giggled. 'Oh, don't be so straight and traditional. She looks gorgeous, and I think could be bi-sexual.'

'How would you know if she was ... ?'

Esme stared into his eyes. 'I wouldn't, unless I am bi-sexual myself. Don't be shocked, dear. I've had two relationships with women, both fantastic experiences, and this is not so unusual in France. We are all adults, no?'

'Maybe, but you cannot have a fling with my boss, it is out of the question.' His face flushed again at the thought of Esme and Karen naked, entwined in each other's arms. Fergus felt shocked, and that everything had turned upside down in a minute. He feared that Esme was too cosmopolitan for him and, as for fancying women, God forbid! What would his mother and Father say? Fergus now dreaded the meal at the Greek restaurant, and thought about faking illness to get out of it.

'Esme, I don't think this meal tonight is a very good idea.'

Esme gave Fergus a quizzical look that said so much. 'And exactly why is that?'

'I'm scared you might start groping Detective Inspector Foster under the table.' He tried to laugh, but it didn't quite work.

'Oh please, I would do nothing to embarrass you. I am, of course, joking. I'm not in love with this Karen Foster, and have just met her. But, I am in love with you.' She wrapped her arms around his neck and gave him a big kiss. 'See, only you, my love, I promise.'

'Well, okay then. You're sure this evening won't turn into an embarrassment for me?'

'Of course not. Come on, let's go home and have some fun before we get ready for tonight.'

Fergus smiled, then laughed. 'Well, if you insist, let's go.'

***

When they got home, Esme went straight into the shower. She then spent an hour licking, sucking, and fucking Fergus, so he would be in a happier mood come the evening. She loved it and could tell that Fergus had as well. She well knew how to spoil a man in bed, and the age-old adage that to keep your man happy was to be cordon bleu in the kitchen and a whore in the bedroom, was never more appropriate than what Esme had just been like with Fergus.

She could see that Fergus still felt concerned about the evening ahead, as he did the buttons up on his designer blue shirt, but at least he was happier. Esme dressed in a black mini skirt with a skimpy silky top that, when she leant forwards or sideways, exposed her braless, firm breasts. Fergus mentioned that it was revealing, but Esme said she dressed like that for him, and that he should take it as a compliment. What Esme didn't say was that she had purposefully dressed like that because she wanted Karen to see her breasts, and maybe she omitted to mention the fact she wasn't wearing any knickers either. When they left, Esme wore a long coat to keep warm and to keep Karen's surprise under wraps. Fergus drove as usual, and Esme—as usual—took the micky because of how slowly he drove.

'You English drive so slowly and with no feeling,' she said, gesticulating with her hands.

'Two things, Esme, I am Scottish not bloody English, and I am a very good police trained driver, thank you very much.'

'What is the point of this training? In France we are naturally gifted drivers, do you not think?'

Fergus shook his head and smiled. 'Yes, Esme, you are the best driver in the world.'

Esme liked that and sat contentedly and quietly for the rest of the journey. They arrived at the restaurant and parked, it was ten past eight—they were late.

Karen and Simon were already inside, and two bottles of wine sat on the table. They sat and chatted as Fergus and Esme entered. Simon sat with his hand in the air waving. Fergus let Esme move in front of him and they made their way to the table near the back of the restaurant. It was then all hellos and how are you's and general bonhomie. Esme waited and made sure Karen was looking at her when she removed her coat. Karen looked gobsmacked, and her eyes had immediately been drawn to Esme's breasts, which moved under the silky fabric. As Esme moved to sit down, one of her nipples poked briefly through the gap at the neckline. Karen herself wore a see-through blouse with a black bra and jeans, she looked chic and sexy, and Esme noticed.

'You look so lovely, Karen. You have great dress sense.'

Karen laughed. 'And you, Esme, are ...' She paused, while she looked at Esme's firm breasts, which moved against the flimsy fabric as she breathed. 'You are very beautiful. Fergus is a lucky man.'

'I'll drink to that,' Fergus chimed in.

They ordered Meze, and Esme loved all the small bowls of different food that filled the table. The wine disappeared quickly, and another bottle was ordered. They had all finished their food.

'Esme, come to the bathroom with me,' Karen said.

Simon spoke up, 'Why do women always go to the loo in pairs? I never understand it.'

With a chuckle, Esme rose from the table and they sauntered off to find the ladies'.

***

As they entered the bathroom they innocently brushed shoulders, looked at each other, and smiled. Karen went into one of the individual cubicles, and when she came out, she found Esme combing her hair in front of the mirror. Karen washed her hands, and then moved behind her and slipped her hands in the side of the blouse and grasped her breasts. She rubbed the nipples gently and Esme moaned. Karen kissed her on the neck and smelt a delicious musky perfume, then she dropped her hands to Esme's skirt, took the hem in her hands, and lifted to reveal a gorgeous rounded bottom. She grabbed the two cheeks and squeezed. Just at that second, the door swung open and a woman entered. Esme just got her skirt down in time, and the two of them headed for the door. On the way, Karen whispered in Esme's ear, 'I want you so much.'

Esme turned and smiled. 'Me too.'

They re-joined the men and the evening went well, which wasn't surprising considering they had drunk six bottles of wine and various shorts. The meal over, they prepared to leave. On the way out, Esme pulled Karen back a little and spoke to her quietly, ' I need a favour from you. Would you ...'

Both couples got home safely and were soon making love in their respective bedrooms. But, while having sex with Fergus, Esme thought of Karen, and Visa versa.

CHAPTER 22

This was the first time Karen had taken Simon with her to one of the 'Surrey get to know you' parties at the Town Hall. She'd always been too scared to take Chau, but now she felt thankful to have a man on her arm. Karen had gotten used to these events by now, and she always followed the same routine: move around, say hello to lots of people, make sure Chief Inspector Park saw she was there, and then disappear early. She'd told Simon this one would be no different, and he had agreed quickly.

When they entered the room, Karen looked around—there must have been about a hundred people, all eating nibbles and holding wine glasses, as they chatted in small groups. She noticed two smartly dressed men stare at her, and they didn't remove their eyes when she held their look. Something about them put her on guard. Danger—she would have to find out who they were before she left. They mingled for a few minutes, and then a hand on Karen's shoulder surprised her. She turned around.

'You're Detective Inspector Foster, I believe.' It was one of the two men—a horrible, slimy man with a weasel face.

'Yes, that's right, and who might you be?' she asked with only a faint smile.

'Philip Black, Commander, Metropolitan Police.'

This announcement shocked Karen. They were here … Black and Fellows were actually here.

'How are you, Detective?' he asked her.

The smile disappeared. 'Fine, thank you. What can I do for you?' She wasn't about to be intimidated by this excuse for a man.

'The new Member of Parliament for Kingston and Surbiton would like a word.'

Karen knew this meant Fellows, and decided to put down a marker straight away. 'Well, I'll be here for another hour, so when it's convenient he can come and find me.'

Black gave her a filthy look that said it all. 'I do think it would be in your interests to play ball, Miss Foster.'

'As I said, I'm not going anywhere.' With this, she slipped her arm into Simon's and walked off.

A short while later, Commander Fellows approached the two of them. 'Detective Foster, or can I call you Karen? Sorry about that, I was busy or, of course, I would have come to say hello earlier. I've heard so many good things about you from Chief Inspector Park that I had to come and say hello. Peter Fellows.' He offered his hand.

Karen shook hands, and then Simon and Fellows did the same. Simon pulled his hand away as quickly as he could without giving too much offence.

'So, you cleaned up Bermondsey and now you're doing the same in Surrey, very commendable indeed.'

'I didn't clean up Bermondsey on my own, and a lot of good officers died while I was there. As to Surrey, it's no different to every police force. There are always messes to clear up and bad apples to find, don't you agree?'

'Of course, but sometimes things are best left alone, or there can be personal repercussions.'

Karen was not going to put up with that. 'Are you threatening me, Fellows?'

'Don't be absurd, woman, I don't go round threatening people. Just take care to stay out of the wrong business.'

Karen's blood boiled. 'That sounds like a threat to me. You want to be careful, it's against the law, as you well know.'

'Well, it's been a pleasure, Detective. I'm sure we'll meet again in the not too distant future.' Fellows spoke to her like she was something unpleasant he had trodden on.

Karen and Simon moved away to get new drinks.

'There is an air of menace around that man. He scares the shit out of me,' Simon murmured once they were out of earshot.

'Don't worry, he'll get what's coming to him, they always do.'

Karen glanced round to see where Fellows and Black were. The Westburgh bitch had joined them. Karen's hackles rose as she remembered the encounter at Epsom nick, and five seconds later she noticed Fellows and Chief Inspector Park chatting like long lost buddies. Karen felt physically sick, and she and Simon sneaked out a few minutes later to go home.

***

Fellows nodded to Park. 'That Foster woman is a menace. Philip, here, tells me she is most uncooperative and even threatened one of his staff. It's really not good enough, you know. Why don't you give her a desk job? That's all she's fit for.'

Chief Inspector Park had to be careful, but he'd been round the block. 'I admit she's a bit headstrong, but she is a good police officer.'

'So, what do you say then, … I understand your position is coming up for review due to your age, … be a shame if you couldn't stay, don't you think?'

Park was caught. Fellows had the influence to get rid of him. 'I think a desk job would suit Detective Foster for a couple of months—she's been overdoing it and could do with the rest.'

'You see, Philip, this is called cooperation between interested parties. Excellent, Park, glad to hear it, and you must come to my club soon for a spot of dinner.'

'Be delighted to, Sir, whenever is convenient for you.' Park couldn't wait to get away from this obnoxious peer.

'Good, I'll be in touch.' Fellows, Black, and Westburgh walked off towards the exit.

***

Sunday afternoon soon came around, and Fergus and Esme were relaxing after making love yet again. Fergus had become more depressed, as the time to take Esme to the

Airport drew closer. He ran his hand down Esme's breast and tweaked her nipple. 'Esme, I wish you didn't have to go.'

'Are you sure about that?'

'Of course I'm sure.'

'Well, in that case, I'll stay for at least another two weeks.' Esme's smile stretched from ear to ear.

'Very funny. What about your job?'

'It's a surprise. I asked Karen to contact my boss and say I was helping with the Mary Bishop enquiry, and could I stay for a further two weeks.' She held her arms out, and then screamed, Fergus jumped and crashed into her and they rolled across the bed and landed on the floor with a thud. Esme didn't care, she was so happy, and a small bruise on her bum was a price worth paying to see Fergus's happy face.

***

On Monday morning, Karen felt nervous and excited at the thought of seeing Esme again. She hadn't felt so excited since the first sex with Chau, a few years ago. A knock sounded at the door.

'Come in.' Karen walked towards the door, expecting Fergus and Esme, whom she'd instructed to come straight to her office upon their arrival, but she got a shock when Jeremy appeared.

'Morning, boss, I just came to say hello.'

Karen wasn't prepared for Jeremy and, for some inexplicable reason, wasn't happy to see him. She made an instant decision. 'Good morning, Jeremy. Look, I don't know what happened the other day, but it's not going to happen again, it was a one off, okay.' She smiled, trying to keep it as pleasant as possible.

'Oh, that's a shame. I enjoyed myself and I think we should do it again.'

Karen spoke more firmly, 'It's not going to happen, so best go and get on with your work.'

'Be a shame if it was to get out, shagging in the office, wonder what Park would make of that?'

Karen took three steps closer to Jeremy until she loomed right in his face. 'I wanted this to be done nicely, but if you insist on being difficult and nasty, I'll fucking well shaft you. Rape is a very serious offence and, believe me, I make a brilliant witness. Especially as I have a sample of your DNA on a tissue, and you know where that's from, don't you?' It was a lie, but it would scare him to death. Jeremy wasn't ready for that and looked shocked, then he backed off.

'Only joking. Have a nice day,' he said and turned towards the door. Just then, another knock came. Jeremy turned to Karen.

'Come in,' she said, feeling relieved at the interruption.

Fergus entered and, behind him, came Esme. Fergus saw Jeremy. 'Hi Jeremy, how are you?'

'Very well, thank you. I was just leaving.' He looked at Esme. 'And who is this?' He smiled.

'This is Esme, from France. She's working with us for a couple of weeks.'

'Doing what, may I ask?'

Before Fergus could answer, Karen stepped in. 'Thank you, Jeremy.' Then she ushered him out of the room. Back to the door, she said, 'Esme, welcome. Come and have some coffee.'

'Wow, you have such a big office,' Esme said, looking around and taking in the size of it. Karen felt overdressed in her dark-blue trouser suit, but she *was* at work.

'I love your work suit,' Esme said, and Karen laughed. They were on the same wavelength.

Janet came in with fresh coffee and biscuits, and they all sat round the conference table, chatting.

***

While Karen admired Esme, the Frenchwoman secretly wished that Karen had hold of her breasts again. Tenseness thickened the air; an erotic atmosphere that only Esme and Karen could feel. Both of them knew that sooner or later they would be naked together, exploring and touching every part of each other's bodies. Coffee finished, Karen and Esme kissed cheeks, and the electricity passed between them.

Fergus showed Esme around the station, and then dropped her back at the Ashley shopping Centre in Epsom town centre. Esme strolled through the centre, spending a lot of time in M & S and Waitrose, where she picked up chicken, red wine, button mushrooms, shallots, and bacon for a 'cock-au-vin'. She loved the clothes and shoe shops, and enjoyed herself.

After a couple of hours, she decided to have a rest and went to the Costa Coffee shop, where she ordered a Latte and sat on one of the stools by the window. She sat sipping her coffee while people watching through the huge windows. She felt happy: her last relationship had ended in disaster and she was so thrilled to be with Fergus—a strong, dependable man and, she hoped, loyal. She took another sip of her hot coffee and nearly choked. She focussed intently upon a man strolling past the window—she felt sure it was Alex. She jumped up from her seat and rushed to the door, walked quickly to catch him up, and grabbed him by the shoulder.

'Stop, Sir. I am a Police officer. You are Alex, from France, yes? I need to question you about—'

Before she could finish, Alex turned and punched her full in the face, breaking her nose. Blood poured out, and the pain felt excruciating. Esme didn't stop, but shouted, 'You are wanted for murder. You are under arrest.' She ducked another punch and grabbed hold of one of his legs.

Alex shouted to add to the confusion, 'It's my ex-wife, she's mad, she's trying to kill me.'

'Help me, please, someone help me,' Esme shouted in reply.

Alex lifted his other foot and kicked Esme hard in the stomach, and though she doubled up in agony, she still didn't let go. And then help arrived. Two of the shopping centre security staff jumped on Alex, and helped Esme to subdue him. More staff turned up and, in the end, six security men had hold of him. Police officers arrived a few minutes later. An ambulance came as well, and took Esme to A & E at Epsom General Hospital—only minutes away.

***

Meanwhile, the police took Alex to the Epsom station and booked him in, and he soon sat ruminating in one of the cells in the basement. It was one of those funny situations where no one really knew what had happened and why. Karen was informed that a man had been arrested and that Esme Delon was in Epsom hospital, but her injuries weren't serious. Karen rushed to find Fergus and they were on their way to the hospital within minutes.

'Esme, you have no authority here. You cannot arrest anyone. You cannot attack people in the shopping centre. We are in big trouble. We'll be sued for this.' Karen couldn't believe Esme had gone for Alex. What she should have done was follow him and call for backup. She continued her tirade, 'You do realise that this man has done nothing wrong. Well, not in this country, anyway. He is innocent of any crime in the UK. We are in such deep shit.'

'I'm so sorry, Karen. In France, these things are not important. He is a wanted man, so I tried to detain him.'

Fergus rubbed her shoulder. 'You were incredibly brave, and I love you for that.'

'Thank you. I knew you would be on my side,' she said, but looked at Karen.

'I'm on your side, too, but we have procedures and protocols we have to follow.'

'Look at my nose—broken.' Esme burst into tears.

'Your nose is beautiful,' Fergus murmured, in an effort to soothe her.

Karen looked to the heavens. 'Fergus, get a grip. Take the rest of the day off, take Esme home, and I'll see you in the morning. Meanwhile, I'll try and clear up this mess.'

Karen rushed back to the Police Station. Mick met her in the CID offices and shook his head when he saw her. 'High powered lawyers are already here, and it looks bad,' he told her.

'Fuck, crazy French police officers, we don't need!' But she laughed. 'Although it does make life more interesting. So, what the fuck do we do now?'

Mick shrugged. 'Release him. Apologise, and pray.'

'I don't think so. I don't give a shit how we do it, but that bastard is staying here, at least for tonight. If nothing else, we are interviewing him in connection with a disturbance in the shopping centre, which means we can keep him overnight and ask him some interesting questions about Mary Bishop.'

'His brief won't let you ask any questions about France.'

'You're probably right. Anyway, I'll give it some thought. Speak to you later.' Karen walked off towards the stairs. Once she had reached her office, she called Chief Inspector Park. It had been the only sensible thing she could do. He knew that Alex had almost certainly killed Mary Bishop, and so she asked for his advice.

'That's right, Sir. He's in custody, but we'll have to let him go in the morning.'

'Well, you've done the right thing by calling me, so well done for that. This is a tricky situation. What happened in France has no bearing here at all. Philip Black has already been on the phone, but I haven't taken the call. Is Alex his real name?'

'We're confirming that as we speak, but his driving licence says he's Trevor Banks.'

Silence followed her words, then Park spoke with zest, 'I know that name. A former Metropolitan Police Officer, sacked for taking bribes, and he's almost certainly working for Fellows and Black. My God, what to do? Okay, look, try to scare him. It's a hell of a long shot, but if you can get a confession then we're home and dry.'

'It won't work. He's a former police officer.'

'You never know. There's nowt as queer as folk, as they say, and you never know 'til you try.'

'Okay. Thank you for your help, Sir.'

'My pleasure. See what you can do and keep in touch.'

CHAPTER 23

At around eight in the morning, Karen looked out of the window of her office and thought about Robert Young. They'd gotten nowhere, and only had the reports of the green and white tracksuit to go on. 'Fucking waste of time,' she said to herself with loathing. She looked out at the road and saw a beautiful, brand new, gleaming silver Mercedes. She admired it and wondered what the male driver did for a living to be able to afford such an expensive car. Then she got the shock of her life, as the car turned into the police station and drove through into the car park. What was that kind of car doing here? She rushed out of her office to the other side of the landing and looked out of the window, down onto the car park. The Mercedes parked, and Karen waited, expecting to see some top brass chief Inspector climb out. When Jeremy Hope stepped out of the car, she was stunned beyond belief.

Jeremy touched the paintwork on the bonnet and stood admiring what looked, to all intents and purposes, like his new car. Karen turned back to her office—she wasn't going to jump to conclusions; he could have borrowed it for the day, but she had to find out …

'Mick, Jeremy Hope has just driven into the station in a brand new Mercedes. Get the registration checked and see who the owner is.'

'What sort of Mercedes is it?'

'Mick, how do I know? It's a Mercedes, for God's sake. Just get on with it.'

Five minutes later, Mick phoned Karen back and confirmed that the registered owner was a Mr Jeremy Hope. Karen's suspicions heightened, but there could be a thousand reasons why he could afford such a beautiful and expensive car. She got stuck back into the paperwork mountain and momentarily put it out of her mind.

***

Jeremy loved his new car. He'd paid a seven-grand cash deposit and driven out of the showrooms with it two hours later. His wife had seen the car pull up outside the house and dashed out to see what the hell was going on. When Jeremy told her it was their new car, she'd jumped in the passenger seat and said, 'Let's go.'

Jeremy had to drive her round to her best friend's to show the new car off. When she enquired as to how they could afford such a good car, Jeremy told her that now he was a sergeant it wasn't a problem. Jeremy, of course, was hoping that at some time in the not-too-distant future, an envelope full of money would once again fall through the letterbox. And if anyone at the station asked questions about the car, he could claim a lucky bet or maybe an inheritance, or something. Besides, he had friends in high places that could make any problems go away.

***

At nine thirty, Karen sat making notes as she got ready to interview Trevor Banks. Finally done, she phoned down to the custody suite to prepare him for interview. Karen had to mentally get up for the interview, because she honestly thought it was a waste of time. Banks was a tough ex-metropolitan police officer and would be a hard nut to crack. On her way to the interview room, Karen stopped off at the CID office and picked up Mick, who was to accompany her. Within two minutes, they stood outside the room.

'Ready, Mick?'

'As I'll ever be.'

They pushed through the door together.

Karen made herself strong, in charge, and confident. 'Good Morning, Mr Banks.' She nodded at the solicitor sitting next to him. 'As you are aware, we are interviewing you this morning in connection with a disturbance at the Ashley shopping centre in Epsom yesterday. We will be taping the interview.'

Mick turned on the tape.

'Would you confirm your name and address, please, Mr Banks.'

'Trevor Banks, 16 Market Gardens, Surbiton.'

'I am Detective Inspector Foster. Also present, is sergeant Mick Hill and Craig Brown, solicitor.' She paused minutely, then continued. 'Mr Banks, I understand you are an ex-metropolitan police officer who was sacked for taking bribes.'

The Solicitor went apoplectic. 'This has no relevance and must be deleted from the tape immediately.' He stared, red faced, straight at Karen.

'I'm sorry, Mr Brown. I only stated that because, as he was a police officer, he is obviously aware of the interview process.' She turned from Brown and looked at Banks. 'Mr Banks, would you describe what happened at the Ashley Shopping Centre, please.'

'It was astonishing. I was walking along, window-shopping, when someone grabbed my shoulder. I thought I was being attacked, and turned and threw a punch, and it was only then I saw that it was a woman. Why she was attacking me, I don't know.'

'Is it not true that the woman who placed her hand on your shoulder shouted that she was a police officer?'

The Solicitor interrupted, 'She is a French police officer, with no power or jurisdiction in the UK. This was a simple case of assault on my client.'

'After you punched and broke the woman's nose, you knew it was a woman and yet you then proceeded to kick her viciously in the stomach, is that not true?'

Trevor's steely eyes glared at her. 'That is totally untrue.'

'Mr Banks, there are eighteen CCTV cameras in the Ashley centre, and I have viewed one this morning that clearly shows you kicking the woman in the stomach.'

'My client has been traumatised by the events and cannot recollect exactly what happened.'

'Mr Banks, when did you arrive back in the UK from France?'

'This has nothing to do with what happened in the Ashley Centre, and my client will not answer any questions other than those that are relevant.'

The interview was going exactly as she thought it would, and she continued. 'Mr Banks, do you know a lady by the name of Mary Bishop?'

'No, I do not.'

Just at that moment, the door opened, and a police constable entered, holding a sheet of white A4 paper. He said, 'Excuse me, Ma'am,' and handed it to Karen. A moment of silence fell as she glanced at the paper and, although she felt like smiling, and even laughing, she managed not to. She turned back to the suspect.

'I wonder, then, why the French Police Nationale have requested your extradition.'

Trevor Banks turned white and was, without question, in shock as he turned to his Solicitor and glared at him.

The Solicitor was not best pleased. 'I have not been informed of this development, Detective Inspector, why is that?'

'I'm sorry about that, but the paperwork has literally just come through.' She held the paper in the air, and the Solicitor made a grab for it, but Karen was too quick for him and pulled it away. Karen was furious. 'What do you think you're doing?'

'I don't trust you. Let me see the extradition request.' The Solicitor was seething.

'Not a chance. You'll have to take my word for it.'

'This is outrageous. I must protest in the strongest possible terms,' the Solicitor spluttered. 'I warn you now, if this is some sort of deception, you will be very sorry. I am asking for the second time, let me see the extradition request.'

'No. Now, the interview will continue. The Police Nationale have requested that you, Mr Banks, be extradited to answer questions about the suspicious death of a British National—one Mary Bishop. Now, I ask you again, do you know a woman by that name?' Banks looked at his Solicitor, who shook his head and said, 'No comment.'

Banks repeated, 'No comment.'

'I have to inform you that the French Police have an eye witness who saw you with Mary Bishop at an address in Cannes.' Karen paused, and then lied, 'With photographic evidence of that fact.'

Banks looked at his solicitor, and looked more worried by the second.

'No comment,' the Solicitor spat out through clenched teeth.

Banks repeated it again, 'No comment.' But he wouldn't hold Karen's gaze.

'I think we could all do with a break. The interview is stopped at nine fifty three a.m.'

Karen looked at Brown. 'We will leave you here with your client. When you have finished, or if you need anything, please speak to the police officer outside the door. We shall resume in one hour's time.'

Karen and Mick left the office and sped towards the CID offices.

'That's given them something to think about,' she said to Mick.

'Certainly has, boss. The, eh, extradition … I hardly dare ask.' He raised his eyebrows.

Karen took the piece of paper and handed it to Mick. He read from the top: *The French Police Nationale are considering a request to her Majesty's Government for the extradition of one Trevor Banks of …*

'So, they are considering,' he said, attaching importance to the word considering.

'Esme got her boss to send it, but at least its sort of official.'

'Jesus, boss, you could get in a lot of trouble for this.'

'Mick, I'm not stupid. The French Government are preparing the official papers as we speak.'

'Thank God for that. So what's the plan?'

'We'll grab a coffee and let them stew for a bit. Banks won't want to go back to France, so maybe there's some sort of deal to be done, but we need to speak to Banks without the Solicitor being present.'

'Easy enough. Just tell them questioning will resume in the morning, and then we have a chat with him on his own.'

'We'll finish our coffees first.' Karen smiled like the cat that had gotten the cream.

The Solicitor was informed the interview would continue the next morning at ten thirty a.m. He left the station on the understanding he would be back in the morning for the next interview. Karen watched as he left, and as soon as he got outside, he got on the phone to report in.

Karen looked forward to re-interviewing Banks. 'Time for us to have a private word with Trevor Banks, let's go.'

Karen and Mick returned to the interview room.

'I was wondering when you would reappear, what's the deal then?'

Karen smiled. 'I forgot for a second that you were a copper once. Why did you do it, Trevor?'

He shrugged. 'Wanted a nice house, car, you know how it is.'

As soon as he said 'car', Karen thought of Jeremy with his new Mercedes. She was momentarily in another world. 'Sorry, but I bet it was a Mercedes, wasn't it?'

Trevor laughed. 'Of course, only the best.'

'And it was silver coloured?'

Banks looked her straight in the eye. 'You're a good guesser, aren't you. So, get on with it, what's the deal?'

'You know already, don't you?'

Banks thought for a second. He had been in Karen's shoes many times. He started off confidently, 'Well, let me see, now. Something like I spill the beans on what I was doing in France and my contacts here who gave me that job and maybe I won't face extradition, how's that?'

'Trevor, well done, ten out of ten, and it was almost word perfect.' Karen put on her tough face. 'Now, let's cut the crap, make no mistake, we will send you back to France if you do not help us, it's as simple as that.'

Banks looked thoughtful and worried. 'Believe me, it's not as simple as that. I'll be killed, … better to be in France alive than dead meat here.'

'You know we can protect you. We need a confession, and information relating to certain individuals, and for that you will get a drastically reduced sentence.'

'You haven't grasped it, have you? There's no hiding place in prison or anywhere else—nowhere would be safe.'

'Well, at least you're safe here.'

'I can't serve my sentence here, but I tell you what, I'll think on it. Tell my Solicitor he's fired, and that I don't want to see him again.'

***

Banks had already made his mind up, but wanted to sleep on it. He didn't want to rot in some stinking French Jail for twenty years. Better to do five or ten here in the UK, and then disappear.

***

The Solicitor's office told Craig Brown that he was no longer working on the Trevor Banks case. He was totally shocked, as was his contact when he rang and told him. The wheels of violence were put into effect immediately ...

The man answered his mobile phone and listened.

He felt sick as he answered, 'I'm telling you, it is not possible.'

The man listened again, then said, 'You're not listening, it is fucking well impossible.'

The man had to listen yet again.

He wiped the sweat on his forehead.

'I have no idea how it could be done, and it would almost certainly end up with me joining him, and I'm fucked if I'm going to do that.'

He listened again and became more and more agitated as the call went on.

'You dare touch my family, I'm warning you, I'll bring everybody down, and I mean it, and that fucking well includes you.'

He went quiet, and a tear ran down his cheek as he listened to the other man.

'All right,' he shouted down the phone. 'Enough, enough.' They had him again; he was theirs. He rubbed his forehead, and could feel a terrible headache coming on.

'Yes. Okay, yes.' Then he lost control. 'Yes, I know, ... all right, I'll do it. Fuck knows how, but yes, I've told you, I'll fucking well do it.' He threw the phone across the room, took a small packet out of his side jacket pocket, took three tablets out, and walked to the kitchen, where he filled a plastic cup with some water and swallowed the pills. Then he splashed cold water on his face. He went to the pill cupboard and took out three 20mg fluoxetine pills; he also took two Paracetamol for his headache, and swallowed the lot with another cup of water.

Back in the lounge, he sat down to think. When he looked at his watch, he saw it was one o' clock, and on his fucking day off. He had the time, but how? How the fuck was he going to do it? It was stupid, but he poured himself a large whisky, sipped it, and the warmth flowing down his throat made him immediately happier. The man on the phone had said there was always a way, and that it was just finding it, finding the key that unlocked the door. He took another sip of whisky, said 'fuck it', and knocked it back in one. There was so much at stake: his family, his lifestyle, his freedom. He ran his fingers through his hair and felt clammy and sick. He got up and strolled to the back door, then went out into the small rear garden and took a few deep breaths. He strolled around, hands in his pockets, thinking, and then he stopped. It had come to him suddenly: he had to get the man out of the station, and there was one easy way to do that.

***

'Time to have another word with our friend, Trevor,' Karen said as she stood up.

'Fingers crossed, eh, boss.' Mick grinned.

'Everything is crossed, believe me.'

DI Foster and Sergeant Hill made their way back to the interview room. They stopped outside the door, looked at each other, and held up their crossed fingers and laughed quietly. Karen pushed the door open and they went in.

Without preamble, Karen addressed the suspect. 'Have you had a cup of tea?'

'Don't pretend you fucking care. For Christ's sake, let's get on with it.' He looked ruffled around the edges.

Karen dropped her smile and sat down opposite Trevor. 'So, what's it to be?'

'I don't want to go back to France. If you can guarantee in writing that I will not be extradited, then I'll play ball. That is the first of my conditions. I want a reduced sentence, guaranteed no more than ten years, serving a maximum of five, and I want to serve that time in the remotest prison in Scotland. I still may not be safe, but send me to Belmarsh and I'd be dead within a week. When I come out of prison, I will need a new identity, papers, the works, and some money. That's it—what do you say?'

Karen sat back and stared at Banks. She so wanted Fellows and Black it had to be worth it. 'You know the score. What can you give us on your contacts?'

'Enough to put the two of them away for a very long time plus, of course, a couple more of their acolytes. I want it written up properly, and my new solicitor—when I get one—will need to check it. Although the food is shit, up to that point I'm happy to stay here, … at least its safe.' He finished up with a laugh.

Karen studied him for a moment. 'I think we could have a deal. I need to run this by the Chief Inspector and the Crown Prosecution Service, so I'll come back to you as soon as I can. Meanwhile, enjoy the good food and luxury accommodation.'

Karen and Mick left the interview room and Karen made for her office to call Chief Inspector Park at Guildford. Park took over and said he would deal with the Crown Prosecution Service, as they were a bunch of useless twats.

***

At six p.m., the police station emptied quickly. The civilians were long gone, and the last one or two officers were making their way to the car park to go home. Two officers were still working in the custody suite, and would finish at eight p.m., when the new shift booked on duty. Some nights were quiet beyond belief, but you could always guarantee a couple of visitors on Friday and Saturday nights. This being Wednesday, it would probably be dead. Eight p.m. came and the two new officers, Constable Wright and Sergeant Jones, took over responsibility for the custody suite. Two prisoners occupied the cells: Trevor Banks, and a drunk called Simon Cassidy.

Time stood still for Wright and Jones, the custody suite was so quiet it was eerie, Banks and Cassidy were sleeping, and the two officers could faintly hear one of them snoring. Two a.m. came around, the worst time of the shift, fatigue had set in, and the endless coffees were not having any effect. Jones and Wright sat at a long wooden desk in an office that adjoined the door to the cells. They were supposed to be working, but in reality were chatting and doing absolutely nothing. And then Jones sniffed the air, twice.

'What's that smell?' He stood up and walked to the door. When he opened it, the force of wind and fire hurled him backwards. He flew across the floor and smashed into the front of the office desk. He couldn't see, but his hair was burnt, and steam rose from his jumper. Wright jumped out of his seat and ran round the desk to see how Jones was, but before he got there Jones shouted, 'Shut the door. You must shut the door.'

Thick, black, acrid smoke had already poured into the office when Wright launched himself at the door. He slammed it shut, but noticed smoke already seeping in under the door, and he pulled his jumper off and covered the gap at the bottom.

'That door won't last long. We need to move.' Wright bent down and helped lift Jones to his feet.

'You all right?'

'Yes. Why the fuck hasn't the alarm gone off? And the sprinkler system's not working either. Press the alarm by the cell door.'

Wright hit the red fire alarm button … nothing.

'It's not working.'

'Dial 999, it's the quickest way.'

The door into the office turned black as the heat and flames attacked it from the other side—the fire and smoke would soon be through.

'They're on their way,' Wright shouted over the noise of the inferno.

Sergeant Jones took control. 'The cells … let's go. Handcuff the drunk, and I'll get Banks.'

They rushed into the cells to find Banks standing by his door shouting. He was panicking. The drunk stirred and stood up, clueless as to what was happening. Jones and Wright handcuffed the two men and brought them out into the small corridor. They turned to see the door into the office collapse and burst into flames. The killing black smoke enveloped the room, and the flames would be on them in seconds.

'Break the glass and open the door,' Jones yelled.

Wright picked the hammer from its holder on the wall, and then smashed the glass. He pulled out the large Chubb key, inserted it into the emergency door, and turned. The door opened and a gust of fresh air rushed in, they pushed the two prisoners out through the door, and walked five yards, then stopped.

'Thank God for that,' Jones said in, between coughs. He looked up as he heard the sound of fire engines screaming up the road at full speed. They were soon unloading gear and rolling out hoses. Jones and Wright turned at the same time to see Trevor Banks suddenly collapse in a heap on the floor.

'Maybe he swallowed some smoke.' Jones crouched down and turned Banks over. He dropped the body like a stone and looked towards the trees, the bullet had entered bang in the middle of the forehead, and blood trickled down his face.

Wright shouted, 'Let's run.'

Jones grabbed his arm. 'Don't bother, it's over, they got who they wanted, and they'll be well gone by now.'

'What do you mean, Sarge?'

'Professional hit, lad, and that's why there was a fire … bastards.'

A while later, the fire under control, police cars, ambulances, and fire engines, filled the front area. Detective Inspector Foster arrived at the scene, already aware that Banks had been shot and killed. Her star witness against Fellows and Black had gone, and this was devastating news. The fire had been localised near to the custody suite, so most of the station remained undamaged. Karen knew immediately that Fellows and Black were behind the shooting, but proving it would be nigh impossible, unless they got a lucky break somewhere down the line.

***

Jeremy arrived home at three thirty in the morning; he'd told his wife that he was going on a secret mission and would only be a couple of hours. Seated in his favourite chair in the lounge, with a large whisky, he couldn't believe how easy it had been. He'd obtained a spare key for a side door into the station, disabled the Fire alarm and sprinkler systems, and then lit the fire with some petrol. Then he'd rushed round behind the other side of the station to await Banks being brought out. Every second had seemed like an eternity, but eventually they'd appeared. He'd taken aim with his new American Remington 700 rifle. The weapon had been hand delivered that afternoon, and was a beautiful rifle with a twenty-six-inch barrel, crowned at the muzzle for accuracy and stability. When the time came, he'd squeezed the trigger slowly and felt the power of the weapon as he fired. He'd watched through the crosswire on the sniper scope as the bullet entered Banks' forehead and he went down instantly, dead. With practiced haste, he'd packed up and was back in his car three minutes later, heading towards the M25.

The whisky went down well, and he laughed, toasting himself. He felt strong, powerful, even invincible, and he felt certain that another envelope would soon be dropping through the letterbox. What would he do with the money?

For certain, they would have an incredible luxury holiday in the Caribbean.

CHAPTER 24

The Bentley purred up the embankment and soon pulled into the Houses of Parliament car park. The uniformed driver jumped out and opened the rear door and, a few seconds later, Peter Fellows emerged, dressed in a Saville Row handmade dark-blue suit with white shirt and blue spotted tie. He'd also bought a new pair of seven-hundred-pound Church black brogues, which were so comfortable he felt like he was wearing his slippers. He stopped and looked around, this was where he belonged, and this was his new home for the foreseeable future. He could feel the history, the power, and he marched forward into the reception area and made for the desk.

'Peter Fellows.'

The lady behind the desk looked at him and raised her eyebrows.

'And what can we do for you, Mr Fellows?'

Fellows couldn't believe that he had to explain who he was.

'I am the new Member of Parliament for Kingston and Surbiton.'

He expected that once he had said that, he would be treated with a little more respect and servility.

The lady pointed towards a desk manned by an elderly uniformed doorman.

'Go and see that chap over there; he'll tell you what you need to do.' She turned away and was soon dealing with the next query.

This wasn't exactly what Fellows had expected but, as always, he could bend with the wind when he had to.

'Good morning, Sir, what can we do for you?'

'My name is Peter Fellows, new Member of Parliament for Kingston and Surbiton, and I'm due to meet up with David Embers.'

'Do you know if he is in the House now? Because his office is across the road in Portcullis House.'

'I'm making my maiden speech in the House today and I'm due to meet up with Embers at ten o'clock.' He glanced at his watch. 'And, unless I'm mistaken, it is now five to ten.'

'I suggest you go to the chief Whip's office; they'll sort you out.' The doorman came out from behind the desk. 'Go straight down that corridor 'til you come to the terrace restaurant entrance, turn right, and then sharp left, go along that corridor, take the first flight of stairs to the first floor, turn left at the top of the stairs, and about two-hundred-yards down you will see a door marked whips, and that's it.'

'Can't you show me the way?'

'Can't possibly leave my post, Sir, more than my job's worth.'

Fellows set off and got lost within a second; people rushed in every direction, and trying to get someone to stop was tricky. He also felt somewhat embarrassed and didn't want to appear a complete fool. He trudged on, desperately looking for someone he might recognise, and at last he struck lucky.

'Toby Marchant, thank God, you've saved my life, I'm meant to be meeting Embers but can't find the whip's office, can you help?'

'No point going to the whips office, old chap, you need to be getting a seat in the chamber, isn't it your maiden speech today?'

'Yes, it is.'

'Follow me, then.' And off he went, as though he was back in the Guards marching at trooping of the colour. Fellows sped after him and soon became short of breath. Five minutes later, they entered the double doors of the chamber, and Fellows felt even more at home. He looked around and marvelled at the green leather seats and the beautiful woodwork. Toby pushed him up to the back and they grabbed two seats that hadn't been reserved with name tickets. Excitement coursed through Fellows, and then he noticed the hanging microphones, he then scanned the chamber looking for prominent members of the Conservative and Labour parties. The number of women who were now members of parliament surprised him. Members of the shadow cabinet, and the Labour leader Harold Stevens looked to be deep in conversation with the shadow chancellor, Ed Argent. Due to good attendance, the chamber soon filled. Right at the last moment, the Prime

Minister, David Macintosh, entered with the chancellor, Keith Johnston, and Jim Smith, the minister of defence. The house went quiet and all eyes followed the Prime Minister to his seat, and then the speaker rose from his chair.

'Order.' The room quietened even more, so everybody could now hear the labour MP, Dennis Bannan, chatting animatedly with the man next to him.

The speaker leaned forward and looked directly at Bannan. 'Would the Honourable member for Hull please shut up so we may proceed?'

Howls of laughter rose from the conservative benches.

'Order, Order.' The speaker then shouted his final 'Order' and the noise trickled to nothing.

'Prime Minister.'

Fellows was entranced: he wanted to walk in and have everyone looking at him, and he could feel the power of the position. When he thought back to school, it was the same atmosphere, and a lot of the same people, and he was going to make his maiden speech—he prayed he wouldn't mess it up.

The Labour leader spoke and things quickly turned nasty, with personal insults flying to and fro. Other members were called to speak, and then Toby nudged him and whispered, 'Whenever you're ready, old chap.'

Preparing the speech had been easy—it was meant to be kept short. But now Fellows had to stand up, and whoever he might be, it was a nervous moment. He raised his hand, but the speaker called someone else, it happened again, but on the third try, he heard the immortal words for the first time from the speaker.

'The Honourable Member for Kingston and Surbiton.'

The house hushed. It gave a certain respect to members making their maiden speech, as it was a momentous occasion for them, and it demanded silence. The members in the conservative benches turned as one to see the new MP perform.

Fellows paused and looked round the chamber. 'Will the Prime Minister join me in congratulating the Metropolitan Police for their steadfastness and professionalism in the face of growing threats from Terrorist organisations from around the world?'

He sat back down and heard several calls of 'Hear, Hear' from the conservative benches. The Prime Minister rose and turned towards Fellows, and the house once again hushed.

'I welcome the Honourable member for Kingston and Surbiton to the House. I agree wholeheartedly that the Metropolitan Police are to be congratulated on their professionalism. Without question making them the finest Police Force in the world.'

More shouts of 'Hear, Hear' came from both sides of the House.

The PM continued, 'I would also congratulate the Honourable Member for his twenty-five-years of service to that institution.' He sat down and Fellows relaxed: it was over. He had enjoyed it immensely and looked forward to when he would be making long speeches and joining in with the banter. Yes, it felt just like being back at Eton.

The House closed and Fellows had coffee with some of his MP colleagues in the Whip's office, and then it was back to the Bentley and off home.

Life was good for Fellows: Trevor Banks had been shot by a supposed professional assassin, and Surrey Police were clueless, as usual; Philip Black had tied up all the loose ends and everything was done and dusted; Jeremy Hope had proven to be highly resourceful and they had given him a further fifteen-thousand pounds for the Banks' job. However, Fellows had now to start the most difficult campaign of his life, which was to reach the ultimate political post in the UK—that of Prime Minister. Utterly ruthless, Fellows wouldn't hesitate to use the same methods of corruption, violence, and bribes as he had used at the Met to get what he wanted.

CHAPTER 25

Karen Foster couldn't stop herself, she had tried, and in fact she had tried so hard she had cried. She'd told herself a hundred times not to do it, … not to go. That it would be a mistake, and she should think of Simon. She *had* thought of Simon, and that was when she'd cried, but it still hadn't stopped her.

She drove back to the Police station from the Croydon Travelodge. Friday had been immense, like a fucking machine that never stopped. He was so huge she felt sore, but she had loved it and wanted more, and for sure, there would be another time.

Karen got back to the office at ten a.m. and grabbed her usual latte, then settled down to do some paperwork. She'd called a progress meeting for eleven, and wanted to make some notes before Mick Hill and Fergus O'Donnell arrived. It all felt so frustrating: so many dead bodies and, added to the list, Trevor Banks. They were getting nowhere. Fellows and Black were, it seemed, untouchable. Every direction just seemed to end in brick walls and silence. If she'd been at home, she would have screamed. Mick and Fergus arrived at two minutes to eleven and Janet organised coffee for all three.

'So we are—and I hate to say, as usual, but it does feel like that—on a boat with no fucking paddle. I want us to review where we've been, where we are now, and what we are going to do following this meeting. One of my favourite expressions comes to mind.' She looked the two of them in the eye. 'It's a pile of shit and, Gentlemen, in case you had any doubts, it is our pile of shit and it needs cleaning up.'

Mick chipped in, 'We're with you, boss, one hundred per cent.'

'I know, God knows what I would do without you two, so let's crack on.'

Karen handed them a sheet of paper each.

'Killing number one: David Kane, well over two years ago, almost certainly killed by a police officer at the Energy demonstration. There is no evidence, nothing, and the Mary Bishop connection has gone, not that she could have helped anyway. The one shred of good news is that we have the phone number connection to Theodore Taylor, but of course, he is in Brussels, so forget him for the minute. Killing number two: Mary Bishop.' Karen shook her head. 'We're certain that Trevor Banks, alias Alex, was responsible for that and he is now dead. Trevor was killed in order for loose ends to be tied up, and just maybe they thought he was doing a deal, because he fired his solicitor, who I have since found out had some dodgy connections, to say the least.' Karen paused for a moment. 'Killing number three: Robert—I still get upset when I think about him, such a future wasted—I think he saw something on the demonstration photos and that's why he was killed. Mick, what's happening with the pictures?'

'I'm still going through them, but it's like looking for a needle in a haystack and we don't even know what we're looking for.'

'So, it's almost a waste of time, then?'

'I hate to say it, boss, but yes.'

Karen thought for a second, 'Okay, bin it. Fergus, how are you getting on with the snitches and our friends?'

Fergus sighed, obviously pissed off at giving Karen no news or, worse, bad news. 'Nothing. This is way above any contacts we have.'

'I thought that's what you were going to say. Let's move on. Mark Heenan and Scotty both died in suspicious circumstances and, according to the Met, both cases are closed—dead ends, again. There're so many dead bodies, I've lost fucking count.'

'Five,' Fergus said.

'It's six, for Christ's sake,' Mick said in a raised voice.

'Fellows and Black—oh, and that fucking bitch, Carla Westburgh, ... did I tell you she called me a cunt in my own nick? Imagine, in my own fucking nick.'

Both Mick and Fergus answered, 'Yes, boss, you told us.'

'Yes, well, she'll get her fucking comeuppance. I'll never forget that cow. Sorry, where were we? ... Right, Fellows and Black think they're bullet proof. Well, let me tell you, they will make a mistake and, when they do, we will be all over them like a rash.'

'I saw that Fellows on the telly, in the House of Commons, giving a speech or something.'

'I didn't know you watched the news, Mick. Blimey, next you'll be telling us you watch Mastermind.'

'Very funny, Fergus, ha ha.'

Karen smiled. 'Okay, boys. Look, one other thing: I was going to ask Jeremy Hope to give us some help, but … Mick, his new Merc?'

'I asked him, and apparently his Auntie died and left him ten grand. It's on credit.'

'You believe him?'

'Yeah. I don't particularly like him, but it sounded convincing to me.'

'Okay, he may know Fellows and Black. I'll sound him out and get back to you. Keep your eyes and ears open. I'm not letting this go.'

Mick and Fergus left the office. Karen relaxed and sat back. She had one card to play, and thought about it for a minute. It would create massive shock waves … she picked up the phone.

It was done.

Time stood still for the rest of the morning as Karen plodded through the mountain of paperwork that never seemed to get any smaller. At last, lunchtime came and she fairly skipped down to the canteen, glad to be away from her desk. She entered and looked round, hoping to see Mick or Fergus, but neither of them were there. However, there was someone she wanted a word with. She queued up, got some Quiche with chips, and approached his table.

'Jeremy, how are you?'

***

Confusion slowed his response. It hadn't been long ago that DI Foster had threatened him with rape charges. He blinked, then said, 'I'm fine, thank you.'

'That, eh, you know, little disagreement we had the other day? All forgotten, okay?'

'Of course, all forgotten.' She must be after something. What though?

As he looked at her, he remembered the sexual frenzy that had come over them both. He'd enjoyed it and wanted more. Karen sat down and tucked into her lunch, and between mouthfuls, made small talk. Jeremy finished ahead of her and pretended to get up.

'Got to go. Very busy at the moment.'

'Wait a minute.' Karen took another small mouthful of food and pushed the plate away. 'I'd like a word.'

'Okay, what can I do for you, now we're best friends again?'

She gave him a big sexy smile. 'That's nice to hear.' Then she shrugged and said, 'So, look, I've got something on. Wondered if you might be able to help.'

'If I can, sure, why not.'

'Have you ever done any work on police corruption? Say, the Met, for instance?'

Jeremy was now more than a little interested. 'Hmm, well, that's a very delicate subject. As it happens, I haven't, but I do hear an awful lot of … shall we say … stuff on the grapevine. You'll have to be more specific.'

'Some senior officers in the Met … I heard some rumours.'

'What are their names?'

Karen seemed unsure, but went ahead. 'Ex Commander Fellows, and his replacement, Philip Black.'

It was Jeremy's turn to look thoughtful. 'Fellows is an MP now. I've heard them in passing, but certainly not anything to do with corruption. Are you sure about them?'

'No. As I said, rumours, only rumours.'

'Do you want me to have a little dig, then?'

'Well, that would be helpful, but keep it on the quiet. I don't want them to know we're looking at them.'

'Mum's the word.'

When he got back to his office, he immediately phoned Black and told him the news. Black called Karen Foster every foul name in the book and finished by saying he was losing patience. Jeremy took that to mean that at some time soon, he could be asked to deal with the Karen Foster problem permanently.

CHAPTER 26

Karen and Esme browsed in the Accessorize shop in the Ashley Centre in Epsom. They'd met at ten in Costa Coffee and then set out to window shop. Karen had been so excited and felt like a teenager again. They had kissed cheeks when they met and immediately the atmosphere changed to one of sexual tension. Karen liked the best of both worlds, what with fucking the man mountain, Friday, and now being smitten with the sensual French Esme. Karen wore jeans and a white see-through blouse, while Esme had chosen a short blue skirt and shirt combination.

Esme looked at scarves and loved a particular multi-coloured green one, so Karen grabbed it and paid for it before Esme could protest. Esme thanked her with a kiss on the cheek, which somehow caught Karen on the lips. While they sauntered round the shop, touching fingers and being playful, the experience felt heady for both of them. They both knew what was going to happen later in the day, and enjoyed the flirting and getting to know each other better. Esme was a tactile woman, and Karen wanted her so much she could barely contain herself. They wandered into M & S, and Esme bought Karen a beautiful bouquet of flowers to take back to her flat. They bought some cheese and French bread for lunch, and then they visited the Perfume Shop, where Karen bought some Eau de Guerlain—Esme's favourite—she was already thinking of where she would put it on Esme's gorgeous body.

It came to midday, and Karen suggested they go back to her place and have some lunch. Esme agreed, and twenty minutes later, they entered Karen's flat. Karen put the flowers in a vase and displayed them in the lounge; they smelled intoxicating and delicious. Neither woman spoke much, as an atmosphere had developed, and the tension was almost unbearable. Back in the small Kitchen, Karen sliced the Brie, while Esme cut the French bread into manageable chunks. Their shoulders kept touching, and in the end the dam broke. It happened. Karen instigated the contact; she couldn't control herself any longer.
'Esme, you know how ...' She put her arm round Esme's neck and stroked her hair.
Esme turned to her and ran her tongue around her lips. 'Stop talking.' Then their lips met. A meeting of bodies and minds. Tongues licked and sucked, and then their hands were all over each other. Esme tore at Karen's blouse, revealing her black bra, which was soon on the floor, followed by jeans and knickers. Esme ripped her shirt and skirt off to reveal beautiful matching white bra and panties. They joined in a tangle of hands and legs, kissing passionately and probing with their fingers. Karen finally pulled away and held her hand out, Esme took it, and Karen led her to the bedroom.

Karen got off the bed and stretched. It had been a wonderful experience—even better than she'd anticipated—Esme was a sensational woman, and Karen couldn't make up her mind whether, if given the choice, she would have Esme or Friday. She laughed: both would be so exciting, and perhaps Esme would like to have a threesome. Esme lay dozing, so Karen went to the kitchen to make some coffee. She enjoyed walking round the flat naked, enjoying the wonderful feeling of freedom. The coffee was on and Karen cursed that she didn't have any champagne. Next time, for certain, she promised herself.

The doorbell rang as she pulled cups from the cupboard. She wasn't expecting anyone, so didn't anticipate anyone coming to the flat. With the door open just an inch, to make sure whoever it was couldn't see her pert breasts and naked body, she asked who was there. But, as soon as the door opened, it was pushed with massive force from the outside, and she slammed against the wall, hit her head, and almost lost consciousness.

Two men, dressed in black balaclavas, burst through the door. One of them grabbed her by the hair and pulled her along the hall carpet, while the other man checked the lounge then went into the bedroom and found Esme. He grabbed one of her legs and pulled her off the bed. She screamed and the man hit her across the mouth with the back of his hand, making her fall back. The whole thing finished in under a minute: Karen and Esme had their mouths taped, and their hands secured behind their backs with plastic ties. The men had thrown them on the bed. The two women lay at the headboard end of the bed, and tried to cover their lower bodies. One of the men stayed in the bedroom, while the other had a look around the flat. Karen could hear drawers being opened and the contents tipped onto the floor. A minute later, the man came back into the bedroom.

'Fuck all.'

'What did you expect? Diamonds?' He turned to Karen and Esme. 'Two fucking dykes. Makes me want to puke.'

The other man studied the two women. 'Nice bodies, though.' He licked his lips.

Karen wondered who the hell they were. Burglars? Somehow she didn't think so. Not rapists, either. The larger of the men moved towards them, took Esme's arm, and dragged her to the other end of the bed. She tried to kick him, but the man slapped her across the face again, and blood trickled down her chin and she lay still.

The two men just looked at them. Karen thought for a second that she and Esme might be executed. If the men were trying to scare them, it was working.

'Listen, and listen well, I'm only going to say this once. You two dyke bitches have one chance and this is it. Leave the Energy Demonstration case alone. Forget it ever happened. You know what I'm talking about.' The man looked at Karen. 'Foster, you're an intelligent woman, and this is your one and only warning. Leave it, or you will both be killed.' He paused and stared her in the eyes. 'Don't think it won't happen. We're the two that injected an overdose of heroin into that Marxist wanker, and we would be more than happy to give you some of the same treatment. Do you understand me?'

Karen felt so scared. The mention of the heroin overdose had her shaking and terrified. She nodded.

The man bent down until they were almost chin to chin. 'Good, now just to make sure you get the message …' He looked at his sidekick.

The other man clenched his fists and smashed Esme full in the face. He hit her four times more. Her eyes had begun to bruise already, and had closed up. Her nose was broken again, after just healing, and blood poured down her face. She cried in pain. The man then pummelled her body, landing sickening punch after punch into her stomach and chest. Esme collapsed and lost consciousness. Karen could barely watch. She, too, cried, but in pain of a different sort. The punching finished and the man spoke again.

'Foster, you sure you've got the message? Because if we meet again, you and your dyke bitch will both die.'

Karen nodded again, and prayed the men would leave now.

The two guys turned and made for the front door. Karen heard one of the men ask the other if he was doing anything in the evening, and if not, they could go for a drink.

Bastards. Callous, no good, fucking bastards. She pushed herself towards Esme, who remained slumped and unconscious. She got off the bed and made for the kitchen, opened the cutlery drawer, and managed to get a sharp steak knife into her hand. Then she turned the knife and sawed at the plastic that bound her wrists. It was tough going, as the plastic was strong, and it took fully forty minutes to cut through. Karen swung her arms to get the circulation moving, then found her mobile and called 999.

Fifteen minutes later, paramedics, ambulance men, and police officers filled the flat. Mick Hill had been one of the first on scene, closely followed by Fergus and a crime scene team. Esme was rushed to Epsom A & E, closely followed by Fergus, who was bound to be in a state of shock. ... Not only did the state of Esme's injuries rock him, but he'd thought that she was out shopping on her own. However, she and Karen had been together.

Karen was a mental and physical wreck and could barely string a sentence together. Chief Inspector Park called but only stayed on the line a minute as he could tell Karen was still in serious shock. Everybody felt rattled. A Detective Inspector and a French policewoman had been attacked during the day, in the DI's own flat. It was incredible. Karen kept quiet about the warning, instead saying they were thieves high on drugs. She would keep it to herself, otherwise Park could well close the case for good. As soon as Karen felt a little better, she got Mick to drive her to the hospital to see Esme. Karen found her awake and compos mentis. Karen told Fergus to take five minutes and get a coffee. She became tearful again when she leaned across the bed, and whispered in Esme's ear. 'Esme, darling, it's Karen. I'm so sorry. I wish it had been me and not you.' Rivers of tears ran down her cheeks. Then Esme moved her hand, so Karen grasped it and felt Esme squeeze. She squeezed back.

'Don't worry. You are bruised up. It will all heal quickly and you will be beautiful again very soon.'

Esme tried to speak. 'T-the ... the men, they come back.'

Karen understood that Esme felt scared, and rushed to reassure her. 'No, there are police guards outside, so no one can come in except past the officers. You are very safe, I promise.' Karen had a flashback and remembered promising Chau that she was safe on the Isle of Wight, and in Hospital, but she had been abducted from both.

'Esme, you are safe, do not worry. Please, just get well, all right, my beautiful girl.'

Esme spoke again, 'Sleep now.'

Karen stroked the hair back from her forehead. 'Yes, sleep, Esme. I'll come back later.'

Karen left the private room and got straight on the phone. She spoke to Esme's Father and told him that Esme was okay, but in hospital. She said that they were to come over straight away and, as soon as Esme was fit to travel, they should take her back to Cannes. She then found Mick and Fergus by the coffee machine and told them the truth.

Mick was more than alarmed. 'Jesus, boss, this is serious. You have to drop it. These people will do anything. It's not worth dying for.'

Karen didn't know what to think. She had the feeling they would do it—a car accident, or she could just disappear one day—she shuddered inside: she liked living and it had really traumatised her.

'Truth is, at the moment, I don't know what to think. I need a drink, let's go.' She marched off towards the exit. But before she got far, she turned round.

'I won't be a minute.' Karen almost ran back to Esme's room, and then approached the two officers outside the door.

'Right, you two. Anything happens to that lady, and I'll have your bollocks, you got that?'

'Yes, Ma'am,' they chorused, and she headed back to the exit.

Two days later, Esme said she wanted to stay, but Karen and her parents insisted she return to France. In the end, Esme gave in, and was soon on a flight to Nice.

Karen went back to her flat and hit the whisky, she then rang Simon, who dropped everything and was on his way. Karen felt bad; not only was she cheating on Simon with Friday, but also now with Esme … her personal life, as usual, was a fucking mess.

CHAPTER 27

The DI had thought long and hard about what to say to Chief Inspector Park, and in the end, Karen trusted him and his judgement, so told him the truth. He had been furious and spluttered that it was disgraceful that an Eton chap should be behaving so badly.

'I'm not sure yet how we're going to do it, but Fellows and his nasty sidekick have got to be locked up.' He paused, before adding, 'And for a very long time.'

'Yes, and we mustn't forget that other nasty piece of work, Carla Westburgh.'

'Yes, let's lull them into a false sense of security. Don't do anything at all. Let them relax, think they're home and dry, and meanwhile we'll put a plan together to smoke them out, and then have the bastards.'

'Do nothing, Sir? How long, exactly, did you have in mind?'

'A month, Detective, and I am also thinking of your health. Put your plan together and come and see me at the beginning of next month.'

Karen left Guildford, somewhat relieved. Although she was champing at the bit to get Fellows and Black behind bars, she was only human, and concerned about her personal safety. She got back to Epsom after lunch, and didn't feel that interested in doing any work, so went on a tour of the station. The repairs had been done and the cell block freshly painted following the fire, and a paint smell wafted round the station, even after a couple of days. On her way upstairs, she bumped into Jeremy.

'I was just coming to find you, boss'

'Come to the office, then.'

Karen sat behind her desk. 'So, what can I do for you?'

***

Jeremy knew what he'd like her to do, but she wasn't up for it, which was a shame. So he just said, 'I've been looking at that Fellows bloke, and can't find anything. He's either innocent, or good at covering things up.'

'Doesn't matter now. That case, if it ever was a case, is closed. I have no further interest in him, so no worries.'

Jeremy immediately thought that Black would be interested to hear that fact.

Karen asked, 'Are you well? You look a bit peaky?'

He tried to cover, 'I'm fine, never better actually.' But in truth, he felt a bit faint and pale.

'Well, if you say so. If you'll excuse me I have—'

'Of course, work to do, I'm on my way.'

He rushed back to his office, locked the door, and took a plastic bag out of a locked draw. He opened the bag and sprinkled the white powder onto his desk, rolled a five-pound note, and snorted the powder into his nose. He snorted again and shook his head; he felt like shit but the coke would soon have him back up. That reminded him, he needed to put in an order with Max, and for a much larger quantity.

He calmed down and placed the call to Philip Black.

'The case has been closed with no further action. I heard it from her own lips myself not ten minutes ago.'

'Excellent, it seems the visit she had has proven to be successful. We can all relax a bit.'

'You should have asked me to deal with her and the French slag. I would have enjoyed it.'

Menacing silence reigned for five seconds.

'She knows you. Let me do the thinking, you just do as you're fucking told.' The line went dead.

***

Karen phoned Esme at the restaurant to see how she was. A lot of the times she called, the line was engaged, and that was because when Fergus was in the office he spent half his time on the phone to her. This time it rang.

'Esme? Esme, is that you?'

'Yes, Karen, how are you?'

'Missing you more than you could ever know.'

Esme laughed a happy laugh. 'I'm missing you too.' Then, after a slight pause, she said, 'And I'm missing Fergus as well.'

Karen didn't know what to make of that, but she liked men and women, so Esme could too.

She wanted to ask who Esme preferred, but thought that wouldn't be fair. Karen felt it better that Esme had a long-term relationship with a man anyway.

They talked about the restaurant, about Esme's mum and dad, and what was happening with investigations at Epsom Police Station. Karen ached to see Esme, but with Simon, Friday, Fergus, and the job, it would be difficult.

CHAPTER 28

(THE MONTH OF JUNE)

Karen had taken Chief Inspector Park's order literally, and she had stopped thinking about Fellows and Black and concentrated on policing the local community. Crime in Epsom and the surrounding area was low compared to nationally, and considerably lower than areas closer to London. The local schools had broken up for summer, and families had jetted off to sunny climates abroad. The only local trouble had been at the Derby, as half-a-million people descended on the Downs for the world-famous horse race. Most of the trouble came from drunks, pickpockets, bike and car thefts, a couple of handbag thefts, and fights.

Karen had met up with Friday once during the month. Although she was happy with Simon Kane, she couldn't resist the temptation of the best fucks she'd ever had. She spoke with Esme and heard that Fergus was going out to see her; she wished she could have gone as well. The police station was quiet and there were some whispered rumours that Guildford were looking at closing it. Karen had immediately called Park, who said it had been looked at but was safe for at least another two years. Karen had visited her parents for a weekend of being spoilt, which made an agreeable change. There had been some lovely summer weather, which had brought out smiles on faces of even the dullest people. All in all, June had been a decent Month. Nearing the end of June, Karen's attention was once again focussed on Taylor, Fellows, Black, and of course, Carla Westborough.

***

Fergus had been shocked by the attack on Karen and Esme. His anger and frustration stemmed from not being able to do anything to bring the perpetrators to justice. Karen had said the two men would pay dearly for their disgusting attack on defenceless women, and Fergus had hoped he would be there to dish out some of his own justice. He'd gone over to Cannes for a long weekend, which had been fantastic. Esme had recovered from the severe bruising in no time at all, and they'd enjoyed good food in the restaurant, and plenty of passionate lovemaking. Because of Esme, Fergus was keen to get back on the trail of Fellows and Black, and so he was raring to go at the end of the month.

***

Esme had been thrilled to get back to Cannes. The attack in Karen's flat had knocked her for six and she wasn't sure she would return to the UK, even with Fergus living there. She had immediately been spoiled rotten by her parents, who cooked her favourite meals, and she had an endless stream of well-wishers dropping in to see her. She'd begged Fergus to visit her as soon as possible, and he'd flown over for a long weekend on EasyJet. They had good food and loads of sex, and Esme felt much better, but still sad when it was time for him to leave.

***

Mick had made the most of the break from the intense case and spoilt his wife and kids. He could be an abrupt, officious, curt, brusque and—when needled—nasty man. But if he liked you and thought you were straight, then he would work with you, drink with you, and—in the end—love you. He was committed to the DI one-hundred per cent, and would take a bullet for her if needs be. He, too, felt desperate to bring Fellows and Black down, and however difficult that seemed, thought it was only a matter of time before that happened.

***

Chief Inspector Park was keen to help Karen, but had to cover his back. He recognised in Fellows a powerful adversary, and to bring him to justice would require every skill that Surrey Police could bring to bear on the case. He had friends in high places, but compared to Fellows, was an amateur. Like Karen, he was determined to see justice done. He spent two weeks of the month on holiday in France, touring the chateaus and tasting wine; he'd never enjoyed himself so much. The other two weeks, he spent cultivating relationships throughout the Metropolitan Police and in certain Political circles.

***

Jeremy was on a downward spiral into drug dependency. The amphetamines, Paracetamol, and Fluoxetine that he took at the Energy demo, had progressed to an expensive addiction to cocaine. He could afford it because Fellows had given him money for the jobs he'd done. He'd become so hooked that he couldn't wait for news of a new job to sustain his habit.

***

Commander Philip Black took his time in everything. Unless it was an emergency, he liked to dot the I's and cross the T's. He was a planner, a schemer, and he looked for the weakness in people. Then he ruthlessly manipulated that to his advantage. Having said this, he was a family man who loved his children and, unfortunately, they had inherited some of his appalling traits. June, he spent planning for the next twelve months in his new position as a Metropolitan Police Commander.

***

Fellows was a man with no friends but many acquaintances, and a man who would do anything to help succour his monstrous ambition. Family wealth had corrupted him at an early age, and he saw it only fitting that he should be the leader and everybody else was there to serve him and his interests. He was successful, and fitted perfectly into the old-school network at Parliament; he would serve the establishment and the establishment would look after him. The summer recess would allow him time to start his insidious campaign of intimidation and threats to gain new followers, who would support him in his ultimate aim. It was all very well to have power in the UK, but Fellows wanted international and worldwide recognition—his ambition knew no bounds. June provided time to establish new contacts, and he sent his wife on holiday to America for two weeks so he could focus totally on his plans.

***

Simon had fallen in love with Karen, and thought he'd found his soul mate in life. He looked forward to a long and rewarding relationship. Although he'd sworn never to marry, he had considered asking Karen. And he'd even thought about the possibility of them having a family together. Simon knew about the previous long-term relationship with Chau, but accepted who Karen was without reservation. It might have been a different story if he'd known about Friday. Simon was happy that they had a break from the continuous discussion about Fellows and Black, and the Energy Demo, but was still ferociously dedicated to seeing the killer of his father facing justice. June proved a great month; he and Karen had picnics, went to the theatre, and generally spoilt each other.

CHAPTER 29

Two cars had been despatched. One carried the box and the other followed at a discreet distance, in case of any mishap on the journey. The black box arrived at Fellows' private house at seven p.m. The housekeeper informed him it had arrived, and he could barely contain his excitement as he took it to his private study to open. He sat behind his impressive oak desk and broke the seal, then pulled the two sides of the top open. He reached in and lifted the files out, then counted them: five. Black had done his job. Five files on individuals that Fellows needed onside to further his career. He checked them one by one, then put a bulky one aside. He took the first file, opened it, and read. The contents filled him with delight.

***

Toby Marchant relaxed back in his chair, having had a huge meal that had reminded him of school dinners. 'My dear chap, that was splendid. You can't beat a treacle roly-poly with lashings of custard.'

Fellows had invited him to his club, and Marchant knew the real reason for the invite would soon become apparent. He'd known Fellows at Eton, and he'd been a scheming bastard then, so Marchant felt sure he hadn't changed.

Fellows leant back in his high-backed armchair. 'So, Toby, you have been an MP for what, six years now?'

'Actually, seven, old chap. It's been interesting. I've seen a lot of change, and have thoroughly enjoyed it.' He laughed. 'Well, most of it.'

'Yes. ... Look, you might be in a position to help me.'

Marchant was happy the dance was over. Fellows was getting to the point at last. He smiled. 'Of course, always ready to help someone from the old school. What can I do to help?'

Fellows leaned across the table and stared directly into Marchant's eyes. 'I want you. Lock, stock, and barrel.' He paused to let those few words sink in.

Toby frowned. 'I don't understand. Spit it out, man. Just what help do you want?'

Fellows stared again, squinting his eyes and looking almost demonic. 'You will serve me. You are mine, now, and you will do as you are told. Anything at all I want, you will do for me, is that clear enough?'

Marchant was shocked and more than a little angry. 'Have you gone stark raving mad? I don't know what you're on, but if I were you, I would stop taking it. You're completely mad.' He moved to the edge of his seat, intending to stand and leave, but stopped when Fellows leaned back in his chair and laughed. When the man returned to his serious face, Toby tensed. Then Fellows said, 'Do you think I'm a fool? I know all about you. About your grubby past. I know everything.'

Now Marchant was worried. Fellows sounded so confident. The bastard had him, but he had to make certain. 'Bollocks. You're bluffing.'

Fellows smiled a sickening sneer. 'Five years ago, old boy, you molested that boy. How old was he? Oh yes, I remember now, six years old, you fucking pervert. All covered up by friends in high places. Very neat little job that, Toby. Would have been proud of that myself.'

'You bastard.' Despite his anger, he slumped back in his chair, defeated.

'Yes, well, I've been called worse. Now look, old chap, I don't care if you want to play with young boys, but I'm guessing your wife and children—not forgetting the great British public—might not agree with me. What do you say?'

'What do you want me to do?'

Fellows relaxed. 'Nothing.' He paused. 'Yet, of course, you must spread the word that I'm a good chap and will go far. And, if asked, promote me at every opportunity. You see, unlike you, I intend to go right to the very top. Now, let's have some Port and reminisce about school, eh.'

Marchant shrugged. Sighed. Then nodded. After all, he could little else but go along with it. 'Jolly good idea. What house were you in?'

Both men now understood their relationship, and it was in both of their interests to get along. They held power. They were the establishment. They were the fabric that held society together. Whatever Toby had done in the past was of no concern to Fellows, and now that he had him in his pocket, life would go on in the normal establishment way that it had done, and would do, for years.

***

The next day, Fellows and Black met up in Fellows' home office.

'Yes, went like clockwork. One down and five to go. Commissioner of Police is a lovely title, don't you think?'

Philip had supplied the copies of the top-secret files, and had broken into a locked office to find and photograph them. They were gold dust. Five rich and famous politicians, who had murky pasts, and had committed crimes that could well see them visiting H M Prisons, if word ever got out. He nodded toward Fellows. 'Yes, it does have a nice ring to it. Everything is going to plan.'

'Any other news? What about that Foster woman?'

'All quiet, Sir, but Jeremy is keeping a close eye on her.'

'How is he?'

'He's developed an expensive coke habit—our friend Max, is supplying him, but I'm slightly concerned.'

'Why?'

'He's addicted and, if that's the case, he'll be unreliable, which I don't like.'

Fellows thought for a minute. 'I wonder if we could get rid of him and the Foster woman at the same time?'

Black sat up straighter. 'Anything is possible, of course.'

'Look, I've got to get the other four on board, and then we can decide about Foster and Hope. Keep an eye on them, and I'll speak to you soon.'

Once Black had left, Fellows got back to the business at hand. He chose to go after the next politician at the unlikeliest of places: his old school. The old boys were having a celebration dinner in honour of a retiring General who had been to the school.

Andrew Parr had been an MP for fifteen odd years, representing Hampstead North, a safe Tory seat. He was on various committees and had served in the shadow cabinet when they had been in opposition. A national figure, all parties universally respected him throughout the House. The dinner was traditional. There would be speeches, and then the port would be handed round, more than once. Fellows had been watching Parr all night to make sure he didn't slip off early, but it looked like he was there for the duration. The dinner finished, several of the old boys went to the bar for a nightcap, and amongst those was Andrew Parr. This provided the opportunity Fellows had been waiting for. Parr went to the bar, and Fellows approached and touched his arm. 'Can I have a word?'

'Of course. Congratulations on your successful campaign, Fellows.'

'Thank you. But it was a safe seat, after all.'

'Yours to lose, old chap. PM wouldn't have thanked you for that.'

'Let's sit over in the corner for a minute, more private.'

Parr looked troubled, but did as requested. They made themselves comfortable, and Parr spoke first, 'So, what can I do for you?'

'Actually, more to the point is what I can do for you.'

'Really? I'm all ears.'

'I know all about your money problems. Friends are bailing you out. I wondered if I could help at all.'

Parr was outraged and scared at the same time. 'Jolly good of you, but everything's fine, thank you.' He got up to leave.

Fellows looked at him and whispered severely, 'It's in your interest to sit back down, old boy.'

Parr looked at him, seemed to come to a decision, and seated himself again.

Fellows continued. 'Seems you got some help with your mortgage. I think that is actually a crime. Did you know that?'

'Yes, well, times must, you understand?'

'Of course, I understand. Then there's the loans for the business and the Government contracts.'

Parr was a beaten man. Fellows knew everything. He was finished. 'What do you want?'

'I need patronage, and you shall help me. In return, I keep quiet and I help you financially. What do you say?'

'I say, better get the brandies in, old boy.'

***

At eight p.m., Fellows popped in to the House of Commons Terrace bar, and silence met him. Although nearly empty, the man Fellows wanted to see was already in there. Richard Small was the member for Clapham South, and had been in the House for a year. He served as junior minister in the Treasury, and could one day be Chancellor. Fellows spotted him sitting on his own with a glass of beer and reading a newspaper. Fellows detested this man before he even spoke to him. He was a grammar school boy and, therefore, did not fully understand the implications of having been to Eton. He marched over to Small's table.

'Peter Fellows. Can I have a word, old chap?'

'Hello Peter, I heard of your great success, well done.'

Fellows looked closely at Small. He looked of average height and thin, had manicured fingernails, and smelt like coconut. Fellows hated him even more.

'How are you finding life, now you're an MP?'

'Oh, I love it, serving my community and the country, I was born to it.'

Small didn't answer, and the look on his face suggested he was barely tolerating Fellows' presence. Well, that would all change soon. Fellows wanted to get away as quickly as he could, so got straight to the point. 'Small, I need your help.'

'Really, with what?'

Small remained cool but cordial. However, this didn't bother Fellows in the slightest. 'I need you onside, supporting me, promoting me in the House, and the country at large. You are on the way up in the Treasury, and I need friends in high places.'

'I'm not your man, Fellows. I already support someone and that won't change.'

'You mean Alistair, your poofta mate?'

'You bastard. If we were somewhere else I'd put my fist in your fat ugly face.'

'So, you're a hard poofta then?' He laughed. 'Look, I don't give a shit if you want to stick your cock up another man's arse, but I'm not sure the PM or the country would be quite so sympathetic, and of course, there is the question of security. Alistair Bolton being a whip an all.'

'You fucking shit. You breathe a word of this to anyone, believe me, you'll regret it.'

'As I said, your private life is your own, but you and Alistair will support me, or it could be headline news in tomorrow's papers.'

Richard Small loved his life in the House and would do anything to keep his relationship with Alistair Bolton secret. He stuck out his hand. 'Friends then, Peter.'

Fellows looked at the hand for a second, hating himself as he shook it. But, needs must. 'Good, you won't regret it. I'll not be speaking to Alistair, unless I have to, but I expect his support, you do understand? Goodnight.' He walked away without another word. As he passed an empty table, he picked up a serviette and wiped his hands.

***

The last meeting Fellows arranged would undoubtedly be the most interesting and challenging. Jim Smith had been an MP for twenty years, had been in the cabinet in Government, and opposition for many of those. He currently served as Minister of Defence, and was a close friend and ally of the Prime Minister. He had been to Harrow school. Fellows had asked for a meeting and had been told to visit Smith in his office at Portcullis House, across the road from the House, on Tuesday at three pm.

'Peter, good afternoon. Congratulations on your recent success.'

'Thank you, Jim, very kind of you.'

'So, what can I do for you?'

'Well, I'll come straight to the point. I am ambitious and need support in the party and House, and I think you might want to help me.'

Smith had been round the block several times and knew trouble was brewing. 'I can always put a good word in for you with the PM.'

Fellows smiled. 'That would be wonderful, but I was thinking more long term and comprehensive.'

'And what would I receive in exchange for this, eh, … what shall we call it … expensive favour?'

Fellows had him already and hardly a word had been spoken. 'My silence about the million-pound bonus you got for the last helicopter sale to Saudi Arabia.'

Jim remained calm and calculating. 'You want to be very careful what you say and to whom. It can get you in an awful lot of trouble. I have a lot of friends and some of them can be very nasty if required.'

'Of course you have some nasty friends, as we all do, but the information relating to the bribe, … sorry, bonus, is in safe hands and, should anything happen to me, it would be headline news within a day. Look, we can work together. I want to progress in the party and the House, you can help, and I keep stum—what do you say?'

'I think you're a fucking little shit, and if you say a word about the bonus you will be out of a job very soon, and kicked out of the party not long after. Now fuck off and don't bother me again.'

Fellows had miscalculated. This wasn't going according to plan. ' I'm a wealthy man and if you need money ...'

'I don't need your grubby money, Fellows. Now, is there anything else?'

Fellows just sat there staring at him.

'I said goodbye, Fellows.'

Fellows stood and made for the door at a slow pace, still trying to think of a way around this bad situation. He opened the door, but then turned around. 'I'm so sorry, Jim. Thank you for your time.'

Fellows strode down the long corridor. He had expected problems somewhere along the line, and Jim Smith had provided exactly that. In a way, he admired the man; at least he had some balls, unlike that faggot Small. He hadn't wanted to, but they would have to teach Jim Smith a lesson by some other means.

CHAPTER 30

Simon and Karen sat and cuddled on the sofa in Karen's flat. They'd eaten a take away Chinese and were now chatting.

'Nothing's going right. Some Detective Inspector, eh?'

'No job's perfect, and remember that's all it is, a job.'

'You're wrong; it's not just a job, as you put it. We're here to protect good people from bad people. Someone has to clean the shit up, and most of the hundreds of police officers do it every day of the week because they want to help. Want to make a better society for us all to live in. That bastard Fellows has won, he's gotten away with murder. Do you understand that? Murder.'

'My Father was murdered, if you remember. You question if I understand? Of course I do, for God's sake.'

'There has to be a way, has to be.'

Simon pulled Karen in closer and hugged her tight.

'There's something I want to ... shit, this isn't easy.'

Karen detected Simon had something important to say. 'What is it?'

'I thought we could make things more permanent. Why don't we sell one of the flats and live together?'

Karen couldn't speak. She hadn't expected that.

He pressed, 'What do you think?'

Karen smiled. 'Truthfully, I'm not sure. Sounds a good idea, but I need to think about it. I would want to stay in Epsom.'

'No problem. I like it as well, so … give it some thought and let me know.'

'I will.' She smiled and kissed him. 'Wine?'

'Yeah, great.' Simon had hoped for a more joyous response, but they weren't kids, so he would wait.

Karen returned with two fresh glasses of white wine.

Simon took his, then asked, 'Why don't we go away soon … long weekend break?'

'Sounds good. I'm becoming more and more agitated because of this whole Fellows and Black business. What am I going to do? I can't leave it.'

'Something will happen, it always does. They all make mistakes, and then you'll have the bastards.'

'Maybe, we'll see.'

***

Three days later, Karen was in her office, trying hard to be motivated. But she felt tired and worn out with frustration, and sitting around doing nothing didn't help. She almost wished she was back in Bermondsey, but that idea soon disappeared as she remembered the list of killed and tortured souls. She'd had lunch and was thinking about going home early and having a few glasses of wine.

It all happened very quickly. Mick phoned to say there was a long-haired yob in the front reception who wouldn't speak to anyone other than Detective Inspector Karen Foster. Did she want him to throw the young man out? Karen's first thought was, *Another waste of time*, but something told her she should see him. She asked Mick to put him in the small adjoining interview room and wait there for her. She wasn't going to put herself in harm's way without some support. Karen picked up a pen and a notebook and trekked down to reception; she didn't feel particularly excited and wasn't expecting a confession from a serial killer. That all changed as soon as she saw the young man through the glass; she recognised him from somewhere, but couldn't quite put her finger on where. Excitement quickened her pace. She breezed into the interview room and sat straight down.

'Hello, your name please?'

'William Cameron.'

Karen laughed. 'I knew you would be Scottish. Where are you from?'

'Dundee, you know it?'

'No, have you just come down?'

'Yes, I got back from abroad two days ago and made my way here as quickly as possible.'

Karen thought hard. 'And you have something for me?'

Mick stood silently by the door.

'Yes, I do.' Cameron picked up the backpack he'd put on the floor next to his chair. He spoke while he was rummaging in the bag. 'So what happened to Scotty?'

'Apparently he overdosed on heroin and a bottle of whisky.'

William shook his head. 'Never in a million years.'

'Exactly my sentiments.' Karen nodded. 'You knew about Mark Heenan?'

'Yes, I heard.' He finally pulled out a folded envelope and handed it to Karen.

It was so thin she wasn't sure there was anything inside, but when she felt further, it felt like a couple of sheets of paper. She put it on the table in front of her. 'I'm guessing he posted it to you with instructions to pass it to me if he should have an accident.'

'Exactly right. I have no idea what's in it, and don't really want to know. It's been sat at my mum's for ages.' He rose from his chair. 'I hope it's of some use.'

'We may want to speak with you again.'

'Okay.' He took Karen's notebook and wrote his mobile number. 'Anytime. Scotty was all right.'

'Yes, I think he was. Thank you, Mr Cameron.'

William gave a half-salute then left.

Mick sat down opposite Karen. 'I could hardly believe my ears. What's going on?'

'Unless I'm mistaken, the contents of this envelope could well bring down Fellows and Black.' She sat looking at it for a while before she picked it up. She didn't want to open it in case it was nothing helpful, and while it was still intact she could imagine it was the silver bullet. She ran it through her fingers, and then ripped a small piece off the corner, stuck her finger in the hole, and ripped along the envelope. With a deep breath, she removed the contents. The top sheet of paper had a message written in black biro ...

Karen Foster. Epsom Nick.

I'm almost certain something terrible will happen to me very soon.

The man in the photo was the police officer who attacked the woman and man at the energy demo. If you get this, then I am dead.

Bring the bastards to justice.

Scotty

Karen glanced up and passed the piece of paper to Mick. She looked back down at the photograph, then gasped, with her eyes popping out at what she saw. 'Jesus, I don't fucking believe this.' She picked up the photo and passed it to Mick, who looked at it and gaped.

'What the fuck is he doing in this?' he exclaimed.

'I think I can answer that, but let's go up to my office.

CHAPTER 31

At fifty-seven, and a career politician, Jim Smith didn't suffer fools and he was incensed that Peter Fellows had had the audacity to try and blackmail him. He hadn't finished with Fellows, not by a long chalk, and would make him suffer. And, as for a career in politics, he didn't have one. Smith was a family man, married with two daughters, and they lived in a million-pound house in wealthy Totteridge in North London. He'd been Minister of Defence for twelve months and absolutely loved the job. Who wouldn't, when you got the chance to drive a fifty-five-ton Chieftain Tank at forty miles per hour across Salisbury plain? Smith had a personal police bodyguard team, as did all cabinet ministers.

By six on Friday morning, Jim was looking forward to the weekend. He'd been invited to Chequers for lunch on Saturday and couldn't wait; there was always a good mix of politicians, businessmen, and even—possibly—some pop star or other. One of the other joys in his life was taking his black Labrador to the park for his morning walk. Felix had been with the family for twelve years and was slowing down a bit, but still loved his daily exercise. This particular morning, Smith left the house at ten past six, accompanied by single, forty-year-old, experienced, plain-clothes police officer, Freddie Lamsden. The park was a ten-minute walk away and Freddie kept a discreet distance from Smith, so he could at least imagine he was on his own doing something everybody else took for granted.

He soon reached the entrance to the park, and scanned the area to see if there were any other dogs about. Not seeing any, he let Felix off the lead and he bounded off down the pathway towards a few trees. Smith strolled along the path, enjoying the fresh morning, swinging the dog lead in his hand. Freddie had fallen about thirty-five-yards behind, and also sauntered, enjoying the flowerbeds and nature. A noise from behind made him turn. A man on a bicycle flew past him at high speed. It was nothing out of the ordinary; cyclists were always cutting through the park and using it as a shortcut to the town centre. Freddie watched as the cyclist maintained his speed, but then seemed to slow down slightly as he approached the Minister. For some reason, Freddie felt concerned and quickened his pace to catch up, but it was too late.

The cyclist lifted something in the air, Freddie broke into a sprint, and screamed a warning. The man brought the claw hammer straight down onto the back of Smith's head and embedded it. The Minister collapsed to the floor, his legs shaking, and blood pouring out of the wound. Within seconds, he died. Freddie gasped for breath as he sprinted to catch the cyclist up, but it was a waste of time, he had no chance. So he stopped and drew his pistol, but he struggled to catch his breath, and his hands shook. By the time he took aim with a steady arm, the man was long gone. Freddie ran towards the Minister, hoping for a miracle. He knelt down and felt for a pulse ... nothing. He stood and pressed speed-dial-six on his mobile. Within minutes, the area would be swarming with police.

***

The cyclist dumped the bike half a mile away, Tony picked him up in his squad car, and they were soon roaring away from the incident, with lights flashing and siren screaming. The area would soon flood with police and MI6 Officers, but they wouldn't know what they were looking for, and it certainly wouldn't be for two Metropolitan Police Officers.

***

The Prime Minister was informed, he gave a suitably impressive news conference on how much Jim had contributed to the party and the country, and he ended by saying that an announcement would be made shortly as to who would replace him. The usual 'no stone will be left unturned' speeches from politicians on all sides followed. All of this news delighted Fellows, even more so as it seemed the security services had no leads. The next morning's newspapers were full of the murder and there were, of course, more calls for capital punishment to be re-introduced.

He would have to reward Matt and Tony well for the job. Fellows would stop at nothing to secure his future in the corridors of power, and Smith had been too much of wild card.

CHAPTER 32

'So, we are agreed?'

'Yes, Sir.'

'Good, when are you going to strike?'

'Tomorrow morning. What do you think the response will be?'

'I should think Fellows and Black will be very, very angry, and of course, we need to keep it as quiet as possible for as long as possible.'

'The two men who attacked Esme, ... I have a feeling, it's nothing more than that ...'

'Spit it out, Karen.'

'I think they're police officers as well, ... it's just a feeling, when you've been around coppers as long as us, you get a feeling, ... the voices, the way they spoke and walked, just said coppers to me. They could try something like the Banks shooting.'

'Get him to the safe house as soon as possible. You, Mick, and Fergus should be enough as long as they don't find out where you are.'

'I'm certain he's using drugs, and that could be a problem, if he's addicted.'

'Play it by ear and see. If needs be, you'll have to get professional help.'

Silence descended as they both thought about the coming day. Finally, Karen spoke, 'I'm looking forward to it, Sir.'

'Good, but remember they will not just roll over for you. They are the most dangerous adversaries you will have ever met. They have killed, and they won't hesitate to kill again.'

'I know, Sir, don't worry.'

'Let me know how you get on. Thank you.'

Karen rushed back to Epsom, and met Fergus and Mick in the car park at Tattenham Corner, on Epsom Downs. Coffees were bought at the shack café and talks held in Karen's car. They went through the plan, and who was going to do what. Karen stressed that it had to be done quickly, so as few people as possible in the station knew what was happening.

Karen got home at six, went straight to the booze cupboard, and took out a bottle of red. But, after holding it for a few seconds, looking at it raptly, she put it back and shut the door. She had to keep a clear, level head for the next morning. Instead, she spoke to Simon. Although she couldn't tell him exactly what was happening, she could say it was an important morning for the progress and future of his father's case. He tried to reassure her that it would all work out. Karen got an early night and set her alarm for seven. It took her ages to get to sleep, but she was snoring softly by ten thirty.

***

When Karen drove into the nearly full police station car park at quarter to eight, she saw Mick and Fergus outside the entrance and joined them, taking Mick's coffee before he had time to complain.

'We all ready?'

Mick nodded. 'Very ready, boss.'

'Good. Have you saved the space?'

'Everything is ready and in place.'

The person they were after had arrived at the car park at exactly five to nine every single day, and they hoped it would be the same that morning. The time got closer and closer and suddenly it was ten to nine. Mick, Fergus, Karen, and one advanced police driver got into position. They were ready.

***

Jeremy swung his car into the car park at four minutes to nine and couldn't believe his luck; someone must have just left, as an empty space remained, right in front of the entrance. He looked around to make sure no one else was near the space, slowed down, and glided into the opening. He was in good humour; he'd had a fix earlier and felt on top of the world. He got out of the car, pushed the door shut, and pressed his key-fob. With the key in his pocket, he turned towards the entrance. As he turned, he saw Mick and Fergus walking towards his car, on the way to the entrance.

Mick shouted, 'Morning, Stirling Moss.'

Jeremy smiled. 'More Lewis Hamilton, I think, thank you very much.'

He didn't see it coming, and it was over before he realised what had happened.

Fergus took one side and Mick the other. Mick stood in front of Jeremy so he couldn't move. Fergus grabbed his arms and slipped the handcuffs on, then tightened them. They took an arm each and led him round his car to the back door of the car in the next space, which Karen held open. Fergus got in first, followed by Jeremy, and then Mick. Hope started shouting.

'What the fuck is going on?'

The front passenger door opened and Karen got in the car.

'What's happening, Mr Hope, is that you are nicked, you useless piece of shit.'

The car pulled out and made for the exit.

'Where the fuck are you taking me? What the fuck is going on?'

'If I hear any more from you, I'll shut you up. I fucking hate bent coppers,' Mick said with real feeling.

'I know people. You don't know who you're messing with. Seriously, when they find out what's going on, … God, I wouldn't want to be in your shoes. Let me go now and we'll forget about it.' His shouts did nothing. He tried again, 'I said, let me go.'

Mick slapped him on his face. Not that hard a slap, but it shocked Hope and he went deathly quiet.

'That's better. A nice quiet little ride in the car, what's better than that?'

Karen chuckled in the front. They drove up to the downs and got on Great Tattenham's, towards Burgh Heath. They took a right at the main junction lights and shot past Asda, then they stopped at the red lights next to the shell petrol station. The light turned green and they pulled away. They were on a dual carriageway with fast moving traffic, and the driver increased speed to keep up. They drove straight across the first roundabout, and then took the first left towards Mogador. It was becoming more and more countrified; they continued down the country lane and, after three-hundred yards, pulled into a long driveway. They had arrived at the safe house. The detached five-bedroom house had an outdoor swimming pool and sat in about an acre of land. Karen knocked on the door, and a middle aged, severely dressed woman opened it.

'I've been expecting you. I'm Catherine, the housekeeper.'

While she held the door wide open, Mick and Fergus dragged Hope out of the back of the car, and into the house. The driver drove the car round to the back of the house and parked it in the three-car garage.

Ten-minutes later, another car picked him up to take him back to Epsom Police Station. Mick and Fergus took Jeremy into the lounge and dumped him on the sofa. Fergus sat on a single chair opposite him. Mick left the room and familiarised himself with the entire property, including the outside. Karen talked to the Housekeeper, discussing how the house was to be run and what was available. The housekeeper would be cooking all the meals and keeping the property tidy and clean. She would do the shopping, but the house had extra chest-freezers, thus negating the need for too many shopping trips. Karen was happy with the set up, and placed a call to Chief Inspector Park to confirm the parcel had arrived in good condition. They would have a light lunch, and then begin the interrogation of Jeremy.

***

Hope himself already felt the pressure. He didn't know where he was or what Karen Foster knew. What he did know was that Philip Black would be alerted to a problem at six p.m. that evening, when he didn't confirm a coded message. Once that happened, the search would begin. He knew so much that they would either rescue him or make sure he couldn't talk. He'd killed Mark Heenan and Trevor Banks, and he would get life. And, because he was a policeman, life would almost certainly mean life. Sweat coated his skin, and he itched. Another two or three hours and he would be climbing the walls. He had coke on him, but he needed his hands to use it. He looked at Fergus. 'I need a pee.'

Fergus lifted him up by the arm and took him to the downstairs toilet. He undid the handcuffs and pushed him in. No windows meant no means of escape. Hope pushed the door, but before it shut, Fergus kicked it and it stopped half open. Jeremy reached down and took the small plastic bag out from the inside of his shoe. He didn't have much time, so he licked his fingers and stuck them into the white powder, and then stuck them in his mouth and sucked. Almost immediately, he could feel the high beginning and felt better. He took his dick out and peed, while sticking his fingers in the white powder once again. He grinned as he peed all over the floor: present for the housekeeper. He hid the coke back in his shoe, and left feeling much better. Fergus re-cuffed him and led him back to the lounge.

'Fergus, you need to think about yourself,' Jeremy said. 'They don't give a shit about you. Help me and I'll make sure you've got so much money you don't know what to do with it all.'

'You slimy piece of shit. Say anymore and I'll smash your ugly face.' Hope didn't make any further comment.

The housekeeper made Tuna and cucumber sandwiches for lunch, and soon two o'clock rolled round.

Karen had chosen the study to interview Hope in. The small room had a solid-looking hardwood desk, and three chairs. Fergus dragged Hope into the room and sat him in front of the table, where Karen already sat facing him, with Mick over to the right side. Fergus shut the door on his way out, and most likely wished he could have been a fly on the wall.

Karen gave Hope a hard look. 'Jeremy, you have got yourself in a lot of bother, but the good news is we can help you.' Karen paused to let that sink in. 'We know all about you, your part in the Energy Demonstration, beating up Mary Bishop, killing David Kane, and then the whole cover up.' She paused again, then said, 'There's nothing we don't know. You're in the shit, big time.'

Jeremy bristled, the coke giving him false bravado. 'You know fuck all, and when my friends have finished with you …'

'Your fucking friends in high places are not here, Jeremy. You think they give a shit about you? If I let you go, you would be dead within a couple of hours. You're finished, washed up, surplus to requirements.'

Hope was more than a little concerned at the predicament he found himself in. He felt sure that Foster would play by the book. They certainly weren't going to torture him, so if he kept quiet, what would they do?

'I know what you're thinking, Jeremy. I can read your mind like a book. But think on this, if you do not help us, I will hand you over to Internal Affairs, and they will conduct a full investigation into your behaviour at the Energy Demonstration. At the least, you'll be kicked out of the service in disgrace. But it's my bet the establishment would want to make an example of you and stick you in the Scrubs for a few years. Fellows and Black aren't here to protect you. I can keep you here for days, even weeks, if I have to.' Karen looked at her watch, and then turned to Mick. 'Has he been thoroughly searched?'

'He doesn't have any weapons on him, but we haven't done a full strip search.'

'Do it now. I'll send Fergus in.' Karen left the study, sure he was using drugs. They needed to find out if he had secreted any on, or in, his body.

Fergus joined Mick and they told Hope to undress. Hope became agitated.

'Look,' he said. 'You can see I haven't got anything on me. Jesus, this is crazy.'

Fergus wasn't having any of it. 'Take everything off, or we will.'

Hope kicked his slip-on shoes off and pushed them a little under the desk, he then fully complied and ended up standing naked, praying they didn't check his shoes.

Mick went through his clothes, checking every item carefully, but found nothing.

'Get dressed.'

Hope was elated he'd got away with it. He dressed, then put his right foot into the shoe, and then his world fell apart.

'Stand back.' Fergus picked up the shoes and turned them over. A small plastic bag of white powder fell to the floor.

'Well, look what we have here.' Fergus leant down and picked up the baggie.

'It's not washing powder, is it Jeremy? Oh dear, you're going to miss this. Shame.'

Fergus left the room, found Karen, and handed her the coke. Meanwhile, Hope sat in the study for the afternoon, and slowly unravelled. The anxiety crept in, he started to sweat, and he felt hot and cold. He had to get that coke back, he needed it, and he would kill for it if he had to.

***

Six p.m. came and the coded call to Black was not made. At ten past six, Black knew there was a problem. First, he rang Hope's mobile and found it switched off. Second, he phoned Epsom police station and asked for him, but was given a tale he didn't believe:

'I'm sorry, Sir, but Mr Hope is not well at the moment, and isn't taking calls. Can I put you through to another officer?'

Black put the phone down and concentrated, then he picked it up and rang Epsom again. He asked to speak to Detective Inspector Karen Foster and this time he was told she was interviewing and not available. One last call and then he would take action.

'Its Commander Black, I want to speak to Chief Inspector Park, it's very urgent.'

'I'm terribly sorry, Sir, he's in conference and is not taking calls. Can I give him a message for you?'

'No.' He hung up.

Black put a call in to Fellows and warned him there could well be an issue with Hope. Fellows said just two words 'Sort it.'

Black called his PA, Andrea Houlihan, into his office. She had been with Black for fifteen years and knew exactly what sort of man he was, but she didn't mind—he paid her well over the going rate to ensure her dedication and loyalty, and she had actually once given him a blow job in the office.

'Andrea, there is a safe house in Surrey that I require the address of. How do I go about getting that?'

'I'll phone Guildford and ask them. What do I say if they ask why?'

Black just looked at her, angry. Then his PA said, 'Oh, I see. Well, it will be on the secret register in the Commissioner's office, so maybe we have a friend who …'

'Thank you. That will be all.'

Black got straight on the phone to his contact in the Commissioner's office and promised him a ten-thousand-pound bonus for the address.

Ten minutes later, Black was on the phone again. The Epsom area had only one safe house, and Black prayed it was the right one. He called Tony:

'Pick up Max, and get there as soon as possible. You three should be able to manage it easily enough. This is the address.'

Black phoned Fellows and told him what had happened.

***

As instructed, the receptionist rang through to Park and informed him that Commander Black had tried to get hold of him. Park immediately rang Karen and told her that he thought Black knew there was a problem, and that she should take extra care.

***

Matt and Tony turned the siren on and sped their way to the pick up point. Max would help them kill Foster, Hope, and anyone else unlucky enough to be at the safe house.

***

Max was unhappy; he'd been gutted when that arsehole Black had rung him and told him they knew about him selling drugs. Max had denied it, but Black said he would be arrested if he didn't do as he was told. Max had given in, and this phone call was the first time Black had rung and asked him to do something. He was to be back-up on a job with other policemen who were on their way to pick him up. He'd been told to wait outside Victoria Station. A police car screeched to a halt right next to him, he opened the back door, and got in.

The driver smiled, then said, 'Hi Max. How long you been with the firm?'

The two officers in the front looked familiar to Max, ... maybe he had seen them at a station somewhere.

'Not long, this is my first job.'

The officer in the passenger seat piped up, 'A fucking virgin no less, I hope you know what you're doing?'

'What's the gig?'

Matt and Tony looked at each other. Matt spoke in a serious tone, 'Well, you'll see soon enough, so might as well tell you. We're going to kill two or more people at a house.'

'We're going to fucking what?'

'You heard me.'

'I didn't sign up to this shit. Stop the car.'

'No can do, pal, orders is orders.'

Max trembled—he'd never killed anyone. 'Who … ?' He stopped as he considered what he was saying. 'Who, exactly, are we meant to be killing?'

'Two coppers and anybody else who's there.'

Max couldn't believe what he'd just heard, and he shouted at Matt and Tony, 'No fucking way am I getting involved in this!'

'You're already involved. The three of us. The A team.' He laughed.

'I'll stay with the car. You can do what the fuck you like. Who are the coppers?'

'You don't need to know. Just do as you're told and everything will be kushty.'

Max thought desperately about how he could get out of this. 'I haven't got a gun, and I don't know how to use one anyway.'

Matt and Tony both laughed. 'We've got a boot full. Don't worry, you just point it and pull the trigger.'

Max looked through the window. 'Where are we headed?'

'Epsom Downs.'

That was interesting. Jeremy Hope was based at Epsom. Oh God, no, it couldn't be. He thought about it. What did he have to lose? 'Not Jeremy Hope, by any chance?'

Matt gave Tony a hard look. 'Yes. Do you know him?'

'I worked with him at a demonstration in London once. What's he done?'

'No idea. We just do as we're told, and I suggest you do exactly the same if you want to remain healthy.'

Max had got the message. If he didn't play ball, then one day someone would be driving to visit him. He heaved a sigh. 'I guess you're right.'

'You know it. Do the job. You get well paid and then forget about it. Now stop fucking talking.'

It wasn't long before Max saw a sign that said Epsom. He was nearly shitting himself he was so worried. He wanted to keep his involvement to a minimum. 'I'll be the back-up, then, just in case.'

'That's fine, Max, we'll take care of it, and you can be the back-up.'

They drove over the downs and towards Burgh Heath, and it wasn't long before they turned down a country lane and slowed down. Matt looked at the Sat Nav. 'About half a mile down the road, bit longer, then park up.'

As instructed, Tony parked the car, hiding it as best he could behind some trees. The three of them got out, Matt opened the boot, and Max stared in astonishment. There must have been ten weapons, from hand pistols to Rifles and machine guns.

'Where the fuck did you get all this?' He picked up a pistol and felt the weight in his hand. It felt strong and powerful, and he had an urge to fire it, and pointed at a tree.

'It's not loaded yet. That one's a Glock 17C. 17 means seventeen rounds. If you like that one, you can keep it.'

'Feels good, powerful, very comfortable to hold. I'll keep it just in case, then.'

Matt gave Max the ammunition, which he loaded into the magazine. Then Matt chose a Remington sniper rifle and a Glock 19, while Tony was happier with just a pistol, and liked the Glock 17.

As they set off towards the safe house, Max made sure he was at the back, as he had no intention of getting involved, unless he feared for his own life. He kept looking at the gun; he loved the feel of it and could understand how some lunatic Americans kept so many weapons. Matt and Tony kept a fast pace and they were soon in sight of the house. They ducked down in the undergrowth about a hundred yards from the back of the property. In front of them, lay a manicured lawn with flowerbeds, and a garden path that led from the back door to the end of the garden. They could see directly into the lounge, which had a huge sliding door almost the entire length of the back of the house. Matt looked through his rifle's telescopic sight, and scanned the room from left to right.

'What's happening?' Tony asked.

'Three people in the room. One man sitting with his back to us. I can see the back of his head over the chair. A woman, older, looks like a housekeeper maybe, and one other man, looks like a copper. There must be somebody else, … wait, someone has just entered the room. It's the Foster woman. Good looking as well.'

'What's the plan?'

Matt rested the rifle. 'It makes sense to take one out from distance—that'll lower the odds a bit and scare the shit out of them. Tony, you go round the property and make for the back door, Max will stay with me, and as soon as you're in position text me and I'll take out the man in the chair. I have a feeling that's Hope, so he'll be the first. Straight afterwards, we'll make for the back door. When you see us move, hit the back door and kill anything that moves.'

Max heard those words and his anxiety levels climbed another notch. Tony set off, keeping under cover as he made towards the back door.

All seemed quiet in the house, Hope sat in the lounge, Fergus was on guard duty, and stood stretching his legs. The housekeeper and Karen had left the lounge; the housekeeper went upstairs and Karen occupied the study, on the phone. Mick ambled around outside the property, at the front of the house, getting some fresh air.

Matt looked at his phone; the tension was palpable. Max sweated, and kept wondering whether this was real or was he dreaming.

Matt nodded at Max. 'Its time.' The text had arrived; Tony was in position.

Matt lifted the old army rifle and slotted it into his shoulder. He adjusted the sight slightly and lined up the shot. The copper still paced the floor, and whom he thought must be Hope still sat in the chair. He lined up the sight directly on the middle of the back of the man's head. It was a simple shot; he applied pressure on the trigger, and pulled. He kept perfectly still as he watched the bullet enter the back of the head. Pieces of flesh, bone, and jets of blood shot into the air as his head disintegrated, the body slumped to the side, and fell out of sight. Matt lowered the rifle and started running; Max hard on his shoulder, still completely terrified.

***

Fergus heard the shot at the same time that Hope's head exploded. He ducked down and drew his pistol, then rushed for the door and ran towards the back entrance.

***

Karen thought she heard a shot and almost jumped out of her skin; she grabbed her gun from the desk and checked the safety was off. She opened the study door slowly and looked out. Worry gnawed at her, as she had no fucking idea what was going on. Then another shot sounded, and this time she could tell it was definitely a gunshot: inside the house, near the lounge. She held the gun out in front of herself and took slow, measured steps towards the lounge.

***

Mick had heard the shot, drawn his weapon, and made his way round the house towards the back, where he thought the shot had come from.

***

The housekeeper panicked and locked herself in the safe room, which was a windowless room upstairs with a massive, extra-strong door. She had the presence of mind to press the emergency alarm, which would bring help, but whether in time or not she didn't know.

***

Tony smashed the window-pane in the door and pushed it open, on edge and ready to shoot anything that moved. He stopped to listen. Someone came along the corridor, so he crouched down and aimed his pistol at the corner the person would come round.

***

Fergus felt scared. He approached the right turn, which would lead him to the back door. He stopped and listened, nothing. He took one step and was killed instantly as the bullet entered the middle of his forehead. He crumpled to the floor and a small trickle of blood came out of the wound and ran down his cheek.

***

Tony heard a noise behind him and turned: Matt stood a couple of paces away, and behind him, came Max. Matt took the lead and stepped over Fergus's body. Max saw the body, then dry-heaved. Tony slapped him on the shoulder, shouting, 'Move.'

***

Mick worked his way around the house until he reached the back door. He crept in. When he saw Fergus lying dead, sprawled across the floor, he felt sick rising in his throat. He recovered quickly, although he felt enraged, … shot in the head in cold blood … someone would pay. He edged around the corner and wondered where Karen was. He stopped again to listen, and could hear someone in the lounge. The first shot had probably killed Hope, so it was likely to be one of the killers checking the room. Mick cursed as a floorboard creaked and he froze on the spot, crouched down, and aimed his weapon at the lounge entrance.

***

Karen moved cautiously along the carpeted corridor towards the lounge, and paused frequently to listen. This time, she heard someone coming towards her. With a supreme effort to keep calm, she presented the gun, ready to shoot any bastard who appeared.

Matt took the lead and turned the corner first. Karen fired and Matt got a shot off as well. Karen's bullet hit Matt in the chest, and he wouldn't last long. Meanwhile, his shot smashed into Karen's shoulder. The impact spun her, and then she went down in a heap. Her gun flew out of her hand and landed down the corridor. As she lay there, reorienting herself, she realised there was another killer and that she was at his mercy.

***

A man came out of the lounge, he turned left to follow after his other two hit men. Mick couldn't believe his luck. He shouted, 'Stop exactly where you are and drop the weapon.' The man turned and lifted his pistol. Mick fired three shots in swift succession and the man fell, all three shots in the chest, which killed him almost instantly.

***

Karen looked up as Max loomed above her, aiming his pistol at her head. In her shock, she couldn't speak. Her time to go had come. She closed her eyes, expecting to die. Then she counted: one second, two, three, four … what was the bastard waiting for? She heard a thud on the floor, and wondered what it could be, … five, six, seven … she felt like shouting 'get on with it, you fucking bastard'. When she finally opened her eyes and looked at the man, he had pissed himself and she could smell the urine. She still couldn't speak, and became wide eyed as she noticed he was no longer holding a gun. The thud had come from him throwing his gun down. A miracle had happened. Then, through the excruciating pain, she heard a shout.

'Stand still and put your hands in the air. I will count to three, and if your hands are not in the air, I will shoot you.'

Max came to life and his hands shot up. Mick grabbed him and threw him to the floor.

'Lie still and do not move.'

Karen moaned in pain. Mick knelt down and spoke, 'Don't worry. Help is on the way. You'll be fine.'

Karen smiled, then started to cry. Through her tears, she said, 'He could have shot me. I thought I was ...' She couldn't finish the sentence. Mick jumped up, then kicked Max in the stomach.

'How many of you?'

Max spluttered, 'Three.'

***

The answer pleased Mick. 'I'll be back in a minute,' he told Karen. Then he ran to the stairs, shouting, 'All clear.' At the safe room door, he said, 'Catherine, it's Mick, come out.' The door opened and she appeared.

'Karen's been injured. See what you can do.'

Mick rushed back downstairs and heard shouting—the cavalry had turned up.

***

Armed officers swarmed all over the house, checking every room. An ambulance arrived ten minutes later and whisked Karen off to St Helier Hospital. She went straight into the operating theatre where the bullet was removed and she was sown back together. After surgery, they put her into a private room with a police guard. She was still unaware Fergus had been killed.

***

Officers drove Max straight to Epsom police station, where he identified himself as a serving Metropolitan police officer. He also informed the custody team that the two dead killers were also serving officers. The custody officers were appalled beyond belief, and contacted Chief Inspector Park at Guildford straight away. Forty minutes later, two squad cars pulled up outside Epsom police station and ten armed Surrey police officers filed in. Mick greeted them; they were extra protection for Max. The officers stationed themselves at strategic points throughout the building, with two joining the custody team. Chief Inspector Park wanted to take no chances, and would, himself, visit Epsom the next day to personally interrogate Max.

***

When he had received no call from Matt, Philip Black didn't panic, it wasn't in his nature. Something had gone wrong and, as yet, he didn't know exactly what. He made a couple of calls and found out that a woman police officer was in St Helier Hospital with gunshot wounds but would survive, so he assumed it was the Foster bitch. He also obtained reports of police officers being killed, and discovered that Surrey Police had gone into lock down, which meant a major incident had occurred, and everything would be shut down, with no communication in or out. Black made a call to Fellows and said one word, 'Armageddon.' Then put the phone down.

***

At midday, the next day, Chief Inspector Park visited Karen at St Helier Hospital. Karen was out of any danger and had recovered enough to have eaten a hearty breakfast, and insisted on making phone calls. Her first call was to Mick Hill, and she heard the terrible news that Hope and Fergus had been killed. She cried buckets for Fergus and then thought about Esme, and who would tell her. Nothing would stop her bringing down Black and Fellows now, and this had hardened her resolve even more. She had a light bowl of soup early, so she would be ready for her visit from Park. St Helier Hospital, from the outside, was more akin to a prison—a ghastly, huge stone building with no personality or charm. The trust had recently spent millions on the interior, which was a step forward. Chief Inspector Park arrived with no less than four gofers at eleven fifty-five. He was shown into Karen's room, while his entourage stayed outside, twiddling their thumbs.

'Karen, how are you?'

'Very well, Sir, thank you.'

He took a seat by the bed. 'Sorry about Fergus. He was a good officer.'

Karen felt tearful again. 'Yes, he was. Has his family been told?'

'Yes, though I understand you are going to tell his partner?'

'Yes. But I really didn't want to do it on the phone. However, I can't see any other choice, so I'll do it when you go, Sir.'

Park shifted in his chair. 'Hope is no longer, but the better news is we have Max Groves in custody and I am going to interrogate him this afternoon.'

Karen pushed herself up, so she could sit more comfortably. 'Sir, you must promise me one thing.'

'And what is that?' he asked with a smile.

'Groves had a chance to shoot me, but he threw the gun away. He'll talk, and when he does, he'll name Black. I want to be there when he's arrested. Promise me, please, for Fergus, Scotty, and all the others. I must be there.'

'I'll do better than that. You will be the arresting officer, even if you are in a wheelchair.'

'Thank you, Sir. I'll be out of here in a day or two.'

'The interviews with Groves will last at least two days, so there's no rush. Now, anything else before I shove off?'

'I hope Groves is well protected, Sir?'

'I sent a handpicked team of armed officers. Epsom is like a fortress; don't worry. So, look, see you in a couple of days.'

'Thank you, Sir.'

When he left, true to her word, she called France.

'Esme, it's Karen.'

Karen was still in pain and had found it so hard to pick up the phone and punch in the numbers. It had taken her ages to actually feel mentally ready for the call. She knew how Esme felt about Fergus, and it would devastate her. The couple had talked about living together and marriage. It upset Karen even thinking about it.

'Karen, so good to hear from you, how are you?'

Karen already felt tearful and could hardly speak. 'Something's happened, Esme. It's Fergus … there was shooting … he didn't make it.'

'Sorry, Karen, it is not a perfect line. Fergus did what?'

'Oh God, please.' Karen's tears flowed in floods.

'Karen, what's wrong? Has something happened to Fergus?'

Karen wailed down the phone, 'He's been shot, shot dead.'

Esme screamed down the phone. Karen cried some more. 'Esme, Esme, I'm so sorry. Esme.' She held the phone away from her ear and the screaming continued unabated. Then the phone went quiet and a new voice came on:

'Karen, I am friend. Esme, we talk later.' Then the phone went dead. Karen continued to cry off and on for the rest of the day, and as soon as she thought she had control she would start again. A nurse gave her a sleeping pill, and eventually she nodded off.

**

At a quarter to two, Chief Inspector Park arrived at Epsom police station, suitably impressed by the heavy and professional security in operation. He had a ten-minute meeting with Mick Hill, and then proceeded to the custody suite. Max Groves was taken out of his cell and taken to an interview room, with two armed guards following him the short distance.

Park sat down opposite Groves, who had elected not to have any representation. 'Groves, you are a disgrace to the uniform. You make me thoroughly sick. Your only saving grace is that you did not pull the trigger when you had Karen Foster in your sights.'

'Just ask whatever you want and I'll tell you what I know.'

'Who is the ringleader in this nest of vipers?'

'Commander Philip Black ordered me to help the other two kill Hope, Foster, and every other person we found at the safe house.'

'And you'll sign a statement to that effect and appear as a witness in court?'

Max blanched, but said, 'Yes.'

'I need to know what Black has on you.'

'I gave Jeremy Hope some uppers on the day of the Energy Demonstration, Black found out, he threatened to kick me off the force, with no pension, nothing.'

Park sat deep in thought. 'Okay, so we need to start at the beginning and tape everything; you know the procedure.' It took three hours, then they stopped for the day. The interviewing would continue again the next day to make sure they had all the details. Park left Epsom, happy in the knowledge they had Philip Black by the balls. If there was one thing Park detested above everything, it was bent coppers. Black would get his, and soon.

***

Karen's recuperation went well, and the thought of arresting Black seemed to speed up her recovery. She looked forward to leaving St Helier shortly.

At the end of the week, Karen was discharged, on a Friday afternoon. A colleague drove her to her flat. Five minutes after arriving home, she received a call from Chief Inspector Park, who told her they had concluded the interviewing of Max Groves and that they had a watertight case against Black. He also mentioned that Groves had no knowledge of anyone else working with Black, which meant Fellows was in the clear, for the time being at least.

***

Black spent the weekend putting his house in order: paper was shredded, reports went missing, phone records were deleted, and computers crushed and incinerated. Money was transferred, and accounts closed; he was good at the detail, and they would find nothing to incriminate him or Fellows. It would be his word against whomever the prosecution put on the stand.

He provided for his family through offshore accounts that had been set up and operating for years. Fellows would keep an eye on the family and make sure they were safe and didn't want for anything. The agreement had always been that whoever was exposed would cover the back of the other. Black knew he would go to prison for a long time, but it had been an exciting journey and life. He would serve most of his time in Administrative protection, as every nark would take great delight in beating, stabbing, and generally making his life a misery, from the second he woke to the second he went to bed.

He took his family out to dinner on the Sunday night—the last supper. It was a merry affair until they were on the coffee and liqueurs, and then he dropped the bombshell that he would soon be arrested and charged with serious crimes. He explained he had made some serious errors of judgement and would be going to prison for a lengthy sentence. His wife and children stayed strong, resilient, and driven, and accepted stoically what Black said. They only wanted to know one thing: did he have the best lawyer money could buy? The evening finished and Black said he would more than likely be arrested on the following morning. The wife and children promised to support Philip every single day through his long trial.

The next morning, Philip got up at seven-thirty as usual. He had his normal breakfast of toast and lemon-lime marmalade, and extra-strong tea. The only difference that morning was the way he hugged his wife and children just before he left the house. After the poignant moment, he left the house as quickly as he could. He settled down in his luxurious Audi A6 for the drive into New Scotland Yard. He wondered what would happen, and it was interesting for him to try to work out the sequence of probable events.

He took his usual route, turned onto the one-way system at Victoria train station, sped onto Victoria Street, past the Cardinal Place shopping Centre, and was nearly at the junction with Palace Street. He slammed on the brakes when a car came speeding out of Palace Street straight in front of him. At the same time, a black saloon car pulled alongside him. He looked in the mirror. Armed men piled out of the car behind him. The neat operation impressed him; it had been well carried out, and professional. He stayed quiet while they opened his driver's-side door and dragged him from the vehicle. An officer pulled his hands behind his back and handcuffed him. Pushed against the door, he felt hands searching his uniform and body and, a minute later, the officer shouted, 'Clean'. The man then turned Black around, and a group of plain clothes and uniformed officers approached him. At the front, stood Detective Inspector Karen Foster. Also in the group were two officers from Internal Affairs, with Mick Hill at the back. Karen stuck her hand under Black's chin and lifted it up.

'Philip Black, I am arresting you on suspicion of murdering Jeremy Hope, Fergus O'Donnell, Robert Young, Scot Ferguson, Mark Heenan, Trevor Banks, and Mary Bishop. You do not have to say anything, but it may harm your defence if you do not mention, when questioned, something which you later rely on in court. Anything you do say may be given in evidence.'

She stepped back and turned to the Internal Affairs officers. 'Take this scum away.' The two officers came forward, took an arm each, and marched Black to one of the waiting cars. They both got in the back with him, then the car roared off, headed towards the most high-secure Police Station in London: Paddington Green.

Ten minutes later, the car pulled into the police station. They took Black to the custody suite and the booking in process began. First, he had to empty his pockets and remove any jewellery. His watch and wallet were placed in an envelope, and he signed a document to that effect. He then filled a form in with his name and address. Then they photographed him, finger printed him, and swabbed his mouth for a DNA sample. He did all this in a cooperative and resigned manner. When he'd finished the process, he sat waiting to be taken to the cells. The desk sergeant became more and more agitated as he stared at Black, then he shook his head and asked, 'Have you got no remorse for what you have done in that uniform?'

Black looked him square in the eye and half-smiled. 'No Comment.'

The case against Black would take months to prepare, but—amazingly—Black was given bail, on condition that he stayed under house arrest and that he surrendered his passport. He was over the moon with that and spent hour after hour in his study preparing his case in minute detail. Since he had given the code-word Armageddon to Fellows he had not even mentioned his name, and it was almost as if they didn't know each other. Fellows had contacted Christian Turner, probably the best criminal defence lawyer in London, and he worked with Black. They made a formidable team and the Crown Prosecution Service were well aware they had a tough job on their hands. The ace in their hand was Max Groves—his personal giving of evidence was crucial to the case. However, bearing in mind he had been selling drugs to police officers, it could be said he wasn't the most reliable witness. But the fact he had been arrested at the safe house and witnessed the murder of Fergus O'Donnell would be critical.

***

Karen tried time and again to speak to Esme, but her phone had been turned off. She finally decided to write an email. It was so difficult, and she still couldn't stop crying. It took an hour to write eight lines, as she kept changing the wording. In the end, she wrote it from the heart, and left it.

Esme, my darling friend,

Words cannot express how I feel for you. I cannot stop crying for you and Fergus. He was a kind, thoughtful, lovely man who was so very much in love with you—he worshipped you as I do. I cannot help now, except to support you in any way I can. I am thinking of you all the time and pray that you can come over for the funeral to say goodbye to Fergus. It will be a difficult time, but you must come and stay with me. Let me know when you can make it and I'll pick you up at the airport. If there is anything I can do for you, please let me know.

Love to Mama and Papa.

All my love to you,

Karen XXX

Karen got a reply the next day.

Karen, my love,

It was good to hear from you. I am sorry my phone is switched off, but I do not want to speak to many people at the moment. Yes, of course I am coming to say goodbye to Fergus, and I would like to stay with you, if possible. I am now crying again. I don't think I will ever stop. It is all I have done for days. Why does life have to be like this? I was so happy with Fergus; he was my dream man. I'm crying again, … maybe we can cry together when I come over. I want to come Thursday, to Gatwick, is that okay? You are a dear friend to me, Karen, and I can't wait to see you. We must *have some red wine, yes! I am crying again, see you soon, my love.*

Esme XXX

CHAPTER 33

The police summoned Philip for interviews at various times. His lawyer made life as difficult as possible for the Crown Prosecution Service by challenging every single act and submission, and taking an inordinate amount of time to reply to any communication. The interviews were all the same: the interviewers would ask a question and Black would give the reply, 'No Comment.' It was exceptionally testing and frustrating to ask fifty questions and get fifty 'No Comments'. Surrey Police found that the mountains of evidence they thought they had, amounted to not very much. Max Groves would go on the stand and swear that Philip Black told him to go with Matt and Tony to kill everybody in the safe house. Black would, no doubt, swear that Max Groves was a drug selling, junkie liar. The case would be tight and, certainly, the outcome could not be easily predicted.

***

Esme arrived at the North Terminal of Gatwick on Thursday at seven p.m. Karen waited as close to the arrivals door as she could, and when she saw Esme push the doors open, she screamed her name, ducked under the silver railing, and ran to her. They embraced, and kissed cheeks warmly. Two seconds later, they were both in floods of tears.

All Karen could say was, 'Esme, Esme,' as she hugged her tighter and tighter and kissed her a dozen times on the cheeks. They moved away from arrivals arm in arm, still sobbing, and made their way to the short-stay car park. Neither of them could stop talking, interspersed with more tears and sobs. They reached Karen's car and, two minutes later, pulled out of the airport, and headed back to Epsom. Karen studied Esme, and thought she looked fragile and tired—not surprising, with the shock of what had happened. They chatted in the car continually and, forty minutes later, parked up at Karen's flat. Karen carried Esme's suitcase inside. A short time after that, they sat in the lounge with a glass of red wine each.

'I thought we would eat out tonight, is that okay?'

'Yes, of course, but I am tired, so not too late, and not too much wine.' Esme smiled, and Karen smiled back. Despite everything, she remained smitten with this tired, but still gorgeous-looking, French girl from Cannes.

'Before we go out, can I have a quick shower?'

'Esme, you don't have to ask. Everything is in the bathroom, so please go ahead. Be careful, as the hot water can be very hot.'

Esme put her glass of half-finished red wine down and disappeared into the bathroom. Karen stayed in the lounge and sipped her wine. The shower hummed as it came on. She closed her eyes and remembered Esme's delicious breasts, but snapped out of it when she heard Esme shout,

'There's no towel.' Karen went to the airing cupboard and took out a freshly laundered, pink, fluffy towel, then went to the bathroom door, knocked, and held the towel so Esme could take it.

'Karen, what is wrong with you? Come in, we are all girls here, you know.'

Karen hadn't wanted to, because she didn't want to see Esme naked. She feared she might just jump on Esme, who very likely might not be receptive to advances at the moment. Esme's bottom greeted Karen when she walked into the bathroom, and before she could stop herself, she spoke, 'That's a lovely arse, Esme. ... Oh God, I'm so sorry, I didn't mean ...'

Esme turned and smiled seductively, and Karen now had the pleasure of seeing Esme's breasts and smooth pussy. Esme took the towel and wrapped it around herself, covering up the carnal delights.

'Yes, Karen, you are right as always. I have a gorgeous arse, as you put it.' Esme brushed past Karen and kissed her on the cheek. 'I must get dressed if we are going out, ... come with me.' Esme went into her allocated bedroom, took the towel off, and handed it to Karen.

'I am so tired. Can you help dry me, please?'

Karen was beside herself. She couldn't take her eyes from Esme's beautiful body. She swallowed, then said, 'Yes, of course.' Then dried Esme's back and shoulders with gentle rubs of the towel. Next, she dried her bottom, and it became increasingly difficult to maintain normalcy. Karen's breathing became strained, and she now had to dry Esme's breasts. She ran the towel over the pert beauties and the nipples hardened. She couldn't take anymore, and threw the towel playfully at Esme.

'See you in a minute,' she said. 'I've got to get dressed myself.'

Karen escaped to her room and shut the door, breathing heavily. Although she still loved Esme, she felt ashamed when she thought of Fergus and the funeral.

Karen and Esme looked casual, but still stunning, as they left the flat and drove into the town centre. Karen fell lucky and got a space right outside the Thai Restaurant in South Street. The waiter wanted them to sit by the window, but Karen walked to the back of the restaurant and sat in the corner.

'I don't want to be on show tonight, and it's cosy back here, don't you agree?'

'I do not mind where we sit, Karen, but now is the time for you to tell me exactly what happened.'

Karen wasn't quite ready to relate the details of how Fergus had been killed. 'Let's get some wine first,' she said, instead, and signalled for a waiter. Karen ordered a bottle of house red, and only then told Esme the story. She didn't add or leave anything out, but told her exactly what happened that day in the safe house. Esme listened without interrupting once and, when Karen had finished, she cried some more. Karen held her hand. 'He was a good officer, one of the best, and you should be proud of him.'

Esme struggled to speak, 'I would rather he was here, than being proud of him. But thank you for telling me the truth.'

'What else could I tell you, other than that?' Karen topped up the glasses with wine. 'I have a day off tomorrow, and I thought we might go into the country and have a pub lunch somewhere.'

'That sounds nice. What time is the funeral on Saturday?'

'Three, followed by a snack and drinks at the station. He was popular and there will be a lot of people paying their respects.'

The food arrived and they ate heartily, drank more wine, and then ordered a second bottle.

'I had planned to drink little; if I get drunk, I will start crying and never stop.'

'There's no rush, ... from here we go home to bed. Oh, I didn't mean together, I mean we go home, oh shit.' Karen and Esme shared a laugh.

The meal was delicious and they managed to finish the second bottle. Karen shouldn't be driving, but it was only a mile, and as long as she was careful.

They got home in one piece and held hands as they walked towards the flat. Esme felt tired after her flight, and

Karen slightly drunk. They stood in the lounge, just looking at each other. Karen moved first and kissed Esme on both cheeks.

'Goodnight, my beautiful Esme.' Then she went to her room and shut the door. She stripped off and got under her duvet. Exhausted, she soon fell asleep.

***

Esme had gone to bed, but couldn't sleep. She lay still, thinking of Fergus, and whether she wanted to stay in the police or work in the family restaurant, and a hundred other things that stopped her from sleeping.

After what seemed like hours, she clicked on her mobile—three a.m. showed in bright numbers. She was upset, depressed, and Karen was next door … she needed her friend. Naked, she crept to the door, opened it, and tiptoed to Karen's door. She turned the handle slowly and let herself in. Gentle breathing came from the bed. Esme approached and, for a second or two, stared at Karen—she was lovely and she looked so comfortable and cosy. Then, slowly, Esme pulled the cover back and slid into the bed.

Surprised to feel Karen's naked body so warm and inviting, she cuddled up to her and placed her arm around her waist. Happiness washed over her, and she felt loved and secure. She moved her hand up and touched Karen's nipple and breast, breathed a sigh of relief, and a minute later fell fast asleep.

***

At about eight, Karen stirred. She froze when she realised that someone was in bed with her. It wasn't Simon, and she had a momentary panic attack at the thought she might have brought a man back, but then she relaxed. Esme's face stuck out from the duvet. Karen yawned and stretched, then snuggled into the back of Esme, feeling her body as they became one. Esme woke and pushed her bottom back into Karen, who kissed her shoulder and moved her hand round to hold Esme's breast—it felt firm and the nipple hardened when she played with it. Karen didn't understand why, but she stopped and got out of bed, then went to make some breakfast. She turned as Esme stood in the doorway.

'Why did you get up?' she asked, in a sexy, sleepy, French accent.

'I kept thinking of Fergus. I can't help it.'

'Don't you remember, you know, between us in the Greek Restaurant? And here in the flat, before? There has always been something, … something really special … magical?'

'Yes, there is something between us, but … the funeral …'

Esme smiled. 'Let's say a fitting farewell to Fergus then, and see what happens after that.'

'Agreed, my darling. Now, how about some bacon and eggs?'

Esme squealed, 'Oh my God, no. Where are the pain au chocolate and Croissants?'

***

The funeral proved to be a tearful affair. Karen and Esme cried from the beginning to the end. Over fifty police officers attended and, as a send-off, it was a great success. Everybody went back to the canteen in the police station for a glass of wine and egg mayonnaise sandwiches.

Several speeches heaped praise on Fergus for his work as a police officer, and for being a good man. After a couple of hours, Karen told Mick's wife to take him home, as he was getting drunk, which she duly did. All things considered, Esme held up well; Simon was a rock for Karen—always there when she needed a shoulder to cry on or a hand to hold.

When it came to six o'clock, and the event had nearly finished, Karen felt relieved. Plates and glasses were cleared away, and four bottles of the red mysteriously managed to find their way to Karen's office.

Simon, Esme, and Karen decamped to the flat in Alexandra Road. Nobody felt like eating anything else, so they opened a bottle of red and sat in the lounge, reminiscing about times with Fergus. Karen told some stories, and Esme talked about how popular he was in France with her parents and at the restaurant. That bottle finished, and another opened, Esme went for a lie down. She'd been through an emotional wringer and needed to rest. When she'd left the room, Simon again mentioned the idea of living together and got a lukewarm response. Karen had given it some thought, but was loath to lose her independence: the fact she could do what she wanted, when she wanted, and with who, would be difficult to give up. On the other side though, she couldn't wait too much longer if she was going to have a family, and the thought of growing old on her own felt like an unattractive proposition. They decided to talk it over once Esme had gone back to France and things were quieter.

***

Max Groves'd had enough of Epsom police station, which wasn't altogether surprising, and felt relieved to be eventually moved to a safe house in Glasgow. Although there had been pressure to send him to prison, common sense prevailed, and it was felt he would be safe in Scotland until the court case.

***

Philip continued to work on his case through July, August, and September. A trial date had been set for October 28th and, as usual, the defence felt this was inappropriate and protested that they did not have enough time to prepare their case. The Judge agreed and the trial date went back to January 18th.

***

Karen worked hard, but everything felt unreal somehow. The sensational story of police corruption stopped appearing in the papers and on television. Life went on to new challenges. It almost felt as if it had all been a dream. Had

Fergus really been killed? Whenever she thought that, Karen would pinch herself and remember all the dead bodies. This whole period of time felt incredibly frustrating. Esme had returned to France, and Karen would visit Cannes for a long weekend in November.

***

Fellows established himself as a suitable candidate for a cabinet post. He didn't care which one. Next, he would focus all his efforts on becoming Foreign Secretary, before the final, huge challenge of Party leader and Prime Minister.

CHAPTER 34

The trial of the year opened at the Old Bailey a week behind schedule. The press bloodhounds latched back onto the case and set up camp opposite the Law Courts. Pandemonium erupted when Philip Black, Barristers, Solicitors, and Court Officers arrived.

DI Foster, dressed in a smart trouser suit, and Simon, in suit and tie, watched from the pavement while Black strutted towards the entrance, surrounded by an entourage of Legal advisors. Karen felt physically sick when she saw the hideous Member of Parliament, Peter Fellows. She pointed him out to Simon. Black followed close behind the group. Simon couldn't take his eyes from Black.

Karen had already secured two seats in the courthouse, and she and Simon followed the crowd into the Chamber. Karen was used to courts, but Simon had, surprisingly, never ever been in one. She watched as he marvelled at the gravity of the surroundings, and the Barristers in their cloaks and wigs. A confusion of noise broke out, mostly people talking, then it went silent. A court official stood at the front and, in a raised voice, announced, 'All rise for the honourable Judge Nigel Hale, Baron Hale of Harwich.'

The judge entered the chamber amongst much solemnity, then took a seat. The Barristers and multitude of Solicitors and Court officials followed suit, and then the press, police officers, members of the public, and other officials who were fortunate enough to be present. Karen and Simon sat halfway back in the chamber and had a clear view of all the proceedings. The judge opened some files and looked at a collection of papers, then picked one up. He looked at the Court official, who announced, 'The state versus Mr Philip Black.'

Karen glanced over at the twelve Jury members: a mixture of nationalities and ages, and a good cross-section of the community. She looked back to the bench: something had happened. The judge leant on his right elbow, holding his chin with his right hand, and looked directly at the Barristers. The judge looked serious. 'Counsel, approach the bench.'

Two Barristers stood and walked to the Judges' bench. They stood right in front of him, and the judge said, 'Mr Fish, you are the prosecutor of this case?'

'Yes, Sir.'

'Well, unless you can give me a very good reason in the next two minutes as to why I shouldn't, I am going to throw this case out of court.'

Fish shifted on his feet. 'Your Honour, the Crown Prosecution Service have spent months on this case at great public expense. They, as do I, believe we have a strong case.'

The judge looked annoyed. 'Yes, you are correct. This case has cost the taxpayer a small fortune, and your case is completely dependent on one police officer. A witness who, by all accounts, could be involved in murder, is a drug supplier, and possibly an addict.' The judge looked at his papers. 'One Max Groves.'

The defence Barrister, Simon Cottrell, leaned forward. 'Sir, may I speak?'

'What do you want? Speak, then.'

'Your Honour, this case should never have come to court, and I advised the Crown Prosecution Service of this on several occasions.'

'Thank you, Mr Cottrell, that is most helpful,' the judge replied in a sarcastic tone. He turned back to Mr Fish. 'Does the prosecution have any new witnesses or evidence? Or are you basing your case heavily on the evidence of this Max Groves?'

Fish looked to be a very worried man. 'Sir, I need to take council.'

'How long do you want?'

'One hour, Sir.'

'Granted.'

The two Barristers marched back to their desks. Mr Fish looked like thunder, while Cottrell smiled at his colleagues. Karen and Simon, like the whole court, were desperate to know what was going on. The air felt thick with tension as the court officer stood and made an announcement.

'The court is in recess for one hour. All stand.'

The judge stood and left the chamber. The prosecution team gathered up their mountain of files and rushed for the exit. The defence team huddled in deep conversation. Simon turned to Karen. 'What the fuck is going on?'

'I don't know, but the prosecution team look like shit, and the defence team are all smiles. It doesn't look good.'

'He can't get off, surely to God. No, it can't happen.'

Karen thought back to a case she'd seen in court about three years ago with similar circumstances. The case hadn't been prepared properly by the Crown Prosecution Service, and the case had been chucked out before it even started. She prayed it wasn't going to happen on this occasion.

'Simon, be prepared, anything could happen.' The noise in the Courtroom rose to incredible levels. Karen and Simon left and went straight to the canteen for a coffee. When they entered, they caught sight of Peter Fellows and Carla Westburgh at a table with two other devious-looking men. Fellows looked up, noticed them, then smiled and winked at Karen. She nearly lost control and felt like killing him right there in the canteen.

The hour felt like a day, then—at long last—the time came for the court to reconvene. Simon rushed to the counter to get some water. They left the canteen, went downstairs, and filed back into the courtroom and took their original seats. An eerie silence lingered as everybody waited to see what would happen next. The last to arrive were the prosecution team, and they all looked sombre.

'All rise for the honourable Judge, Nigel Hale, Baron Hale of Harwich.'

The tension felt extraordinary when the judge entered and sat.

He looked around the court, and then settled his eye on Mr Fish, the prosecuting Barrister. The judge looked angry. 'Mr Fish?'

Every eye in the courtroom turned and focussed on Mr Fish, who rose slowly from his chair and looked the judge in the eye. 'The prosecution will withdraw, Sir.'

Pandemonium struck when the court erupted into a barrage of shouts and screams. The judge allowed it to carry on for five seconds, then lifted his gavel and brought it down hard. He did this three times and, eventually, the court hushed. The judge looked at Philip Black. 'You are free to go. Case dismissed.'

'All stand,' the court officer boomed. The judge left for his chambers.

Well-wishers swamped Black, all wanting to shake his hand. Karen couldn't move. Simon stared at Black with deadly intent. Karen looked at Simon and saw the fire burning in his eyes—he was no longer with her. He stood and gripped the back of the seat in front with both hands.

'No. I'm not going to let this happen. It's not fair. He's responsible. He's a killer. Justice? What the hell sort of justice is this?' He let go of the bench and felt in his right-hand jacket pocket. 'It's not right.' Then he shouted, 'Murderer! Killer! Black, you are the devil and are going to hell.'

Simon ran towards the party around Black, and shouldered one man firmly out of the way as others shouted warnings. But it was too late, Simon had the bread knife from the canteen in his right hand, which he lifted and plunged into Black's neck, pushing and ripping as hard as he could. Arms tried to stop him as he pulled the knife out and plunged it back in again. Blood sprayed in every direction from the Carotid and Vertebral Arteries being sliced open. Simon continued to plunge the knife in until his eyes and face became covered in blood. He dropped the knife and court guards pushed him to the floor. A smile of happiness lit his face, and he shouted joyfully.

Karen couldn't believe what she'd just seen. It had all happened so quickly that she had not moved an inch. The next thing she knew, Mick Hill was holding her up. He dragged her from the blood and gore spreading across the floor, and almost carried her down the long court corridor until he came to an office with some empty chairs. He took Karen in and sat her down, then knelt in front of her. 'Boss, Karen, are you all right?'

Karen managed to mumble, 'Take me home. I need to be at home.'

'Are you sure you're okay? You've had a terrible shock.'

'No, Mick, take me home, please. Now.'

Mick bundled her up, took her out to his car, and sat her in the back, where she lay down, curled up, and fell asleep within minutes.

***

Police, security guards, paramedics, and ambulance crews swamped the courtroom. Black had bled to death quickly, and now the courtroom—being a crime scene—had been sealed off. Everybody, including Peter Fellows, left the courthouse in a state of horror: it had been the most unnerving spectacle.

***

Mick took Karen into her flat and put her to bed. Karen dreamt that Simon attacked and stabbed Philip Black to death. When she awoke, with a start, she looked around, and felt glad to see she was in her own bed. But where was Simon? She called his name, but no answer came. Might he be making breakfast? She swung her legs over the bed to get ready for work, thinking it was early in the morning. But when she looked at the clock by the bed, it said six p.m., and she felt totally confused. Someone said her name. Mick stood in her bedroom doorway.

'Mick, what the hell are you doing here?'

Mick looked so concerned that Karen couldn't understand it. 'Have you seen Simon?'

'He …' Mick started to speak but wasn't sure what to say. 'He's been arrested and taken to Strand police station.'

Karen tried to understand, but couldn't grasp what Mick was saying. 'I don't understand. What the hell's going on?'

'He stabbed Philip Black in the courtroom. The injuries were fatal. Simon has been charged with murder.'

Karen shut her eyes. It wasn't a dream; it was a nightmare. Simon did stab Black in the courtroom.

Tears flowed. 'What are we going to do? We have to help him.'

'The only thing we can do at the moment is make sure he gets a good lawyer. The one that got Black off would be a good start.'

'He would cost a fortune.' She lay down and curled into a ball. 'Mick?'

'Yes?'

'Tell Esme what has happened, please, as soon as you can.'

'I'll do it tonight, don't worry. And I'm cooking dinner.'

Karen laughed in between crying. 'It's not your cooking, but I'm really not hungry. I won't be able to eat anything, believe me.'

'Okay, in that case, I'll be in the lounge.'

'No, go home to your family, they need you as well.'

Mick seemed hesitant. 'Are you sure you'll be okay?

'Fine. I'm going to sleep. I'll see you soon.'

'Okay, I'll be on my way, but if you need anything call, okay.'

'I promise, and thanks for everything. I appreciate it.'

When the front door slammed, Karen jumped out of bed and stumbled to the kitchen. She opened the booze cupboard: Red Wine, Whisky, or Pernod? She plumped for the wine to start with, opened another cupboard, and took out a huge wine glass that could almost take half a bottle. Three-quarters filled, she took a long slow sip, sat at the tiny kitchen table, and drank until it she'd emptied it, then filled it up again, emptying the bottle.

It was a long drunken night. Phones rang all over the place, but she didn't answer any of them. One of the calls was from Esme, whose answer-phone message sounded frantic with worry. Karen woke up at six o' clock in the morning, on the floor in the lounge. Red wine had spilled on the carpet, and the room stunk like a brewery. She dragged herself up, only to collapse onto the sofa. Her head throbbed, so she went to the bathroom and took two paracetamol out of the cabinet. Her mouth felt disgusting so she gargled some water and spat it out in the sink. To do something about her dehydration, she headed to the kitchen and drank greedily from the box of orange juice, letting it spill and dribble down her chin. She still felt like shit and shambled back to bed, got under the duvet, and went back to sleep.

She woke again at two p.m., having had a deep sleep, and was horrified to feel a wet sheet. She'd peed the bed. Mortified, she stumbled up and went to the bathroom, but her bladder was empty. Next, she went to the kitchen and drank a large plastic cupful of water. Wobbly on her feet, she sat down at the table. Even though it was still early afternoon, she felt like a drink. A bottle of Pernod stood by the sink, and she picked it up, pleased to feel it still half full. She got a clean tumbler glass from the cupboard and stuck some ice in it from the freezer, then took the remains of the orange juice and poured it over the ice. Then she added a generous measure of Pernod. The smell hit her, making her stumble. She wasn't in the mood for fucking about with drinks, and drank until she held an empty glass. She refilled the glass and sat sipping from it, wondering when her life had first gone wrong. She finished the Pernod, then moved onto the last bottle of red wine. Once she'd finished that, there was nothing.

***

Esme arrived at Gatwick at seven p.m. and Mick Hill picked her up. He drove her straight to Karen's flat, where they banged on the door, but got no reply. Mick got in through the open bathroom window and opened the door for Esme. The whole place stank of stale booze, vomit, and urine. Esme rushed from room to room. Karen lay on the floor in the kitchen, in a puddle of urine and vomit. Esme checked for a pulse, and relief flooded her when she found one straightaway. She called to Mick and they lifted her onto a chair.

'Go and run the shower, then come back and help me,' she told him.

Mick did as asked, checked the shower wasn't too hot, then returned to find Esme struggling to undress Karen.

She looked up and said, 'You hold her up while I get her clothes off.'

Mick didn't move. 'I'm not sure.'

'Just get on with it. She won't remember a thing.'

Mick lifted Karen under the arms and held her upright. Esme pulled her trousers and knickers off, followed by the blouse and bra. She smelt terrible. They hauled her to the bathroom. Esme undressed right in front of Mick and climbed into the shower. Mick pushed and Esme pulled, and eventually Karen was in the shower. Esme washed her thoroughly, and then Mick lifted Karen out.

'Start drying her. I'll get some linen and will make the spare bed.'

Mick grabbed a towel off the rack and did his best to dry Karen. Esme soon came back. She had found some pyjamas for herself and a flannel nightie for Karen. They dressed her and carried her to the clean second bedroom. Esme tucked her into bed and, within a minute, she was snoring away.

Mick left. Esme opened all the windows, and then tidied up. The washing machine was soon on and the urine and vomit covered floors cleaned. Within an hour-and-a-half, things looked and smelled much better. Esme found some car air fresheners in a drawer and placed them in the lounge, kitchen, and bathroom. She did a quick tour and was satisfied with the results. Next on the list was to prepare some soup. A search showed near-empty cupboards: no vegetables or anything else to make something fresh. So, with dismay, she settled upon the six cans of Heinz tomato soup she'd found. Then she smiled; it must be Karen's favourite. Esme sat in the lounge and checked on Karen every half hour. By ten p.m., Esme felt exhausted. Unsure what to do, she hesitated, but in the end got in bed with Karen. She squeezed in and soon fell fast asleep.

CHAPTER 35

(ONE MONTH LATER)

'The Honourable member for Kingston and Surbiton,' the speaker of the House announced.

Peter Fellows rose from his seat and looked around him. He had recently received some specialist training in public speaking and he now put the theory into practice. He made sure as many eyes as possible were on him before he spoke.

'I am here today to remind the House that there are brave men and women who give their lives in service to our great Island country.' He paused for effect.

'Hear, hear,' rang out throughout the chamber.

'I name the latest of these as Philip Black, who gave his life in service to the Metropolitan Police. He died at the hands of a lunatic terrorist in a Crown Courthouse, of all places, a few weeks ago.' He paused again and surveyed the House, thinking he was Churchill giving a wartime speech. 'Does the House agree with me that extra pension benefits should be given to the wives and husbands of these innocents who are killed whilst working in the line of duty?' A chorus of 'Hear, hear,' rang once more throughout the chamber. He felt pleased with the speech, and sank back into the green leather seat.

The first MP's to support Fellows were Richard Small, Alistair Bolton, Toby Marchant, and Andrew Parr. Fellows smiled from ear to ear, then he heard a name called he was unfamiliar with.

'The Honourable member for Dartford and Thanet.'

Ex-Chief Inspector Park of Surrey Police had retired and now worked as a Labour MP. This would be his maiden speech in the House.

'It is with regret that today, on my maiden speech to the House, I must criticise one of our major institutions, that being the Metropolitan Police.' He paused as chaos erupted.

First up was Peter Fellows, screaming, 'Shame on you. Sit down, sit down.'

The noise became deafening as MP after MP shouted Park down every time he tried to speak. The speaker of the house screamed for order, and eventually Park sat down and the noise abated. The speaker rose from his seat with a stern look. 'Members of the House have to listen to honourable members and not shout them down. I am issuing a warning to all members of the House; if it continues you will be removed and suspended from the House and face severe censor.' He sat back down.

'The honourable member for Dartford and Thanet.'

Park once again rose from his seat.

'The Metropolitan Police is an institution that is endemic with Racism and Corruption.' He looked around and his eyes met those of Fellows. 'I myself have reason to believe that certain officers in the Metropolitan Police have committed heinous crimes in the past six months, and this includes murder.' An audible gasp came from the members. Fellows climbed to his feet, shaking with rage. Through the red mist of fury, he heard the speaker say:

'The honourable member will SIT DOWN IMMEDIATELY.' Fellows slumped back.

Park spoke again, 'I charge this House to fully investigate the report that I am sending to the Prime Minister today.' Park then regained his seat.

Fellows looked up to the Public Gallery to garner some moral support from his wife, but to his horror he saw the woman sitting next to his wife—the bitch detective from Epsom, Karen Foster. He turned back, swearing that the piece of shit Foster would have a serious accident in the not-too-distant future.

***

'Are you sure about this, Esme?'

'I said so, didn't I? Speed up. I can't wait.'

Karen laughed. 'God, you're worse than me.'

'We're a team. As good and as bad as each other, because we love each other—simple.

'That was a mouthful, ... five minutes and we'll be there.'

'You sure he'll turn up?'

Karen burst into laughter. 'Look, when I told him I was bringing a friend he was ecstatic and started jerking off over the phone.'

Esme smiled. 'Did he, you know, finish over the—'

'Oh, I see, ... I've no idea. I said goodbye and put the phone down.'

Karen pulled into the car park, and they were soon knocking on room eighteen and were let in. Karen led Esme to the bed and they both sat down. Karen held Esme's hand and spoke to the man.

'This is my friend, Charlotte. She doesn't believe how big you are.'

The man undressed to his white boxers and stood waiting.

Karen whispered to Esme, 'Pull his boxers down.'

Esme stood, then knelt at the huge man's feet. She put her thumbs into the side of the man's shorts and pulled them down slowly. They got lower and lower, and then a huge, thick, long cock sprang out and nearly hit Esme in the face. She fell back and howled with laughter.

'Oh my God. Oh my God, look at it, it's like a massive tree trunk.'

Karen laughed, and Friday showed his sparkly white, perfect teeth in a broad smile.

'Now, you two better show me what you got.'

Karen and Esme took their time to undress, then kissed and fondled one another, while Friday saluted and moved to join the party.

THE END

OTHER TITLES AVAILABLE FROM AUTHOR CHRIS WARD

SERIAL KILLER: DI Karen Foster, Book 1
http://tinyurl.com/p5ld9dx

THE BERMONDSEY THRILLER TRILOGY:

    1.   BERMONDSEY TRIFLE
http://amzn.to/1l3B3up
    2.   BERMONDSEY PROSECCO
http://tinyurl.com/nebwtys
    3.   BERMONDSEY: THE FINAL ACT
http://tinyurl.com/nbuahoj

***

About the Author

Chris Ward was born in West Bromwich in the Black Country, which resulted in him following in his father's footsteps and becoming a lifelong West Bromwich Albion supporter. He moved south at an early age and lived his childhood in Purley, Surrey, and at Boarding School in Ashtead, Surrey. He left school not knowing what he wanted to do and ended up at college for two years learning how to cook. He then worked at the BBC for three years cooking for the stars as well as on an Iranian missile base in the Persian Gulf. He left catering after a few years and moved into Food Sales. He then spent thirty-odd years in sales and marketing before starting his own food marketing company. Chris still works as a marketing consultant, which fits in well with his writing. Chris has published five books: the first, a memoir of his boarding school days. This was followed by three books in the Bermondsey Gangster Trilogy: Bermondsey Trifle, Bermondsey Prosecco, and Bermondsey: The Final Act. Serial Killer came next, featuring DI Karen Foster who was in the three Bermondsey Books. Blue Cover Up is Chris's latest crime novel, featuring DI Karen Foster. Interests include cooking, eating, wine, sport, reading and, of course, writing. Chris is married and lives in Epsom and has loads of kids!

Printed in Great Britain
by Amazon